Educated at a co-educational Quaker boarding school, Rebecca Shaw went on to qualify as a teacher of deaf children. After her marriage, she spent the ensuing years enjoying bringing up her family. The departure of the last of her four children to university has given her the time and opportunity to write.

Village Gossip is the seventh novel in the Tales from Turnham Malpas series.

VILLAGE GOSSIP

The peaceful lives of the inhabitants of Turnham Malpas are disrupted when a visitor comes to stay. Hugo — an old friend of Jimbo and Harriet's at the Village Store — is a famous actor and is recuperating from a serious illness. But he finds country life boring, and when he meets Caroline, the Rector's wife, he is instantly attracted to her. Soon he agrees to direct and star in a village play, with Caroline as his leading lady. When Peter, Caroline's husband, becomes aware of the attraction between her and Hugo, he has to use all his powers of patience and diplomacy to contain a potentially heart-breaking situation.

REBECCA SHAW

VILLAGE GOSSIP

Tales From Turnham Malpas

Complete and Unabridged

ULVERSCROFT
Leicester

First published in Great Britain in 1999 by
Orion
London

First Large Print Edition
published 2001
by arrangement with
The Orion Publishing Group
London

The moral right of the author has been asserted

British Library CIP Data

Shaw, Rebecca
    Village gossip: tales from Turnham Malpas.—
    Large print ed.—
    Ulverscroft large print series: general fiction
    1. Turnham Malpas (England: Imaginary place)—
    Fiction 2. Pastoral fiction 3. Large type books
    I. Title
    823.9'14 [F]

    ISBN 0–7089–4352–7

Published by
F. A. Thorpe (Publishing)
Anstey, Leicestershire
Set by Words & Graphics Ltd.
Anstey, Leicestershire
Printed and bound in Great Britain by
T. J. International Ltd., Padstow, Cornwall

This book is printed on acid-free paper

Inhabitants Of Turnham Malpas

Nick Barnes
  Veterinary surgeon
Roz Barnes
  Nurse
Willie Biggs
  Verger at St Thomas à Becket
Sylvia Biggs
  His wife and housekeeper at the Rectory
Sir Ronald Bissett
  Retired Trades Union leader
Lady Sheila Bissett
  His wife
James (Jimbo) Charter-Plackett
  Owner of the Village Store
Harriet Charter-Plackett
  His wife
Fergus, Finlay, Flick and Fran
  Their children
Katherine Charter-Plackett
  Jimbo's mother
Alan Crimble
  Barman at the Royal Oak
Linda Crimble
  Runs the post office at the Village Store

Georgie Fields
Licensee at the Royal Oak
H. Craddock Fitch
Owner of Turnham House
Jimmy Glover
Taxi driver
Mrs Jones
A village gossip
Barry Jones
Her son and estate carpenter
Pat Jones
His wife
Dean and Michelle
Her children
Revd Peter Harris (MA Oxon)
Rector of the parish
Dr Caroline Harris
His wife
Alex and Beth
Their children
Jeremy Mayer
Manager at Turnham House
Venetia Mayer
His wife
Neville Neal
Accountant and church treasurer
Liz Neal
His wife
Guy and Hugh
Their children

Tom Nicholls
Retired businessman
Evie Nicholls
His wife
Anne Parkin
Retired secretary
Kate Pascoe
Village school head teacher
Sir Ralph Templeton
Retired from the diplomatic service
Lady Muriel Templeton
His wife
Dicky Tutt
Scout leader
Bel Tutt
School caretaker and assistant in the Village Store
Don Wright
Maintenance engineer
Vera Wright
Cleaner at the nursing home in Penny Fawcett
Rhett Wright
Their grandson

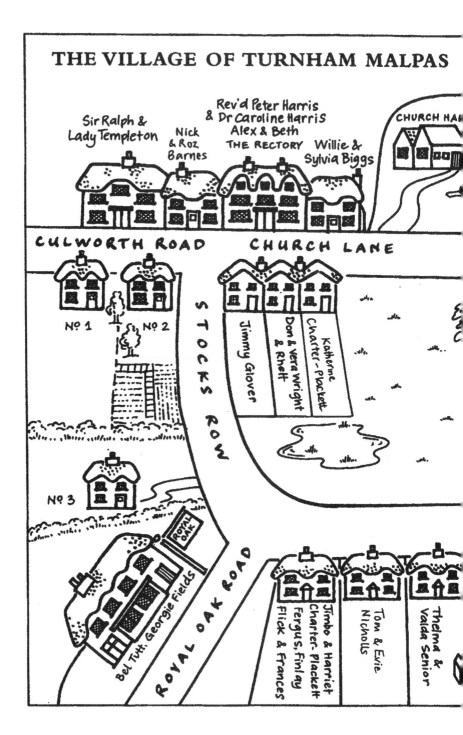

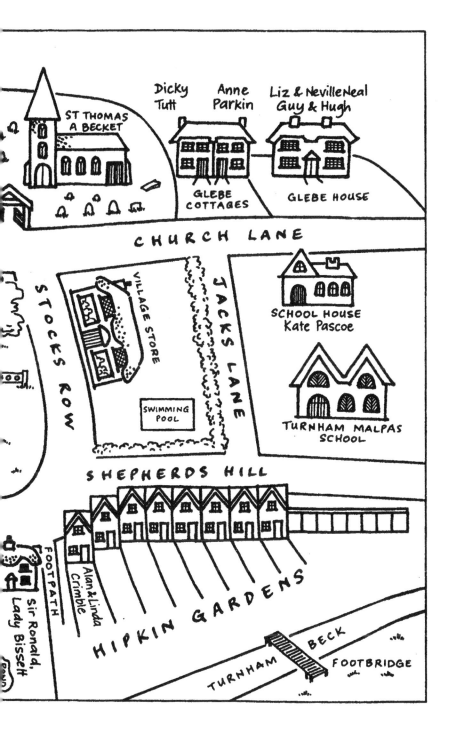

1

His foot propped on the brass rail running along the bottom of the bar, a gin and tonic in hand, Peter toasted Caroline: 'Happy birthday, darling!'

She clinked her glass with his and smiled up at him. 'And the same to you.'

Peter bent down to kiss her. 'I say this every year, and I say it again; how many married people are there who celebrate their birthdays on the same day?'

'Somewhere, someone knows the answer to that, I suppose. Do you remember how sentimental you used to wax about our marriage being 'written in the stars', 'this was meant to be since the beginning of time', et cetera, et cetera, all because our birthdays were on the same day?' Caroline grinned up at him.

'Don't mock. I meant it and still do.'

'I know you do, and I'm eternally grateful that you do.'

'Always will mean it, no matter what.' Peter put his glass down on the bar and surveyed the crowded bar. 'I don't think we could have chosen a busier night.'

'You're right there.'

The Royal Oak had been in business since, as the villagers often stressed, the beginning of time. The thatched roof, the ancient white walls bulging slightly more than they had done five hundred years ago, the huge open fireplace which boasted a real log fire in the winter months, and the mighty oak beams all leant a feeling of timelessness, of permanance, of a kind of security which encapsulated the feeling everyone had about their village.

From the other side of the bar Georgie called out, 'I've just realised it's your birthdays, isn't it? Next drinks on the house, OK?'

Peter thanked her. 'Where's Dicky tonight?'

'Night off.' Georgie turned away to serve yet another customer. 'Yes, sir, what can I get you?'

Caroline, enjoying a birthday which some months ago she had thought she would not live to see, said to Peter, 'Harriet and Jimbo are late. I wonder if our table's ready? I'm starving.'

'So am I. I'll go see.' He threaded his way between the tables, stopping for a word now and again.

'Evening, Rector, 'appy birthday!'

'Thank you, Jimmy.'

2

'Your birthday is it, then? Many more, sir, many more.'

'Thank you, Don, Vera.'

'Many happy returns, Rector, and that's from Sheila too.'

'Thank you, Ron.'

He left a swathe of smiling faces behind him. Caroline, watching, smiled inside herself. He might have his ups and downs with them all but at bottom they were on his side. What a difference he had made to them since he had arrived. Stirred them up and no mistake. She hoped they'd never need to leave, because her roots had gone deep down here in this village and you couldn't ask for more than that. Her eyes lit up when she spotted Peter signalling from the dining-room doorway that their table was ready.

'But, Peter, what about Jimbo and Harriet? They're not here yet.'

'They've rung. Crisis with the children; they're just leaving.'

'Oh, brilliant. I wonder what's wrong?'

'No need to worry,' he smoothed away her frown with a gentle finger. 'Fran has had a temper tantrum.'

'Oh dear.'

Bel was in charge of the dining room tonight, a slimmer, more light-footed Bel of late. She beamed at the two of them and they

3

couldn't help but notice what a lovely heart-warming smile she had.

'Good evening! We've given you the best table, seeing as it's a celebration. Jimbo and Harriet are on their way. Happy birthday to you both.'

'Thank you, Bel.' She handed them each a menu and padded away to attend to other diners.

The door between the dining room and the bar opened and Harriet and Jimbo walked in. Her dark hair damp and curling, her slightly sallow skin flushed with anxiety at her late arrival, Harriet waved when she caught sight of them. Jimbo stood behind her, smoothing his hand over his bald head which gleamed in the light over the tiny reception desk in the doorway. More round than he would have liked, Jimbo was a commanding figure. Energy, both mental and physical, exuded from every inch of him. 'Sorry we're late!'

Peter stood up to pull out Harriet's chair for her. 'Good evening, Harriet!'

She reached up to kiss him. 'Happy birthday, Peter. Happy birthday, Caroline! How useful of you to have your birthdays on the same day. It halves the remembering!'

'To say nothing of the cost!' Jimbo took Caroline's hand and kissed it. 'Happy birthday, my dear, and many of 'em.' He

4

squeezed her hand and she knew exactly what it meant. A gesture of delight at her survival. Tears came into Caroline's eyes. She blew her nose and remained quiet for a while, listening to the chatter and pretending to study her menu.

'Fran Charter-Plackett! She's so amenable, fits in without a murmur with anything we plan and then suddenly wham! bang! she's on the floor drumming her heels and screaming like a hell cat!'

'Jimbo, darling! She did have good reason, or so she thought.'

Peter asked what the reason was.

Harriet explained. 'We've a guest coming to stay tomorrow, and Fran's having a practise go on the put-u-up in Flick's bedroom tonight. We'd talked about it and I'd put her favourite sheets on the bed, done all I could, but when it came to it . . . '

The mention of a guest brought Caroline's head up from the menu. 'Who've you got coming?'

Jimbo wagged a finger at her. 'Wouldn't you like to know!'

Harriet protested. 'Jimbo!'

'If Caroline guessed until this time next week she wouldn't get it right!'

'You're teasing me! Come on, tell!'

Harriet laughed. 'It's a college friend of

ours. Compared to Jimbo and me, who've only managed to rise to the dizzy heights of running a Village Store . . . '

Peter interrupted her, scornful. '*Only* . . . Considering the success you've made of it . . . '

Harriet silenced him with a finger to his lips. 'Hush now. Wait for it.' She intended to pause to increase the dramatic effect but couldn't wait to see their faces. 'His name is *Hugo Maude*.'

A silence greeted her announcement. Caroline stared open mouthed. Peter stared, not believing he had heard correctly.

Caroline, stunned, stammered out, 'Hugo Maude! Not *the* Hugo Maude!'

'The very same!' Jimbo smiled at her astonishment. It was lovely to see her so taken out of herself.

'You mean Royal Shakespeare-Broadway-Stratford-Hugo Maude?'

'The very same!' Harriet glanced at Peter, amused by his more controlled reaction.

Caroline, seized with amazement, said, 'How long is he here for?'

'As long as it takes.'

Bel came for their order.

'With salad?' They all four nodded. 'Jacket potatoes, sauté potatoes?'

Jimbo began to ask for saute potatoes but

6

hastily changed his order to jacket when he caught Harriet's eye.

'House wine, or something special?'

Peter asked for something special.

When Bel left, Caroline said, 'How long *what* takes?'

'The poor lamb has been terribly ill. Some ghastly virus he picked up when he went with the RSC to Tokyo, it came close to finishing him off. So Jimbo and I thought we'd ask him for a quiet stay with us away from the press and such, so he could recuperate properly.'

Caroline persisted with her questioning. 'How come we've never seen him before?'

'Too busy. Never stops. Acting dominates his entire life.'

Caroline nodded her head in complete agreement. 'To be able to act as he does it would, wouldn't it? Only to be expected.' She paused. 'Shall we have a chance to meet him, do you think?'

Harriet grinned. 'I expect so. In fact I promise you shall, but I'm not planning anything until he's been here a few days. I don't know just how ill he is.'

'Oh, of course. Yes. I see.'

Peter said. 'You know that's something we've never done.'

Jimbo looked puzzled. 'What is?'

'We've never used the stage in the Church

7

Hall for serious acting. At least not while we've been here.'

Harriet thought for a moment and then said, 'We've been here three years longer than you and you're right, it certainly hasn't, not for years.'

Quickly picking up on her thinking processes, Jimbo wagged a finger and said, 'No, we are not. Definitely not.'

'Not what?'

Jimbo looked at Peter and answered him by saying they were not going to encourage Hugo to act in a play. 'The man has been very ill and he's here to rest. He's a dear sweet man and he doesn't deserve us begging him for help. It could be the last straw.'

Harriet replied briskly. 'Such a thought never entered my head. Just the same, a village dramatic society would be a very, very good idea, wouldn't it, Peter?'

'It would. A real challenge.'

Peter felt a tap on his shoulder blade. He turned to find Mrs Jones at the next table, twisted around in her chair, wanting a word.

'Good evening, Mrs Jones, and good evening to you, Vince.'

Mrs Jones, obviously bursting with infor-mation, stopped just long enough to greet him and then said, 'Sorry to be interrupting, Rector, but I couldn't help but overhear what you were saying.' Harriet snorted her surprise at such a monumental disregard for the truth. Mrs Jones turned her chair round and squeezed in between Peter and Caroline. 'The last time we had a play on the stage that wasn't done by the Scouts or the Sunday School was in 1953. It was the Queen's Coronation and we did an 'istorical pageant called . . . now what was it called, Vince? 'Royal Progress' or 'Queens Through the Ages', or something like that. Blinking good it was too. The old rector, Mr Furbank, was Prince Albert. I was Brittania, and Vince here was the Prince of Wales, wasn't yer, Vince?' Before Vince could reply she had launched herself into a list of the people involved, followed by an appraisal of the play's reception. 'Two nights we did it and they came from all over. Penny Fawcett, Little Derehams and even some from Culworth, would you believe. And you know what a stuck up lot they are.'

Their food came and they had to excuse themselves. Mrs Jones stood up and turned her chair back to her own table. The four of them ate in silence while they absorbed what she had said.

Peter broke the silence by saying, 'So you see it would be a good idea, wouldn't it? With or without Hugo Maude.'

Jimbo, helping himself to a lavish portion of butter for his jacket potato, said, 'Yes, but not until the winter, when Hugo's gone and then it'll give us something to brighten the long winter evenings.'

'But who the blazes in this village can act? Even more to the point, who the blazes would we get to direct?' This from Harriet who, despite Jimbo's warning, really longed for Hugo's help.

'Exactly. Who? Not me for a start.'

Peter looked at Caroline in surprise. 'Not you? But you did lots at Medical School and at school. Portia, wasn't it? And lots more which won't spring to mind.'

'We'll see. It's all so long ago. And there's the children. Baby-sitting and that. I can't always rely on you with your meetings and things.'

Peter patted her hand. 'Don't you fret about that. Sylvia and Willie would gladly sit in, as you well know.'

Jimbo, realising how much Peter wanted Caroline to be involved, agreed. 'Our boys are getting big enough to be left for a while looking after the girls, so long as we're not too far away. So between us we'd manage something. Rest assured.'

Peter flashed him a look of gratitude. 'It's settled then, a play we shall do. A serious play, not some amateurish cobbled together thing, but a real play.' He raised his glass and invited them to join him in a toast.

'To the play and the players.'

'That sounds terribly grand. When shall we have the inaugural meeting?' Harriet asked.

Caroline parried Harriet's question with one of more immediate importance to herself. 'When shall we be introduced to Hugo Maude?'

'At church on Sunday, if he's well enough. He never misses. Finds the whole thing movingly dramatic.' Harriet apologised to Peter. 'His words, not mine.'

'Sunday it is then.' Caroline drained her glass and asked Peter for more. He refilled it, thrilled to have lighted upon something which he hoped would fill Caroline's heart and mind and above all give her faith in her future.

★   ★   ★

Caroline stood gazing at him, dumbstruck. He was lean, too lean really, with a head of thick dark hair, left full at the sides which made for just a hint of curl above his beautifully shaped ears. He'd been intro-duced to Peter now and they were talking animatedly. There couldn't have been a bigger

11

contrast between two men. Hugo was shorter than Peter, but then with Peter being six feet five, most men were. Not only was he shorter than Peter he was also much more lightly built. One couldn't imagine Hugo on a squash court or running three miles before breakfast like Peter did.

Caroline couldn't help but admire the profile which had been displayed on theatre billboards and in magazines and newspapers all over the world. Beautifully balanced, at once tender and arrogant, elegant and virile.

She was being ridiculous. At her age, swooning over an actor! Come on.

Harriet tapped her arm. 'I've never seen you so excited by a man. You've usually only eyes for Peter.'

Caroline looked at Peter and then back at Hugo. 'I can admire from a distance, can't I? After all, he is famous. You can see he's under strain.'

'He's been very, very ill. And I mean ill. It was a case of 'will he or won't he?' at one stage. Lost a stone and a half in weight. It's left him very feeble.'

'I see.' By now Hugo was talking to Sheila Bissett, whose face was almost the colour of the dreadful purple hat she was wearing for church this summer. Above the babble of the congregation gathered about the church

12

porch, Caroline heard Sheila say, 'Well, of course, you must come to one of my coffee mornings. It may only be a small village but we do know how to do things proper.'

This offer was greeted with enthusiasm by Hugo. 'My dear Lady Bissett, of course I shall be delighted to attend. It will be the highlight of my social whirl.' Hugo looked across at Harriet and made his excuses to Lady Bissett.

'Oh! he's coming over. I'll introduce you.'

Her eyes fixed on Hugo, Caroline muttered, 'I feel ridiculously nervous. Perhaps I shouldn't.'

Harriet did the honours and stood back a little to watch. Hugo took hold of Caroline's hand and raised it to his lips.

'My dear Caroline, what a privilege.' His voice, more suited to Stratford than Turnham Malpas, turned Caroline's knees to jelly. This gesture of his, this kissing of her hand and the holding of it for longer than was really necessary brought the eyes of the entire congregation to rest on her.

She blushed, and she hadn't blushed for years. When in her consulting room, people confided in her the most intimate details of their lives and she never batted an eyelid, never blushed, never ever. And yet here she was behaving like an empty-headed teenager.

'How do you do? I'm so sorry to hear that

you've been so ill. We'll have to hope that the peace and quiet here will . . . '

'I shan't *hasten* to get well, not with charming people like you in the village.' Caroline appeared to have been poleaxed.

Harriet felt the need to intervene. 'Caroline's a doctor.'

'In that case, if I'm taken ill I shall be able to rely on you to cool my fevered brow.'

'I don't know about that, you see . . . '

Hugo dismissed her hesitation with a sweeping gesture of his hand. 'I won't hear of you refusing to come to my aid. I cannot forgo the thrill of your stethoscope pressed to my manly chest.' There were muffled giggles from someone way behind him and Caroline blushed even redder.

'I was going to say that it's not medical etiquette for me to attend another doctor's patient.'

Hugo struck a pose, one hand on his heart and the other clasping his forehead. 'Not even in an emergency! Am I cast out from all medical assistance to die miserably and alone for the sake of *etiquette*?' The last word, delivered with passion, and loud enough to wake Jimmy's geese on the village pond, fell on the delighted ears of the entire congregation. It had been some time since they had enjoyed so much free entertainment.

Harriet, catching the appalled expression in Jimbo's eyes, said abruptly, 'For heaven's sakes, Hugo, you're not that ill. Come on home, the children need feeding. Help me round them up.'

Hugo gave Caroline a huge wink, bunched his fingers, kissed them and trotted meekly after his friend.

With his mother on his arm Jimbo passed close by Caroline as Hugo left. Jimbo's mother wore severe disapproval across every inch of her perfectly made-up face. She and Caroline had long ago patched up their differences but it appeared that in one brief moment of time their friendship had been shattered. With a sharp nod of recognition replacing her normally gracious conversation she swept by. Jimbo raised his eyes to heaven and shrugged his shoulders apologetically.

The congregation began to disperse. Peter had disappeared inside to remove his surplice, Willie was waiting to lock up, the twins were chasing each other among the gravestones and Caroline realised it was time she remembered her duty.

'Alex, Beth! Come quickly now! We'll get the kettle on, Daddy will be wanting his coffee.'

'Mummy! That man kissed you.'

'Yes, Beth, he did.'

'What will Daddy say?'

Ever at the ready to pour scorn on Beth's statements, Alex replied, 'Daddy won't mind. After all, he only kissed her hand.'

'I know, but he shouldn't. He's cheeky. She's my Mummy.' Beth squeezed hold of Caroline's hand and kissed it herself.

'And she's mine, and I say he can kiss her hand.'

'Well, I don't. I shall ask Daddy if he minds.'

'No, darling, don't do that. Mr Maude is an actor and they're inclined to be a bit . . . '

'Bit what?'

'Well, they're inclined to exaggerate everything. They go a bit over the top.'

Alex studied this statement while Caroline unlocked the Rectory door. 'It was only your hand. So it's nothing really.'

'You went ever so red, Mummy.'

'Did I?'

'Yes, you did. Red like a beetroot.'

'Thanks. Do you both want coffee, or orange, or what?'

While they argued with each other as to what they would have Caroline filled the kettle and began to get out the mugs. She heard the front door slam. 'Ready for coffee?'

'Please.' Caroline turned to look at Peter.

He was standing in the kitchen doorway looking at her. Her heart flipped. She loved him so. Compared with Hugo ridiculous Maude he was a gem. His wonderful thatch of red-blond hair, his vivid blue eyes, his fair skin, the width of his shoulders, his energy and his love for mankind, all set her trembling with love for him.

Beth pulled out a chair. 'Sit next to me, Daddy. I'm having coffee too, Mummy, please.'

'And me!' Alex pulled out a chair the other side of Peter and sat on it. 'Daddy! Did you know that Mr Maude is an actor?'

'He is indeed. I've seen him once, a long time ago. In London. In *Macbeth*.'

'What's *Macbeth*?'

'A play by Shakespeare.'

'Was he good?'

'Oh yes, very impressive. In fact very good indeed, I think the best I've seen.'

'Mummy says actors behave like that.'

'Like what?'

'Kissing people and that.'

'Yes, they do. Very emotional they are.' Peter looked up at Caroline and winked as she handed him his coffee.

She had to laugh. 'He really did make me feel a fool.'

'I could see that. This coffee's welcome.

17

What shall we do this afternoon? Do we have any plans?'

★ ★ ★

Hugo's plan to retire to his bedroom and lie down for the rest of the afternoon suited everyone. Harriet, because she'd had more than she could take of him at the lunch table; Jimbo, because Hugo had grated on his nerves and he was forced to admit to a tinge of jealousy which didn't sit easily on his shoulders; the children, because they couldn't get a word in edgeways as he wouldn't stop talking; and Grandmama, because she knew he spelt trouble with a capital T.

'Have you two girls finished? If you have your Grandmama has something for you in her handbag which you can take into the sitting room and play with.'

Five-year-old Fran jumped up and down with excitement. Flick, at twelve, recognised the subterfuge and wished she couldn't see through her Grandmama's every move. But it would only be boring conversation about Hugo and the threat he posed to one and all, so she might as well fall for it. 'Lovely, Grandmama. Come along, Fran.' They retired with some magic tricks in little plastic bags, leaving the field clear for Grandmama's tirade.

'That man . . . '

Jimbo hastily said to his son, 'Fergus, close that door just in case.' When Fergus had reclaimed his chair, his Grandmama continued. 'That man is a charlatan, a chameleon and a sham. The sooner he leaves this house the better.'

Finlay chuckled. 'Wow! You're getting quite poetic, Grandmama.'

He received a withering glance. 'This is not a laughing matter, young man. Jimbo! You must get rid of him.'

Jimbo caught Harriet's eye and acknowledged the warning in them. 'As a matter of fact I quite like the chap. In any case, Mother, it's up to Harriet and me who stays in our house. He poses no threat here.'

'No threat? You must be blind.' She thumped the table with her clenched fist. 'Blind! He wants kicking out. Convalescing indeed. More like out of work or, as they euphemistically call it in the acting profession, resting.'

Finlay chuckled again. 'He is.'

'He is what?'

'Resting.' He pointed to the ceiling. Grandmama, as he was well aware, didn't have much of a sense of humour. She snorted. 'Sometimes you talk in riddles.'

'Mother-in-law! He almost died he was so ill. He lives alone, he needs a family to care for him. Don't worry. Before long he'll get an offer he can't refuse, he'll go dashing off and we shan't see him again for years. He's a close friend of Jimbo's, isn't he, darling?' Jimbo nodded. 'And of mine too. It's the least we can do.'

'Jimbo! Are you head of this house or not?'

'I am.'

'Then take my word for it, he is trouble. If you'll excuse me I'll be off now. I have two friends coming for afternoon tea and I need to get organised.' She collected her handbag and offered her cheek for Jimbo to kiss. 'Cast this viper out from your bosom, Jimbo. Listen to your mother for once. Bye bye, Harriet. Thank you for yet another delightful lunch, I do look forward to Sunday lunch with you all. Bye bye, boys.' She opened the dining-room door, went through it and then came back in. 'And another thing. Caroline Harris had no business to let him kiss her hand. Disgraceful behaviour outside church, with everyone watching. She blushed like a schoolgirl. I expect Peter will have something to say to her about that and no mistake.'

★　★　★

On summer Sunday evenings Peter and Caroline had dinner together after Peter returned from Evensong. With the children tucked up in bed they enjoyed an intimate meal, which Caroline always took a great deal of care over. The wine had been chilled, the steak was almost ready, the sauce bubbled very gently in the pan and the vegetables were already in the tureens in the oven keeping warm, when she heard Peter's key in the door.

'I'm back and I'm seriously in need of sustenance.'

'So am I! I've opened the wine. Won't be a moment.'

Peter came into the kitchen. He'd removed his cassock and was wearing his dark trousers and clerical collar with a grey short-sleeved shirt.

'Take your collar off, you look hot.'

He undid his back stud and peeled off his collar, placing it with the stud on top of the fridge freezer. 'Quite a lot there tonight.'

'Makes a change.'

'It does indeed. Just as I begin to think I shall suggest finishing with Evensong I get a good congregation and I have a rethink.'

Caroline gave Peter a cloth. 'Here, take the

vegetables in. I've served the meat straight onto the plates.'

Peter put down the tureens on the dining table and picked up the bottle of wine. 'Where on earth did this wine come from? Chile! Oh my word.'

'If there's one person I don't like it's a wine snob.'

'Sorry! You're quite right. If I like it, what does it matter where it comes from.'

'Maybe you had a big congregation because they all hoped Hugo Maude would appear.'

'Well, he didn't.'

'I'm in trouble because of him.'

He looked up, his mouth full of steak, and mumbled, 'Why?'

'Grandmama Charter-Plackett doesn't approve of me any longer because of what happened outside church.'

'No wonder.'

'Living in an ancient village like this one, they can get too . . . what's the word I'm looking for?'

'Don't know. Shall I finish the peas?'

'Yes, I don't want any more. Too narrow minded. In fact, almighty prim. They need their horizons widening. All he is, is a bit of fun. Liven us all up. I hope he stays for a while.'

'So do I. But, darling, please be very circumspect won't you? Rector's wife and all that.'

Caroline put down her knife and fork, drank a little of her wine and muttered, 'Here we go again.'

'I beg your pardon?'

'I said, 'Here we go again.''

'Sorry, but you know . . . '

'I know. By the way I'm going back to work as soon as I can get a job. I've decided. General practice. I like that best.'

He restrained himself from being protective, there was nothing more sure to make her go ahead finding a job than him putting the brakes on her. 'That's a good idea, darling, you must be feeling better.'

'I can hear the disapproval in your voice, but I am feeling better and it's ridiculous for an intelligent woman of my years with my professional qualifications not to be using them.'

'Of course. I quite agree. But Sylvia's cut down her hours. How will you cope?'

Caroline said, 'I wouldn't be full time, not like I was when the twins first went to playgroup. Probably just filling in for sickness and the like.'

'Well, that might be different then. You could do, say, three full days.

23

'Well, I haven't got a position yet so we'll wait and see.'

'Are you sure? You've been so ill.' He reached across the table and took hold of her hand. 'I've only just got my confidence back about the chances of your survival. It has been a dreadfully challenging time for my faith, your illness.'

Caroline gripped his hand. 'I know, darling, I know. But I am well and, touch wood, I'm definitely here to stay. OK?'

'And the children, they haven't been the easiest of offspring, have they? Will you manage, do you think?'

'They take after their father, don't they?'

Peter pretended to scowl. 'Hey, less of that!'

Caroline laughed. 'Well, they do. Alex is so like you in his ways, and Beth just follows whatever he does. When I think of your stories about what you got up to when you were a boy, he's going to be just like that.'

Peter answered her abruptly. 'I would have preferred it if you'd spoken with me first, before you decided.'

'What?'

'Going back into practice.'

'What do you mean? I've just told you now. You knew what I would be doing. I should have gone back long ago. How long have I had off? A year? No, more than that. It's ridiculous.'

'No, it isn't. You don't have to work. If you want to be at home then at home you will be. I love it. You being at home.'

Caroline went to stand behind his chair and put her arms around his shoulders resting her cheek on his. 'Peter! I know you do, but there isn't enough for me to do.'

'There is, now Sylvia is doing fewer hours.'

'The children don't need me like they did. Not like when they were tiny.'

'I see. You've exhausted the mother bit so now you can wander off footloose and fancy free.'

Caroline, shocked by his attitude, drew away from him. 'That is absolutely uncalled for and quite untrue. You've upset me.'

Peter stood up and went to look out of the window.

'I beg your pardon. I shouldn't have said that. I'm ashamed of myself.'

'You should say it if that's how you feel.'

'I don't, not really. But I hate your preoccupation when you're working. You bring your problems home and I feel shut out.'

Mockingly, with half a smile on her face, Caroline answered, 'Oh dear! Poor little boy! Not got my full attention. Oh dear!'

Still looking out of the window Peter said, 'I suppose in part it's this old-fashioned idea that as the man of the house I should be the one earning the money. When you're in practice you earn far, far more than I do and could ever hope to do and it hurts, which is ridiculous but true. It kind of rankles. But I'm sorry for what I said.'

'And so you should be. If I want to work, I shall. I find it so *satisfying*, don't you see? You have a brain, you know how stultifying it can be not using it. Why do you think you do so much study and reading and writing articles for the papers? You're really a very scholarly man. The congregation hear only the tip of the iceberg of your learning. Well, it's the same for me, I need to use *my* brain too. And this business about the money. Your private income boosts your stipend enormously and we agreed when we married that your remuneration by no means equated with what you have to do, and that we wouldn't use it as a yardstick. Here you are doing that very thing.'

He didn't reply. Caroline went to stand behind him. She laid her head against his back and put her arms around him again. 'We musn't argue about this. I love you dearly. I love the children to bits. But I just need that something more to make life really worthwhile. And don't worry about my health. I'm fine and I wouldn't go back if I didn't feel up to it.'

'But before when you worked, the children were so distressed . . . '

'I know, darling, I know. But they're older now and they understand better. But I'll give you the promise I gave you before. If they get upset I shall stop working. Right? They come first. So do you, for that matter. Can three people come first?'

Peter turned to face her. 'I want only the best for all the ones I love. I love you, so very much.' He looked her full in the face, adoring her fine creamy skin, the long straight nose, the deep brown depths of her eyes, and the way her dark hair curled almost childlike around her face. He pulled her close to him, bent his head and kissed her. A kiss which turned into a paroxysm of tiny kisses around her mouth, and then her throat. His eagerness for her was overwhelming.

'Peter! We musn't! Wait till we've eaten our pudding and I've cleared away.' Caroline tried to push him away but he had her held in a firm grip. 'Please! We can't come down in the morning to the kitchen in a mess. Sylvia will be absolutely appalled and will wonder what we've been up to. Please!'

Abruptly he released her. 'No, you're right.

I'm sorry. Please forgive me. I beg your pardon.'

'Oh God! We have got our wires crossed. You haven't to apologise to me for wanting me! Right now *I* want *you*! It's just the timing that's wrong. Hey!' Caroline reached up to kiss his cheek. 'Am I forgiven?'

'For wanting to clear up in the kitchen?'

'No! Do I go back to work with your blessing?'

Resignedly Peter acceded the point. 'Of course you should go back to work if that's what you want. You don't need my permission to do as you choose. I'm not going to turn sulky about it. You wouldn't be you if you didn't want to go back to doctoring.'

'Exactly.'

'Yes, exactly so.'

Caroline thought she detected a sigh. She ignored it and cleared the table, then came back from the kitchen carrying a strawberry gâteau.

Peter's eyes lit up. 'That looks fabulous! Did you make it?'

'Of course. We'll have some now and then the children can help us finish it off tomorrow.'

As he finished the last mouthful Peter laid down his spoon and fork and sighed. 'That was brilliant. Superb. Let's do without the coffee. We'll clear up and then I'm taking you to bed.'

Peter left the dining room carrying the pudding plates and she stood gazing out of the window, listening to him stacking the dishwasher. However much he disliked it, she was going back, but she wouldn't let him suffer. He of all men needed support, because of the relentless, unrewarding, lifelong task he had undertaken when he was ordained. He deserved all her love.

Caroline carried their unused coffee cups into the kitchen. Peter turned to look at her. 'That was a lovely meal. It's fun eating with the children, but this meal on our own on Sundays is very pleasant.'

'Indeed it is.' There was a pause and then she said. 'You are right.'

'About the meal, you mean?'

'No, about me having to be circumspect.'

'Ah!'

'Sorry I let it happen. But he is fun.'

'He is. Great fun.'

'But I will be careful. Will this dish fit in the dishwasher or shall I wash it in the sink?'

'Leave it to soak. The cat flap's open, the back door is locked. Everything is shipshape and Bristol fashion and now we're going to bed.'

By the time Caroline had finished in the

bathroom, having let Peter take first turn while she made sure the children were nicely tucked up and she had indulged herself remembering how once she'd longed to have children in bedrooms to check on before she went to bed, and how she wished she had more than she had, Peter was already sitting up in bed. As she walked towards him he swung his legs out to sit on the edge and began unbuttoning her shirt.

'I promise I won't let work get in the way of . . . damn it!' Caroline stood between his knees and pulled him close and kissed his mouth deeply and pleasurably, adoring his taste and the sharp, fresh smell of the soap he'd used. Heart and soul, mind and body she loved him. 'I love you so very much. I wouldn't willingly do anything to harm you and yours.'

'And I love you. Every single inch of your body, every single inch of your mind. Every single inch of whatever it is that's you, I love.'

By this time her shirt was off and he was unzipping her skirt. She kissed the top of his head. 'Somehow, every single centimetre wouldn't sound nearly so passionate and meaningful, would it?'

Peter pulled at her skirt. 'Wriggle out of it. That's it. Whoever invented tights?'

'A nun?'

'I'm sure stockings were much more fun. Just think of me undoing those lacy suspenders! One by one.'

'Gladly.' She helped him finish undressing her. He got back into bed, lifted the duvet for her and she slid under it and lay beside him. She relaxed against his naked body, enjoying the gentle exploratory touch of his fingers, and feeling amazed yet again that he never failed to create this wondrous sensation in her. She grinned and said, 'Peter?'

'Mmmmm?'

'I'm glad it was you I married, because I find your vigorous sexual appetite so gloriously satisfying.'

2

On Mondays Peter always went to Penny Fawcett, so it was Caroline who answered the telephone in his study when it rang just before half-past nine.

'Good morning, Turnham Malpas Rectory, Caroline Harris speaking.'

'It's me, Harriet. I'm in a hurry. What night are you free this week?'

'I'll check the parish diary. Hold on.' She gripped the receiver between her jaw and her shoulder and took a lopsided view of Peter's diary. 'By the looks of it, unless something comes up today, Peter's only free night is Wednesday. Why?'

'Wednesday it is. I'm having a dinner party. Will you come?'

'Love to!'

'Eight for eight-thirty?'

'Lovely. Nothing special is it, not birthday or anything?'

'No, just for fun. See you.'

Caroline put down the receiver. Dinner party. Lovely. Just what she needed. What should she wear? Harriet and Jimbo had seen just about everything she had. Should she?

. . . Yes, she would.

Sylvia was in the kitchen filling the washing machine with bed linen.

'We've had an invitation to dinner from Harriet and Jimbo. On Wednesday. Will you be able to sit in for us?'

'Delighted. It's ages since you went out to enjoy yourselves. What time?'

'Eight o'clock.'

'Fine. You won't mind if Willie comes too?'

'Of course not. I'm off into Culworth this morning. Is there anything you need?'

'Nothing I need, but you did say you'd see about some new sheets for the children's beds.'

'I did. I'll get those while I'm there. I shan't be back for lunch but I shall be home before you leave.'

'That's lovely. Have a good time, enjoy yourself. You could do with a change.'

'I'm looking dreary, am I?'

Sylvia contemplated Caroline. She looked her up and down, especially at her face, her lovely grey eyes taking in every contour. 'You're looking so well, so wonderfully well. But people your age need to be in the swing of things, and what with caring for the Rector and those two lovely holy terrors of yours and all the things you do for the church, you do get bogged down with good deeds. So go swing a loose leg and enjoy yourself. I'll answer the phone and things.'

'Thanks, Sylvia. I do appreciate all you do for us. How we would have managed without you when the twins first came I do not know.'

Sylvia switched on the machine and, with her face turned away from Caroline so she wouldn't see the tears beginning to rise in her eyes, ordered her off the premises quick smart.

Caroline took her bag from the hall cupboard, checked she had her car keys and her credit cards, and left by the back door to get her car out of the garage.

Driving to Culworth was the easy bit, parking when she got there was a whole different ball game. A huge new car park had been provided by the council a matter of only a year ago, but already it wasn't big enough to cope. Eventually she found a space in the station car park.

Culworth wasn't exactly a metropolis as far as fashion shopping was concerned, but there were a couple of dress shops still calling themselves 'boutiques' which she favoured, one in the market square and the other in Abbey Close.

Coming to the market square she tried that boutique first. Madame Marie-Claire could find nothing to suit her. Caroline left amidst a hail of apologies.

The other boutique, named 'Veronique', at least gave Caroline a choice. In the curtained cubicle with its gilt chair and wall-to-wall mirrors Caroline tried six dresses. One was red and close fitting and up-to-the-minute and outrageous. She remembered another red dress, not hers but someone else's, worn in defiance at a dinner party at Harriet's many moons ago, when she, Caroline, sick with longing to have Peter's children had offered him a divorce when they got home. The black? Too severe. The green? Bilious. The blue? Too safe. The other black? Too matronly. Silvery grey? Didn't suit her mood.

'Look, Veronica, I like this red the best, but I've got to have time to think about it. I shall be back, because I must have something new to wear, but it is a bit daring, isn't it, for me?'

'Maybe it's right for your mood, though. Whatever you've purchased here in the past has been elegant but cautious. But this . . . this says something, doesn't it?' She held the slim red dress up in front of her and swirled it around and made it look as though it was doing a tango all by itself.

'It does. And that's the trouble. Dare I?'

'The colour is very flattering, your dark hair and eyes, you know. If you were fair like your daughter then I would say no because it would obliterate you. But this . . . oh la la!'

Caroline loved it. 'I'll go have lunch and then I'll come back. Is that all right? Do you mind, keeping it on one side for me?'

'Not at all, for a valued customer like you, Dr Harris, anything is possible.'

'I'll pop into the Belfry for lunch and have a think.'

At twelve-thirty the Belfry Restaurant was rapidly filling up. A waitress signalled an empty table in the corner by the window. She wended her way between the tables, took off her jacket, hung it on the back of her chair and sat down facing the crowded room. She remembered sitting here at this very table when she'd tried to tell Peter she had cancer and realised she couldn't find the words. The menu didn't seem to have changed much. A shadow fell across it and she looked up ready to apologise to the waitress because she hadn't yet made up her mind. But it wasn't the waitress, it was Hugo Maude.

'It is Caroline, isn't it? What an amazing coincidence. I decided to come out this morning to get out of Jimbo and Harriet's hair for a while and they suggested here for a quiet lunch. They didn't say I should find you lunching here. May I?' He put his hand on the back of the other chair and raised his eyebrows at her.

'Of course.'

'Do you often eat lunch alone?'

'I can't remember the last time I had lunch alone in Culworth. I came in to . . . '

'Yes?'

'Have a change of scene.'

Hugo put his head to one side and studied her. 'And why not? Have you ordered?'

'No, not yet.'

'I'm having the lamb cutlets. I perused the menu in the window before I decided to come in.'

'I will too, then. Are you enjoying your convalescing?'

Hugo's face became bleak. 'I need applause, you know. Pathetic, isn't it? A grown man. I miss it very seriously indeed. It kind of feeds me.'

'It's applause you deserve, according to Peter. He saw you in *Macbeth* some years ago. He thought you were brilliant.'

'Peter? Who's Peter?'

'My husband.'

'Not the Rector?' Caroline nodded. 'Amazing. He has real presence, hasn't he? He should have been on the stage.'

'You're joking. The only place he wants to be is where he is. In the pulpit.'

'Truly amazing. But you've no children?'

'We have two, a boy and a girl.'

The waitress came and Hugo ordered for the two of them. 'Wine also?'

'No thanks. I'm driving.'

'No wine, then. Mineral water, please.' He smiled at the young waitress and she must have found it devastating for she blushed to the roots of her hair.

Caroline couldn't resist taunting him. 'You really are a charmer, aren't you? Do you do it deliberately?'

Hugo looked appalled. 'Of course not. I'm just naturally charming. But what about you? I find you very interesting.'

'How can you? You don't know me.'

'But I'm very sensitive to the people I meet. It's all part of being an actor. We have to get into the characters we play and the habit somehow creeps into real life. I can *feel* people's auras, and yours is reaching out to me. How did you come by the children?'

'What do you mean?'

'Well, I sense they're not yours. The emphatic way you replied and the slight hesitation as you chose your words.'

Caroline, avoiding his glance, said quietly, 'No, they're not mine.'

'Ah! Sorry. Obviously I've touched on a sore point. You'd feel better if you accepted it, welcomed the situation, faced up to it instead of covering up about it. It happens all the time, people adopting children, you know. But there's something different about this, isn't there? I can't quite put my finger on what it is, but you're shielding someone, aren't you?'

'I think you'd better eat both our lamb cutlets because I don't want mine. I think you're behaviour is quite insufferably rude to someone you've only just met. You must think that your fame gives you *carte blanche* to offend, *carte blanche* to ride roughshod over people's feelings. Well, you're not riding roughshod over mine, thank you. I'll pay my half on the way out.' Caroline gathered her things together and rose from her chair, almost blind with rage.

Hugo rose too and held out a restraining hand. 'Please, please accept my apologies. I'm so sorry. Believe me, I really am.'

'Too late, I'm afraid.' Her anger infuriated her. How could she be so foolish as to make such an undignified exit from such a public place. That was twice now that he'd made her feel a fool. But he'd cut right to the core of her, for she was shielding Peter, let there be no mistake about that.

She strode lunchless into 'Veronique' and bought the red dress without even trying it on again.

'You'll love wearing it,' Veronica said.

'You're right, I shall.'

After a great deal of deliberation Caroline bought an elaborate Indian silver necklace in the ethnic shop at the corner of Deansgate and a lipstick in Boots, tried on several pairs of sandals hoping to find a pair suited to her new dress, but didn't, and went home to Peter.

She put her car away and entered the Rectory through the back door. One glance at the clock told her that Sylvia would already have left but that she still had half an hour before she collected the children from school.

Caroline dumped her purchases on the kitchen table and couldn't resist another look at the dress. She flicked it out of the carrier and held it in front of her. Her conclusion was that she must have had a brainstorm. What was she thinking, buying a dress like this? She would look a complete idiot wearing it at a dinner party in the country. Caroline flung it down on the table. She heard laughter coming from the study and went to stand in the hall to hear better.

It was Hugo talking to Peter. She hoped he

wasn't using his amateur psychoanalysis on Peter. Better take the bull by the horns.

As she opened the study door she said, 'I thought I heard a voice I recognised.'

'Hello, darling, had a good day? Hugo's called to return your jacket, you left it in the restaurant.'

'Oh! Thank you. I hadn't realised. Thank you very much.'

Hugo bowed slightly. 'Not at all, my pleasure.' A silence fell.

Caroline filled it by offering to make tea before she went to meet the children.

Hugo refused. Peter accepted.

'I'll go make one, then. Won't be long.'

She could hear Peter seeing Hugo out and heaved a sigh of relief.

Peter came in the kitchen for his tea. 'You know he really is very pleasant. Considering his fame, he is a very modest chap, doesn't push it in your face like some would.' He saw her making a sandwich. 'That's not for me, is it?'

'No. It's for me.'

'I thought you'd had lunch with Hugo.'

'No, I walked out.'

'Walked out? Why?' He saw her shopping on the table. 'That a new dress? It looks extremely eyecatching.'

'It is. I walked out because he got me very

angry and I'm not telling you why.'

'Oh, I see. I won't ask, then.'

'No, don't. Here's your tea. I'll move my shopping.'

Caroline devoured her sandwich with one eye on the clock.

Peter drank his tea. 'I'll collect the children, if you like.'

'Thanks. We've been invited to Harriet's on Wednesday. I checked the parish diary, you're free and Sylvia's promised to sit in.'

'Oh good, I shall look forward to that.'

'Yes, I expect you shall.'

'Shall I be taking you in that dress?'

'You shall. If I dare to wear it. Not quite the thing for a Rector's wife, is it, do you think?'

Peter heard the challenge in her voice. 'I don't see why not.'

'Oh good. Because I'm wearing it, and damn the lot of them.'

'My darling girl! What lot?'

'Your parishioners. Your prim, narrow-minded, gossiping, trouble-making parishioners, that's who.'

'What's brought this on? It's not like you to be so miserable. We'll talk about it, shall we, when the children are in bed?'

'We won't, you've a meeting.'

Peter stood up. 'Must go get the children.

42

So I have. Damn meetings. Well, tonight then, when I get back.'

'Perhaps.'

★   ★   ★

Wednesday evening came round all too quickly. Sylvia had admired the dress, though privately she thought it unsuitable for a Rector's wife, but it appeared to be something Caroline needed and as far as Sylvia was concerned if Dr Harris wanted to wear it, it was all right by her. When she saw her actually wearing it Sylvia was very surprised, it was even more out of character than she had first thought. But the Rector seemed pleased with it, so it must be all right. 'Have a good time! Forget everything and just enjoy yourselves!'

When Caroline and Peter left the Rectory to walk to Harriet's they met a total of four villagers on their way. They all greeted them with something just short of surprise.

'Evening, Rector. Evening, Dr Harris.' This from Anne Parkin who typed for the parish.

'Good evening, Caroline! How lovely you look.' This from Muriel who was popping round with a cake for her new neighbour. 'Enjoy yourselves.'

Barry Jones heading for the pub gave

Caroline a thumbs up, his face twitching with a grin. 'Good evening, Rector. Dr Harris. Nice evening!'

Jimmy also heading towards the pub raised his cap and at the same time eyed Caroline from head to toe. He grinned and commented, 'Going somewhere smart, eh? Wish I was thirty years younger! You're a lucky man, Rector.'

'I am. You're right.'

Peter and Caroline were the last to arrive. Gathered in the sitting room when they went in were Gilbert and Louise Johns, Craddock Fitch, Jimbo's mother, and Liz and Neville Neal. Their drinks were being replenished by Jimbo.

He broke off to greet the two of them and said 'Wow!!' when he saw Caroline's dress. 'Give us a twirl! Wonderful! Quite wonderful. Harriet will be jealous. What will you have to drink?'

'Vodka and orange, please. You like it then?'

'Like it? I should say.'

Peter said, 'So do I. It's revealed a whole new side of my wife, has this dress. I'm beginning to feel old-fashioned.'

'Well, you're not darling, you're just right. Thanks, Jimbo.' Caroline took her drink and went off to speak with everyone. Grandmama was barely civil, but Craddock Fitch made a great fuss of her and made her laugh which she badly needed.

Harriet came in to say dinner was almost on the table and where was Hugo?

'Not down yet.'

'Go give him a call, Jimbo. You know what he's like.'

'I'll just finish in the drinks department and then I will.'

Harriet sorted them out as to where they should sit and Caroline found herself between Gilbert and a vacant chair which she presumed was meant for Hugo. Trust Harriet to place him next to her. She was determined not to let him get under her skin. Never again. She would behave as if their contretemps in the restaurant had never happened.

Just before Harriet served the vichyssoise Hugo came in.

'So sorry. Am I late? I fell asleep by mistake.' It wasn't only Caroline who was charmed by his smile. She noticed Louise go gently pink and despite her misgivings about him Grandmama succumbed too.

Jimbo did the introductions. 'This is Hugo Maude, who requires no introduction to you. My mother you already know, this here is Louise, sitting next to Caroline is her husband Gilbert, county archaeologist and church choir master, this delightful creature is Liz Neal, wife of Neville Neal, right here, Neville is an accountant and the church treasurer, and of course you've met Peter, and last but not least Mr Fitch the owner of the Big House you glimpsed between the trees yesterday.'

Hugo went around the table shaking hands and kissing as he thought appropriate. Caroline's hand got a small squeeze and she received a kiss on her cheek too.

Jimbo and Harriet were practised hosts, the food delicious, and the evening went by in the most enjoyable way. There was plenty of laughter and Hugo provided that extra bit of zest needed when it was a dinner party where everyone knew everyone else and the conversation might have become moribund. He told some splendid theatrical stories which everyone except Grandmama enjoyed. She was occupied casting scathing glances at Caroline, the last of which Peter had intercepted. Then it was Grandmama's turn to grow pink, because Peter, who could do no wrong in her eyes, gave her one of his sad smiles. Well, if he didn't mind Caroline dressing as though she was out to catch a man then who was she to complain. But that gown really was an eye stopper, not at all suitable for someone in her position. What was it Harriet was saying, she'd missed that. She watched her spoon some more raspberries into her mouth and heard her mumble, 'Don't you think it would be a good idea? In all the years we've been here we've never done a play. Have we?'

An energetic burst of conversation answered her query. Peter's powerful voice overrode everyone else's and they all stopped speaking and listened to what he had to say. 'I think it would be an excellent idea. It might be the beginning of the Turnham Malpas Amateur Dramatic Society. We have the stage in the Church Hall, we have the lighting, it's all yours for the asking. There's hardly ever been a show of any kind put on except the Gang Show each year.'

Harriet said, 'Hands up all the people who would be willing to take part.'

Grandmama refrained from volunteering and so did Mr Fitch. Another notable exception was Louise.

Caroline said, 'Well, the baby is very young. I can understand you not wanting to be in a play, it takes so much time rehearsing and things.'

Gilbert answered for her. 'It's not that. Well, it is in a way. We're expecting another baby, you see.'

Grandmama was scandalised. 'Another

47

one. Good heavens, you've only just got one.'

'Congratulations!'

'That's wonderful.'

'You must be pleased.'

'Oh we are. Gilbert wants four.'

'Four! Good heavens. Does your mother know?' Grandmama downed the last of her wine and signalled to Jimbo she needed a refill.

The conversation broke up for a moment and it took Harriet some time to get it back to the play. 'I did think we might ask . . . ' she nodded her head in Hugo's direction. 'How about it, Hugo?'

He'd been preoccupied entertaining Caroline and took a moment to realise he was being addressed. 'How about what?'

'How about helping us with the play? Directing it even? What say you?'

'Me? It can't be done in a fortnight, you know, and I wouldn't want to outstay my welcome.'

Jimbo charitably suggested that if he was helping with a village play then he wouldn't be outstaying his welcome. He could stay as long as it took.

Harriet, poised on the brink of victory, beamed at him. 'Well? Say yes. We'd be so proud to have you on board.'

'What play would you want to do?'

Suggestions flooded out across the dining table. 'Blithe Spirit', 'Absurd Person Singular', 'Arsenic and Old Lace', 'Noises Off', 'The Odd Couple'. Ideas ebbed and flowed.

'Well . . . what do you think?' Jimbo asked Hugo.

'Yes, yes, mmmmm, I'll have to think about it. If I say yes can I be leading man and producer?'

'If you wish. Why not?'

'We haven't asked you to do something which is kind of not the thing for a famous actor to do, have we? I mean, we wouldn't want to put a spanner in the works or anything.' Caroline smiled at him.

Hugo smiled back and for a moment the conversation came to a standstill. Caroline recollected herself and picked up her glass of wine intending to take a sip, but Hugo took it from her, held on to her hand and said, 'My dear Caroline, how thoughtful of you to consider me.'

Grandmama cleared her throat loudly and it broke the moment.

Hugo raised his glass to them all, drank from it, put it down and began speaking. 'It would be wonderful to do something just for fun. I don't mean to diminish the idea by making it sound as though I wouldn't be taking it seriously because I would, take it

49

seriously, I mean. But just for once to work at something which didn't demand high profile action on my part would be wonderful. After all it isn't as if the whole world is going to know, not like they do when it's Stratford or the West End or something. We can just quietly get on with it can't we? Money isn't a problem . . . ?'

'It certainly isn't.' Mr Fitch shook his head. 'I should be proud to be associated with such an enterprise. Proud, yes very proud and I would like to commit myself here and now. I will underwrite whatever expenses you may incur. Yes, I certainly will. Who knows, this could be the beginning of something big.' He beamed at everyone around the table and accepted their thanks with delight. 'Now, Hugo, what do you think to that?'

'I am humbled by your generosity. Humbled indeed I am. We shan't be incurring massive expense, I would keep a stern eye on that side, believe me. Now, if I agreed to . . . '

'Something quite appalling has occurred to me.' Caroline's strangled voice drew their attention. 'How on earth can we expect Hugo, who has worked with most of the famous names on the British stage, how can we expect him to work with *us*, a load of complete amateurs? What presumption. We ought to be ashamed of ourselves even thinking of it. I'm sorry, so very sorry that we've put you in such an embarrassing position. Please accept our apologies. We all got carried away.'

A deathly silence greeted her outburst. Hugo was the first to break the deadlock. Very quietly he said, 'Please believe me when I say I would be honoured to work with you all. This business of the virus, I did have a virus certainly but it was exacerbated by the fact that I was also having a complete nervous collapse brought on by overwork. This rest I'm having, the media believe it to be because of the virus, which it is but also it's because I have run out of steam. After years of working like a maniac it is very difficult for me to do *nothing*, but I daren't, not yet, go back on the professional stage because it could be the end of not only me as an actor but the end of *me*. Producing this play would be heaven. You'd all be helping me to resuscitate myself. The decision is yours, but I hope you say you will.'

Jimbo raised his glass and toasted Hugo. 'Thank you for being so frank with us. Neither Harriet nor I had any idea how ill you have been. If we can help in any way then we will, and we'd all be honoured and privileged to work with you.'

'Coffee. I think I'll get the coffee. Anyone prefer tea?' They all wanted coffee. With

Caroline's help Harriet swiftly cleared away the pudding and retreated to the kitchen to attend to the coffee making.

Harriet banged about making the coffee saying as she worked, 'God! that was awful. I'd no idea.'

'Awfully brave of him to admit to it, don't you think? I feel dreadful that I forced him into having to come out with it.'

'You musn't, you did right to bring us all up short. It was presumptuous of me. I can't think what gave me the idea. I must have been mad. I've put the cups out on the side there. We just need the spoons, they're in the cupboard in the dining room.'

'You have to like him, don't you?'

Harriet grinned. 'He's a darling. An absolute darling, but don't tell Jimbo I said that. I'm amazed he's so agreeable to the whole idea.'

'It must be Hugo's charm.'

'Well, he's certainly got plenty of that, so just watch yourself.'

'Me? Come on, for heaven's sake.'

'Yes, you. Carry the sugar in, will you?'

★　★　★

Caroline and Peter fell into bed at midnight, having left the party well before the end in

52

deference to Sylvia and Willie.

'Peter, we can't both of us be in it, can we? That would be impossible, finding a sitter every time.'

'No, we can't, not both of us. But you could.'

'Do you think so?'

'Oh yes. With my height I'd be quite out of place on a stage.'

'Have you ever done anything on stage before?'

'Never, and I don't intend to.'

'Hugo says you have such presence he can't understand why you're not an actor.'

'Well, that's one bit of his amateur psychoanalysis that is way off the mark.'

'You think he does that too, do you?'

'Oh yes. He does. Has he been practising on you?'

She was on the brink of telling him about the incident in the restaurant but stopped herself just in time. 'I'm nearly asleep. It's the wine.'

Peter reached over to kiss her goodnight. 'God bless you.'

'And you.' Caroline was nowhere near ready for sleep but not for anything would she tell Peter what had made her leave the restaurant in such anger. Nor did she want to tell him how Hugo fascinated her. Nor that

Hugo wanted her to be his leading lady in whatever play he decided upon. Nor that she was looking forward to the rehearsals with more enthusiasm than she had felt about anything for a long time. Not since . . . well, she wouldn't think about cancer now. Not now. She would put that right at the back of her mind once and for all and get on with her life.

3

A note had been put through the Rectory letterbox addressed to Caroline. Peter picked it up and propped it against the vase on the hall table. He didn't recognise the writing, but then Caroline was always getting notes about one thing and another. When he heard her come back from seeing the children to school he called out, 'There's a note for you, darling, on the hall table.'

'Thanks.'

' She came into the study with it in her hand. He watched her tear it open.

'It's from Hugo. There's a meeting about the play on Monday night. You're free aren't you, if I remember rightly?'

'I am. In fact I've three evenings free next week. Almost unprecedented. Shall we have an evening out together while we have a chance?'

'Why not?'

'There's bound to be seats going at the Royal. Culworth isn't exactly at the forefront where theatre-going is concerned, is it?'

'There might be rehearsals planned. Let's

wait until Monday night before we book. Just in case.'

Peter patted his knee. 'Come and sit on my knee for a moment.' With his arms encircling her and her feet tucked into the kneehole of his desk he said, 'This play is really important to you, isn't it?'

'Yes, it is.'

'I'm glad. Something completely different from church meetings and children. There's a light come back into your eyes I haven't seen for a while.'

'Is there?'

'Yes. I hope, no, I *know* you'll do marvellously in this play. I shall be so proud of you. You must throw yourself into it and forget all about us. Go for it, you know. What an opportunity for you and for the village. He's such a generous man, doing this without a thought for his reputation.' They sat quietly for a few moments then he said, 'Love you, must get on.' He kissed her and tipped her gently off his knee.

Caroline had to make absolutely sure he didn't mind her being involved with the play.

'Of course not. Why should I mind?'

'You shouldn't, I suppose, I don't know why I asked. You hold me by the tightest of bonds and yet I am totally free.'

'Good. That's how it should be.'

'Do you feel free?'

He had to smile. 'No. I'm bound hand and foot to you. I'm not free and never will be, not even in the life hereafter.'

'Oh God! What a responsibility that is for me!'

'You musn't feel like that, because for me it's pure joy.'

She held his face between her hands, looked deeply into his eyes and briefly saw into his soul; he was alight with love for her. Right at this very moment, love like his she did not deserve. Why she didn't deserve it she didn't rightly know, but there were stirrings inside herself she couldn't analyse, and what was worse didn't want to analyse. It was as though she was at a crossroads, not knowing which way she would turn. Unable to find anything to say in reply to the look in his eyes, she tapped him lightly on his shoulder. 'I've some addresses to call at to collect jumble for Saturday, I'll be a while.'

'I'll have gone by the time you get back.'

After she'd left, Peter sat gazing out of the window. He watched Vera wave to Sylvia as she passed her house. Saw Jimmy setting out with Sykes at his heels. Caught sight of one of the weekenders in shorts and the briefest of tops setting off to the Store by the looks of the large shopping bag she was carrying. The busy life of the village went on, day in day out, despite the trials and tribulations which beset it. He thought about Hugo who could turn out to be a trial and a tribulation without doubt. Though what a lovely chap he was; friendly, caring, very charming, obviously in need of a respite from his demanding life and what better place was there than here in this village amongst friends? It was ridiculous to worry about the man, but somehow Caroline's enthusiasm for being in Hugo's play worried him.

Deep in his heart he became filled with a dark foreboding.

4

It had been quiet all evening in the Royal Oak until the crowd from the meeting came in. But then it was always quiet on Mondays in summer, a fact for which Georgie and Dicky were quite grateful. Summer weekends were hectic, good for business as Georgie always said with a laugh, but frantic nevertheless. Both she and Dicky were pleased with the way things had gone since Bryn left. In fact they were excessively pleased with themselves. The last eighteen months had been far harder work than Dicky could ever have contemplated, but with Jimbo Charter-Plackett teaching him how to keep the books and do the ordering and Bel helping at the bar when they were desperate, they were managing to keep their heads well and truly above water.

It was the first chance Dicky had had to get a close look at this newcomer they were all talking about. Georgie had swooned over his good looks and his reputation when she'd seen him in the Store, and he could see at first glance that she was right. He was handsome and not half.

'Good evening, mine host! Drinks all round on me. What shall you have?' Hugo looked at each in turn and they gave Dicky their orders. Georgie, unable to resist a chance to speak with such a famous figure, came to give Dicky a hand.

'Good evening, Mr Maude.'

'Mr Maude indeed! Hugo, please. I am amongst friends, surely. You are?'

'Georgie Fields.'

'Lucky man is Mr Fields, very lucky indeed.' He grinned at Dicky who let the mistake pass.

'Let's put two tables together then we can all sit round. Do you mind, Georgie?' Under the devastating beauty of his smile Georgie capitulated. Putting two tables together usually meant the group got very rowdy and she normally demurred if the idea was requested. It was the way Hugo's lips opened so generously, showing those immaculately straight teeth, with just one slightly crooked one which gave him the appearance of a boy, not a man.

'Of course. Dicky, give them a hand, will you?'

In no time at all Dicky had pushed two tables together and placed the tray of drinks in the middle. There was a lot of laughing and joking and sorting out of where to sit and

60

who's drink was which. In the middle of it Caroline appeared from the lavatories. Instantly Hugo stood up. His expressive face broke into a warm smile for her which was observed by almost everyone in the bar.

'Caroline! What would you like to drink?'

'Just an orange juice, please.' Harriet pulled up a chair next to her and patted the seat. 'Sit here, look.'

Caroline's orange juice arrived in front of her with a flourish. 'Thank you, Hugo, that's lovely.'

Harriet nudged her. 'Well? What do you think?'

'About what?'

'The play!'

'I think it's going to be brilliant. A wonderful choice.'

'So do I. And it's really rather thrilling doing what is its first real outing on the stage in its present form. If it gets eventually to the West End, well . . . '

'Exactly.' Caroline sipped her drink leaving the others to make all the going with the one liners and jokes. She was in a quandary of the first order. Reading through the script which Hugo had so painstakingly photocop- ied on Jimbo's copier she had been appalled at the intimacy between herself and Hugo demanded by the play. Not that she had to be

61

naked or anything like that, after all they couldn't go that far in a Church Hall. There were limits, even today. But they did have to kiss frequently, and mercifully the curtains closed on the scene where . . .

Heaven alone knew what the parish would think. If there was a moment to withdraw that moment was right now. This instant. Right now. She'd drop the bombshell immediately. As though in answer to her doubts there was a brief lull in the conversation. She put down her glass and said her piece.

'I'm afraid I'm going to have to withdraw, or take a different part. I think this part is beyond me. So, I'm sorry, but there we are.' There were gasps of disappointment all round the table.

Liz Neal said, 'Oh please, you're so right for the part, do do it, please.'

Neville agreed, 'You're so right for it, Caroline, you can't let us down.'

'I can and I will, I'm afraid.'

Hugo said loudly enough for the entire clientele to hear, 'Afraid. That's what the problem is. You've said far more than you know when you said, 'I can and I will, I'm afraid.' You are afraid, afraid of the challenge, afraid of Peter, afraid of what the parish will say. Maybe even afraid the bishop might hear what you've been up to. Tut tut.'

Caroline almost cringed at his words, they were so close to the truth.

Harriet was livid. 'Hugo! really. Be quiet, just shut up. If Caroline feels she can't do the part then that is that, it's not for you nor anyone else to query her motives.'

'Why not? This play could be the making of her.'

Harriet snorted. 'She doesn't need 'making'. Her life has been a complete success without your assistance. Now shut up and find yourself another leading lady.'

'I only meant the part would give her a chance to face up to herself.' He took Caroline's hand in his. 'My dear Caroline, I'm so sorry if I have upset you. I know I'm outspoken, and I apologise. You're not used to the cut and thrust of the theatrical world . . . '

Harriet interrupted. 'Not 'cut and thrust'. Bitchiness would be more accurate. You're making matters worse, so be quiet.'

'That's all right, Harriet, I can fight my own battles. I don't want to do this part because I . . . well I just can't do it.'

Hugo, seeing that bullying was getting him nowhere, changed his tactics. 'Go home and think about it. Sleep on it, as they say. You're so right for the part, you see. I can't see anyone else in it.' He addressed the other members of the cast. 'When she read tonight I knew it in my bones. You can all see her in the part, can't you?'

He looked at them each in turn and they half-heartedly agreed with him. 'You see. They all feel the same.'

Caroline said, 'I'll sleep on it then. Yes, I will. Give you a decision tomorrow. Though I'm quite sure Liz or Harriet would be just as good.'

'Oh no, we wouldn't.'

'I'll leave now, if you don't mind.' She stood up to go. 'Goodnight everyone.'

'Goodnight. Goodnight.'

Hugo followed her out. 'I'll see you to your door.'

'For heaven's sakes there's no need for that.'

'There is. I owe you an apology.'

'For what?'

'For trying to bully you. It wasn't fair.' He turned to face her and took hold of each of her hands. 'I know you will be great. You and me together, we'll make this play. I know it's only a small-time production, but that's no reason for not doing the best we can.'

'If that's all it is then I will think about it. I'll tell you in the morning. It's all very well you saying I ought to ignore my responsibilities to Peter and . . . the diocese and such, but they're there and I can't avoid them.'

By now they'd reached the rectory door. Caroline searched for her key. Hugo took it from her and put it in the lock.

'There. In you go. Sleep tight.' He gave her the lightest of kisses on her lips, stroked her arm comfortingly and pushed open the door for her.

★ ★ ★

'True as I'm 'ere I saw 'em. He'd been holding her hands and then he kissed her. I wouldn't be telling the truth if I said he'd made it last a while because he didn't, but he kissed her, right there under the Rectory lamp, plain as day for all to see.'

Sylvia sat up in bed appalled. 'Willie, are you sure? It's dark, you could have been mistaken.'

'I'm not. Shall I turn out the light?'

'Yes.' Sylvia snuggled up to Willie. 'I can't believe it of her, though when she went and bought that red dress I knew there was something afoot.'

'Holding her hands he was. Couldn't hear what they was saying but actions speak louder than words.'

'Oh I know. But there, let's be honest. You know what these actors are like, kissing and that. I bet they'd kiss someone who had the plague if it meant a part in a film or something.'

'Daresay they would, but what's he wanting from Dr Harris, that's what I'd like to know.'

'Willie! You don't think . . . '

'Maybe. Something to entertain himself with while he recups, or whatever they call it.'

'Whatever will the Rector have to say?'

'Whatever it is, he'd better say it quick before it's too late.'

'She's been in a funny mood for a while. That cancer business took her back and not half. It was the children, you see. She couldn't stand the thought of them being left without her, and her not seeing 'em growing up. She loves 'em that much.' Sylvia dug under the pillow for her handkerchief and wiped her eyes. 'And so do I, I love 'em too. I've never had a happier time in my life since I went to work there.'

''ere 'ere. What about since you married me?'

In the darkness Sylvia smiled. 'You're all part and parcel, aren't you? Went there to work, met you and that. It's all one and the same. If I suspect he's up to something more than producing a play I'll kill 'im. So help me I will. I'll kill 'im.'

'Sylvia!'

'I mean it, and I wouldn't care how many years I spent in prison, it'd be worth it.'

'Right scandal that'd be. What would you say when they asked you why you did it?'

Sylvia thought for a moment. 'I'd say it was a crime of passion, 'cos I'd fallen for 'im and he was ignoring me! It was jealousy, that's right, that was my motive. Jealousy.'

Willie was affronted. 'Sounds as though I'm not satisfying you as I should.'

'You're all right on that score, it's just a ruse so I don't have to tell the truth.'

'Which is?'

'I killed him to stop him ruining a very happy marriage. They love each other, at bottom. It's just that she's feeling trapped at the moment. If only . . . '

Willie rolled over and put his arms round her. 'Never mind, old love. It'll sort itself out.'

'Not easily, I'm afraid. You have to admit he's very appealing, very sexy and so good looking. There's something about his smile which is so attractive. He's kind of all male and all man and yet child all at the same time. It makes him very irresistible.'

'Any more of that and I'll be doing for 'im miself!'

'Oooo, Willie! You never would.'

'I would.'

★ ★ ★

'So, darling, what's this play called? Is it one I know or something Hugo's dreamt up?'

'Not dreamt up, no. It's a play written by a new playwright. It's been done once in Reading, or somewhere, and it flopped. Badly. It's been rejigged, bits cut out that didn't work, et cetera, and now Hugo is convinced the chap's got it right and he's dying to have a go with it. I read parts of it last night at the meeting and . . .'

'Yes?'

'Peter.'

'Yes?'

'Peter, it's quite . . . well, anyway, the part he wants me to take means a bit of kissing and that, and I wondered what you thought about it.'

'I see. What's it called?'

'*Dark Rapture.*'

'Mmmmm.'

'I know I'm being completely ridiculous and if I wasn't your wife it wouldn't matter two hoots really, but I am and that means complications and I've got to have you on my side before I say yes. Well, I did say yes and then I got cold feet last night in the bar and said I wouldn't do it.'

'What do the others think?'

'Hugo asked them and they kind of half-heartedly said yes, they wanted me to do it, so he took it as a definite yes, which it wasn't. You know how moral Harriet can get. She told him off.'

'Would you like to do it?'

Caroline nodded. 'Yes, I would. It feels like an affirmation that I'm taking life on again. I know it's only a village play, but . . . '

'Then do it, so long as there's nothing you have to do which will be against everything you've ever stood for. There's no nudity or anything, is there?'

'Oh no, of course not. There couldn't be in a Church Hall, could there? There's the opportunity for naked flouncing about and it probably would be done that way if it got to the West End, but we're not doing it like that. And we're cutting out the worst of the swearing because I insisted it couldn't be said on church premises. Perhaps I'm being overly careful, I don't know. Nowadays anything seems to go.'

'Can I see the script?'

Caroline hesitated for a moment and then said, 'I'll go get it.'

Peter spent an hour going through the script. He had certain misgivings but that was only when he read it from the point of view of Caroline in the leading part. Otherwise the play was good, and in a strange, convoluted way had a strong moral theme to it. In the end good triumphed.

Peter could hear Sylvia singing as she worked upstairs, he called out 'Sylvia, where's Caroline?'

'Gone to the Store, Rector, she won't be long. Is there anything I can do?'

'No, that's all right. I'll speak to her when she gets back.'

Peter had a while to wait before Caroline returned. When she'd entered the Store a sudden silence had fallen and she became aware of sidelong glances at her, which she found puzzling.

'Jimbo, is Harriet here?'

'In the kitchens. Go through.' He raised his straw hat to her as she slipped past the till. At least he was looking her straight in the face if no one else was.

The kitchens at the back of the Store had been made by opening up a series of small rooms to become two big kitchens. One for outside catering and one for making the confectionary and savoury products with which they filled the Store freezers. Caroline herself had been grateful for their homemade quality on more than one occasion when she'd been too busy to cook.

Harriet, wearing her white overalls and the

net cap she wore in deference to the hygiene regulations, was elbow deep in a huge mixing bowl.

'Hi! Come to see me? Won't be a minute. Go get a coffee from the machine and I'll be with you in a trice. There's a couple of chairs in the freezer room. Take a pew there.'

Caroline did as she was told, found the chairs and sat down to wait. She should have waited for Peter's opinion before she'd come to see Harriet, but she had the feeling that whatever he said she'd still agree to doing the play. Hang whatever anyone else thought, she'd a right to please herself for once.

'Right. I'll just pour mine into a cup. I hate these plastic cups but there's no alternative when it's for the customers — the washing up, you know. Here, let's pour yours into one too. There, that's better. Well?'

'Well?'

'Oh, I thought you'd come to tell me something.'

'Oh, I see. Yes. I've decided. I'm doing it.'

'Wow!! This coffee's hot! Jimbo must have just brewed it. I'm glad. Very glad. Really pleased. It's going to be so exciting.'

'Peter's reading the script.'

'Oh. Right. Is that a good idea?'

'We are doing it in the Church Hall, so . . .'

71

'Of course. Yes, you're right.'

'Hugo doesn't know, I haven't seen him yet.'

'He's not feeling too perky this morning so he's having a lie in.'

'Right.'

'Caroline, you are sure you're doing the right thing? I mean, don't say yes and then change your mind half way through, will you?'

'Of course not. I've decided I'm doing the play no matter what.'

Harriet looked at her, curiously surprised by her emphatic reply, said as though she was still convincing herself she was right to do it. 'You are sure, aren't you? I mean it's not . . . well it's not Hugo, is it, by any chance? I do know him for the absolute charmer he is.'

'I am almost forty, Harriet. For heaven's sake, a husband and two children whom I adore. I'm quite insulted really that you should think that I might be so stupid as to . . . '

'What?'

'Take a liking to him. I swear things will not get out of hand. Honestly.'

'OK then.' Harriet stood up. 'Sorry, got to get on, must go. Stay and finish your coffee.'

'Harriet, tell me, has Hugo ever been married?'

'No. But he's had dozens of female 'admirers', believe me. He's far too gorgeous to have escaped someone's clutches, don't you think?'

'Of course. Yes. Here, let me rinse the cups.'

'Nonsense, they can go in with the rest.' Uncharacteristically for Harriet she gave Caroline a kiss on her cheek. 'Take care. Take care.' And Caroline knew she wasn't referring to her crossing the road.

Mrs Jones was working in the little mail order office when Caroline walked by on her way out.

'Hello, Mrs Jones. How's things?'

'Fine, thanks. And you?'

'Fine, thanks. Lovely weather.'

'It is.' She snapped off the sticky tape on a parcel she was wrapping and called Caroline back. 'Dr Harris!'

Caroline came back and stood inside the doorway. 'Yes?'

'I wouldn't mind giving a hand with this play. Backstage and that, of course. Our Michelle would like to help, too. There'd be plenty of things to do besides acting, wouldn't there?'

'Of course. I'm sure there would be. I'll tell Hugo. He'll be delighted to find things for you to do.'

'I'm a dab hand with a needle and sewing machine if it's costumes.'

'Right. Well, it takes place in the nineteen twenties so I suppose, yes, we shall need a wardrobe mistress. I'll ask Hugo if that's all right, I'm sure he'll be pleased.'

'Then that's that.'

'Oh, but I think we should check with . . . '

'Michelle and me, we'll be in charge of costumes.'

'If it's all right with Hugo, yes, that will be lovely.'

'It's all right, is it, this play? I mean, it's not disgusting? I wouldn't want our Michelle to be involved if it was.'

'The Rector's reading it this very minute.'

Mrs Jones laughed. 'Oh, well, if he says yes then it's OK. My Barry's been roped in by Mr Fitch to do the scenery, did you know?'

'No, I didn't. He'll be excellent for that job, won't he?'

'Of course. And Mr Charter-P's put Pat in charge of refreshments, two nights you're doing it, eh?'

'Friday and Saturday.'

'Right. Well, I'll get to the library and I'll get some books out on costume. Charleston and that.'

'That sounds wonderful. We need all the help we can get.'

74

'If Mr Fitch has his way there'll be a play done at least once a year. And why not? Time we brightened ourselves up. All the talent we've got in this village, we could get famous.'

Caroline said she thought fame might be a bit too ambitious.

'Just wait till the press get onto it. The famous Hugo Maude, no less. And he's lovely, isn't he? Came in here the other morning and sat perched on that cupboard there chatting away as if we'd known each other all our lives. I told him things I've never mentioned to a living soul and he understood, truly understood how hard life can be.'

'He is very understanding.'

Mrs Jones gave her a piercing look. 'We'll have to mind our Ps and Qs, though. We're all taking a fancy to him, not just . . . '

'Yes?'

Rather lamely Mrs Jones said, 'Not just the young ones.' She neatly lined up the parcel she'd just sealed alongside the edge of the table, half started to speak again and then changed her mind, cleared her throat, picked up a list and began to study it.

Caroline wished her good morning and went through to the Store.

Dottie Foskett was standing, arms folded, propped against the chill counter listening to her cousin Vera Wright. 'So, just as I was closing the curtains — after all, you have to be careful these days even in a village, come to think of it, even more so in a village — when I sees 'em arriving at the Rectory door step. Believe it or believe it not he kissed her, and I don't mean a peck on the cheek like we've all started doing since we joined the Common Market — I mean, I blame the French for it — right on her *lips*. Then he stroked her arm and she went in.'

'But it was dark that time o' night, you couldn't see.'

Vera nodded her head. 'Oh yes I could, 'cos the light comes on when you stand by the door. Lutronic or something, it is. So I saw 'em right enough.'

Dottie gave her a nudge. 'You're only jealous. You wish it was you he was kissing!'

'Make a change from my Don, I must say. He's lovely though, isn't he? He's got a face to die for. That good looking I can understand anyone falling for 'im, I really can. And his voice all sexy and that. I fell for 'im when he was on telly in that saucy serial a while back. Saw 'im almost naked, not his vital parts o'course, but near enough. Strips real well he does.'

Dottie's reply was scathing. 'You're forgetting how old you are.'

76

'I can still dream, can't I?' She leaned towards Dottie and confidentially whispered, 'I'm thinking of volunteering me services, behind the scenes and that. Might get a chance for a quick cuddle if I play me cards right.'

Dottie chortled, and in a loud, scandalised voice she said, 'Vera! You are a one, you really are. Quick cuddle! It wouldn't be the likes of you he'd give a quick cuddle to.' Neither of them had noticed Caroline paying for her shopping at the till. 'From what you saw, any quick cuddles have already been spoken for!'

The two of them reeled with laughter. Caroline lifted her carrier from the counter, put her purse away and marched red-faced and embarrassed out of the Store. How dare they speak of her like that! Anyone would think she was some empty-headed teenager. What else could it be but a purely professional partnership? And she'd put her heart and soul into making a real fist of it. She'd show them.

5

Vera, having collected some cigarettes for an old gentleman at the nursing home, went to wait outside the Store for the bus to Penny Fawcett for her afternoon cleaning shift. She couldn't believe her good luck when only a minute after she'd arrived she saw Hugo heading up Stocks Row towards the Store. This could be her moment. Though her knees went to jelly and her tongue appeared to have stuck to her teeth she said, 'Good afternoon, Mr Maude.' She ran her tongue round her teeth to wet them again while she waited for him to reach her.

'I don't believe I've had the pleasure.' She found her hand clasped in his and as through a thick fog heard him say, 'Please, call me Hugo.'

'It's Vera Wright. I live opposite the Rectory with me husband Don and me grandson Rhett. He's a gardener up at the Big House.'

'Indeed. He works for Mr Fitch, then?'

'He does, and a harder taskmaster you couldn't hope to find.'

'A very generous benefactor though.'

'Oh yes. He is. He's footing the bill for your play, isn't he?'

'Not *my* play, my dear Vera . . . may I call you Vera?' Vera nodded. 'Not *my* play, *our* play.'

Melting before his charm Vera pulled herself together sufficiently to say, 'I was wondering about helping. Behind the scenes, o' course. Not on the stage. Amongst all my other jobs I'm in charge of the sewing where I work. I could help with anything like that.'

'We shall be needing help with the wardrobe. Look, we're having a meeting, just for half an hour, for people willing to help behind the scenes immediately before the first rehearsal on Friday. How about coming along to that? I'll listen to your ideas and we can . . . '

'My ideas? What ideas?'

Hugo explained about the play and it needing nineteen twenties' costumes.

'All straight up and down and no . . . yer know.' She shaped her hands over her ample bosom and instantly wished she'd hadn't drawn attention to it.

'Well, yes, that kind of thing.'

The bus ground to a halt in front of them.

'I've got to go,' she said. 'What time?'

'Seven o'clock. Church Hall. Friday.'

'Yer on.' Vera climbed aboard and showed

her weekly season ticket to the woman driver, who, as she stamped on the accelerator, asked her who her new boyfriend was.

'Jealous, are yer? I've just been taken on as his wardrobe mistress.'

Someone guffawed at the back of the bus. '*Bed* mistress'd be a sight more comfortable, Vera.' The bus was in uproar. Vera felt like crawling under the seat not sitting on it. Honestly, you couldn't have a decent friendship with anyone round here without they all thought you were going to bed together. That was the last thing she had in mind. Then she recollected the warmth of his hands as he'd held her own, the tenderness of his eyes and the way his hair grew in a widow's peak and the width of his proud forehead. A tremor ran down her spine. He really was gorgeous. Vera stared out at the passing countryside and pulled herself together. All those bloody sheets to put through the ironer today. And if that old bat in number seven did it in her bed again today she'd give her notice in. Well, perhaps not. She'd have a few days off sick instead. Anyhow, she'd got what she wanted, a chance to work behind the scenes.

★　★　★

At a quarter to seven on Friday evening Vera came downstairs ready for off. Don, who was finishing his tea and contemplating a good read of the paper before he went off to work, looked in amazement when he answered her remark that she was ready for off and could he clear the table when he'd finished.

'I thought you said you were going to a meeting at the Church Hall.'

'I am.'

'The last time you wore that suit was at our Brenda's wedding.'

'There's no point in it hanging in the wardrobe year after year. I might as well get me wear out of it.'

She went to stand in front of the living-room mirror.

'Yer 'air! Yer've had it done.'

'I know. Surprise surprise! He's looked at me!! I swear if I walked about naked yer wouldn't notice, because you never look at me. Not really look.'

She admired her hair, that mobile hairdresser who came twice a week to the village had done a good job, though she didn't expect it would stay like this for long, knowing her hair. This pink suit still looked smart. Well, if yer were wardrobe mistress yer had to let people know yer knew what yer were talking about. She'd show 'em. They'd all have a surprise.

'I look all right, then?'

'Yes, I've got to say you do. A bit of all right, you are. Definitely.'

Her delight at Don showing some interest in her braced her for the forthcoming challenge. She picked up her navy handbag which she'd already filled with notebook and pencil as well as her purse and the pink lipstick that matched her suit, slipped her feet into those excruciating shoes which had killed her all the way through Brenda's reception, and set off for the Church Hall.

Expecting that there would only be a small select band volunteering their help Vera had a shock when she opened the door to the Church Hall. At first sight it appeared that the entire village and then some had come to volunteer their services. The Jones family had arrived in its entirety, three generations of them, and it looked as though Mrs Jones meant business because she had some big books in a carrier bag and was about to put them on a table at the side. Then she spotted her Rhett. The cheeky little monkey! He'd said he was going out but never a word about coming to the meeting. Wait till she got a chance for a word. And there was Miss Parkin from Glebe Cottages, and Mrs Peel, well she needn't think Hugo would be wanting her to trill about on the church organ 'cos he wouldn't. Just behind her Rhett she spotted Kate from the school and Dottie too, heaven alone knew what contribution Dottie thought she'd be able to make. She had to stop counting. This was ridiculous. Anyhow, Hugo had said she was wardrobe mistress and that was exactly what she was going to be.

Despite the pinching of her shoes she strode masterfully across to where Mrs Jones and Hugo were looking at the books. One glance over their shoulders and she realised that things were being taken out of her hands.

'What's this?'

Hugo turned to speak to her. 'Vera! You've come. Look at these ideas Mrs Jones has for the costumes. Aren't they brilliant? It's the colours we shall have to be careful with you know, Mrs Jones. Remember that black and white Ascot scene in *My Fair Lady*? That was so effective. Utterly divine!'

'Black and white, is that what you want me to do?'

Vera bristled. 'I don't understand this. I thought *I* was in charge of the costumes? Wasn't that what you said?'

Hugo, recognising that someone who came armed with illustrations of just the styles he was after was a much surer bet than someone who'd come with nothing, drew upon his

83

considerable diplomatic skills.

'No, no. I merely used that to illustrate how important the contribution of the wardrobe mistress is. Mrs Jones, these designs are wonderful, now can I rely upon you and Vera here to source some materials, bring me snippets and we'll have a serious discussion next week about colours, et cetera? How about that, Vera?'

Disappointment flooded Vera's very bones and she could scarcely hold back her tears. One look from Mrs Jones' gimlet eyes, one glance at her triumphant posture, was enough. She drew back her handbag and swung it in Mrs Jones' direction. It missed, but caught Hugo on the shoulder. With the additional weight of the notepad inside it and rather a lot of loose change in her purse, it caused Hugo to stagger. He clutched at the table to save himself, and made one of the costume books slide off onto the floor and land noisily at Vera's feet.

Vera was devastated. 'Oh, Hugo! I'm so sorry. Look what you've done now, Mrs Jones. Look what you've made me do. It's all your fault, muscling in on my job.'

'It's not *your* job. It's not *my* job. I just brought these . . . '

'Well, you can stuff the job right where it hurts. I'm not working with you, not at any price. It's either me or you, not both. You're a bossy interfering old bag, that's what you are. Think you're something special, don't yer? Well yer not. You're like the rest of us . . . ordinary. I wanted this job and I bet you knew I did so you got them books on purpose to impress. You're a bitch.' She tapped Mrs Jones on her collar bone to emphasise her point.

'Well, really! All I've done is . . . '

'Ladies, please. Please. Let's come to some amicable arrangement, shall we? I think . . . '

But Vera wouldn't stay to listen to his pleas. She'd been made a fool of, and her distress was too much to bear. She kicked the book, twice, for good measure and then marched out with Mrs Jones' protests ringing in her ears.

'Well, Hugo, did you say she could be wardrobe mistress?'

'No, I didn't. I said she could come along to the meeting and give a hand, I never said she was it. That was her mistake. Somehow or other we've got to heal the breach, don't you know?' He put his head to one side and smiled at her, and Mrs Jones' heart melted. 'I'll sort something out. Don't you fret.' She rather boldly patted his arm. 'She can help me, be my chief assistant.'

'Good idea. Right, I'll start the meeting.'

Shattered by the unexpected violence his project had brought about he strode more purposefully than he felt to the stage, sprang up on to it, and stood in front of the curtains with his arms raised.

'Ladies and gentlemen! Thank you. Thank you.' They all stopped talking and turned to listen to him. 'I'm amazed and delighted at the number of people who have turned up to volunteer their services. I have a list here of the backstage people we shall need. As I'm producing as well as acting I shall need really reliable people as back-up. Hands up anyone at all who has experience of theatre work, either amateur or professional.'

Hugo rather suspected there would be no hands put up and he was right. In that case then, here goes, he thought.

'Scenery. Barry Jones. Any ideas for an assistant, Barry?'

'I wondered about Sir Ronald, he's a very practical chap.'

'Is he here?'

'No, but you could have a word tomorrow, he's at home at the moment.'

'Right.' Hugo made a note on the list on his clip board. 'Lighting?'

With one voice they all said, 'Willie.'

'Willie it is. Are you here, Willie?'

'I am, and yes I'm willing. Long time since

them lights was given a proper airing, but I'll do my best.'

Barry Jones gave Willie a verbal reference. 'You did wonders when we had that Flower Festival a few years back. Very subtle the lighting was. He'll do a good job, Hugo.'

'Willie. Lighting. Now, props. That means someone who knows every piece of furniture, every flower, every ornament, et cetera, needed for each and every scene, someone who can find all we need by begging borrowing or stealing — well, not literally, but you know what I mean. Any ideas?'

There was a silence and then a voice from the back piped up. 'I'll do that. I've finished my exams, be glad of something to do.' Dean Jones, Dean Duckett that was, waved a hand to everyone. 'If you'll tell me what you need.'

'Of course. You're . . . ?'

'Dean Jones.'

'Excellent. You're stage manager, then.' Hugo jotted down Dean's name and continued on down his list. 'Now, publicity. This means programmes, posters, tickets, advertising. Who have we got? Any offers?'

There was a brief silence and then Anne Parkin spoke. 'I'm quite good at lists and things. I'm not creative, but I could do publicity and printing and such. If that's all right.'

'Wonderful. Your name?' He leant towards her in the most endearing manner and cupped his hand to his ear.

'Anne Parkin.'

'Anne Parkin it is. Now. Next. Costume is Mrs Jones and Vera Wright.'

A voice at the back said, 'You'ope!'

'I can assure you it will be. A small contretemps, soon be ironed out. Now.'

'You'll have your work cut out sorting that little problem, believe me. How about it, Mrs Jones? Willing to let bygones be bygones?'

'You mind your own business, Jimmy Glover.'

'Mr Maude! I'm Sylvia Biggs. You'll need someone to make coffee and that when you have a break from rehearsing. How about me? Might not manage it every night, 'cos I may be needed at the Rectory. But I'd be glad to be involved, and I'd find a substitute when I couldn't.'

'You can have no idea what music that is to my ears. The cast rely deeply,' there was a lot of emphasis on the word 'deeply' and they all felt it in their bones, 'on cups of coffee to revive them. Absolutely essential. In fact the success of the play could be said to relate directly to the quality of the drinks provided during rehearsal! Wonderful, Sylvia.' He bunched his fingers and kissed them in

Sylvia's direction. 'I'll put your name down.'

Willie nudged Sylvia and mouthed, 'Why?'

Out of the corner of her mouth Sylvia said, 'To keep my eye on what's going on, of course.'

'He's embarrassed you.'

'No, he hasn't.'

'He has. I'll come every night as well. Keep an eye on you.'

'You daft thing, Willie Biggs.'

'He's got a sight too much charm 'as Mr Hugo Maude. Just 'ope he doesn't turn out to be Mr Hugo Fraud.'

Sylvia giggled. 'You're in top form tonight I must say. But I can see you're jealous.'

'I'm not. Have you done? Let's go.'

'In a minute. Let's wait for instructions.'

Hugo had completed his list and wanted to get on with the first rehearsal. 'Thank you very much, ladies and gentlemen. I'll be in touch with all backstage people within the next few days and have some in-depth discussions with each of you regarding duties, expenses, what's needed, et cetera. We haven't much time left to get the show on the road, but we will do it if we all put our shoulders to the wheel! Thank you so much everyone.' He pointed to Michelle Jones standing at the back with Dean. 'Got a small part for you if you fancy it.'

Michelle looked around, realised Hugo meant her, blushed bright red and pointed to herself saying, 'Me?'

'Yes, you. Fancy it? Stay for rehearsal if you do.'

'Yes, please.'

Hugo searched the crowd and pointed to Rhett Wright. 'Hi there! You in the green top and jeans. Yes, you. Fancy a part?'

Rhett nodded.

'Not a lot to learn but every part is vital to our success. Fancy it?'

'Right. Yes, I'll do it.' Rhett rubbed his hands together with delight. 'Great, just great.' Then he remembered his grandma and some of the gloss went off the evening. She'd never forgive him.

★ ★ ★

And she didn't. When Rhett got home, Don had gone to his night shift and his gran was sitting in front of the electric fire drinking a shandy. By the looks of the cans on the table it wasn't her first.

'Where've you been till this time?'

'Well, Gran, Hugo offered . . . '

'Shandy?'

'Thanks.' He waited till he'd sprung the can open and taken a drink before he

90

continued. 'Hugo's offered me a part. Just a little one, like, but it's a part.'

Vera lunged at him and missed the side of his head by a whisker.

'You traitor, you. You should've left when I did. I've never been so insulted in all my life. Never. That Mrs Jones. Since she took over the mail order at the Store she's thought herself a cut or two above the likes of you and me. With her 'Jimbo' this and her 'Jimbo' that. I can remember when she was only too glad to clean at the pub when her boys were all little. How low can you get? Cleaning at a pub. I could tell her a thing or two about her Kenny and Terry that'd make her toe nails curl up. They are disgusting.'

Rhett eagerly demanded 'Are they? What do they do then?'

Vera scowled at him. 'I'm not telling you.'

'I am eighteen, nearly nineteen.'

'So you may be. What's this part then? Not that I'm interested.'

'I'm Dr Harris' son, and Michelle's her daughter.'

'Michelle? Another feather in Mrs Jones' cap. Is there no end?'

'Here's the script. Look.'

Vera gave it a sideways glance. Her lips trembled and she blurted out, 'Just once in my life I thought I'd grab the chance to work with someone who had genius. Real genius. They're few and far between are people with genius, do you know that? Your grandad and me, we've grubbed along all our lives, struggling just to make ends meet, not improve ourselves, but to keep the wheels oiled. Then yer mum went off the rails and we got you.' She patted his arm apologetically. 'I don't mean we didn't want yer Rhett, because we did, you were such a good baby, but just when we thought we could start to make progress you came along and I had to give up me job. I 'aven't regretted one minute having yer, but yer did 'old us back. Yer mum promised us money every month but o' course, as yer can imagine, that lasted for about six months and then . . . yer know the rest.' She wiped her eyes and gazed at the imitation flames curling round the imitation coals on the fire.

Rhett said softly, 'I'm sorry, Gran.'

'Nothing for you to be sorry about, love. But when the idea came to me to be wardrobe mistress I knew I longed to be involved with something beautiful. D'yer know what I mean? Something special, something people would admire me for. I know exactly where I am in the pecking order in this village and it's bottom. Bottom. Even Pat Duckett that was, she used to be at our level, talking over the fence and moaning about 'aving no money and now look what's happened to 'er. A new husband, a grand big house, a car now and a right good job with the Charter-Plackett's catering service. And where am I? Still at the bottom of the pile. I could truthfully say I yearned for that job with the costumes.'

'Look, if it means that much to you, how about eating humble pie, apologising and getting stuck in. Hugo announced that you and Mrs Jones were doing the costumes together.'

Vera looked at him through her tears. 'Not Pygmalion likely. Yer see you make beautiful things all day long in that garden. Yer in touch with beauty, and I never am.'

'You've flowers in your garden.'

His answer was a shrug of his gran's shoulders. 'Say a few of your lines for me, love, will yer?'

Rhett said he wouldn't, he'd be too embarrassed.

'All right then.' Wistfully Vera went back to thinking about the dresses. 'They'll have lovely materials for them dresses, I could right fancy handling materials like that. Touching it and holding it soft like against yer cheek. Lovely. All pretty and beautiful. All beads and embroidery. And the colours, them illustrations in 'er books! All pastel colours, yer know. Peaches and silver greys and soft greens and turquoise. Wonderful! And having that lovely, lovely man saying how pleased he was with them. That would be great. Yer see Rhett, yer grandad's a good man, faithful and that, never a word out of place, but he lacks sparkle. Yes, sparkle. And after all these years, so do I. But making them costumes, that'd make me sparkle and not half.' She stared into the distance and Rhett saw such a lovely smile on her face, a smile like he couldn't remember seeing before. Vera sighed. 'Still, there yer go. Mrs Jones has got the job and good luck to her. Go get me slippers, Rhett, me feet are killing me.'

★　★　★

Mrs Jones popped into the Store the next morning to finish off some orders she hadn't had time to do the previous day. Jimbo handed her a coffee as she swept through. 'Thanks, Mrs Jones. That's what I like to see. Enthusiasm. I hear you've had a promotion.'

'Promotion?'

'Yes. Wardrobe mistress. Hidden talents, eh?' Jimbo smoothed his striped apron, red and white this morning, raised his straw boater to her and bowed.

94

'Don't know about promotion, but it caused a commotion. That Vera Wright. Huh! Thinking she could do the costumes. That's likely!'

'She's had a hard time has Vera. She needs a leg up, you know.'

Humbled, Mrs Jones continued on to the mail order office. While she sorted and checked and packed the orders, one to Bristol, another to Newcastle, two to Devon, and yet another and another, she pondered on what Jimbo had said. The uproar had not been her own fault, but wild horses wouldn't make her go to Vera and suggest she helped despite the quarrel. Not likely. Never. The orders finished, she marched them to the post office counter and handed them to Linda.

'There you are, Linda. Six. There's your list. OK?'

'Thanks.'

'I'm off now. Off to Culworth on the lunchtime bus. Got some materials to look at. I know just where to go.'

'Exciting, isn't it? If I was more free I'd have a go too. Just imagine acting with that wonderful man. He could butter my bread anytime!'

'Linda! He's full of charm but he's not like that. It's only good fun and part of his lovely nature.'

'Oh yes. That's not what I've heard.' She leaned her elbows on the counter and put her face close to the grill. 'On Monday night . . . '

An old man from Little Derehams elbowed Mrs Jones aside. 'Hurry up. I need my pension. I'm catching the lunchtime bus to Culworth.'

'All right. All right. Keep yer hair on.'

She served the angry pensioner and by the time they'd argued about her rubber stamp not being clear enough and whether or not she needed a new one and she'd do better if she didn't gossip so much, Mrs Jones had to leave to make sure she didn't miss the bus.

Rhett, who'd gone round to see her about his gran's disappointment, missed her. He knew he owed his gran a lot. Everything, if the truth be known, because he might as well not have a mother for all she cared. And some days that hurt. Now he'd missed Mrs Jones so his idea had fallen on stony ground. He thought over his conversation with his gran last night and how she'd revealed more of herself than she'd ever done before. He thought about beauty. She was right. He touched and saw beauty every working day. Flowers, plants, fruit trees, vines. The scent of them after the rain, the mingled pleasurable aromas he inhaled greedily when he opened the glasshouses first thing in the summer. The smell of soil freshly turned with his spade, the crumbly moist feel of it; the new paths he laid, feeling his way, making the patterns with the stones; the satisfaction of . . . Then it hit him: energising shock waves ran through him right to his toes. Of course. The stones. He'd repair the crazy paving at the back of Gran's cottage, extend it a bit here and there and buy her a little plastic table and chairs so she could sit out. There were those old pots at the back of the kitchen garden wall that Mr Fitch wanted rid of. Greenwood Stubbs would let him have those for nothing and he'd buy some plants and . . . His head full of ideas, he pedalled furiously up the drive to the Garden House to find Greenwood. This would be the surprise of his gran's life. He'd see to it that she had some beauty.

6

True to his word, Hugo went to see Sir Ronald Bissett. He rang the bell and waited. Lovely old cottage, thatched roof, roses around the door, the lifelong dream of thousands of town dwellers. A cottage in the country for himself? No, not quite his scene.

The door opened and Sheila Bissett was standing there beaming, dressed as though expecting visitors.

'Hugo Maude, you remember me? Good morning, Lady Bissett.'

'Do please call me Sheila. Everyone else does.'

'Sheila, then. Is your beloved in?'

Sheila asked, 'My beloved?'

'The renowned Ron. His name's been volunteered to help backstage with the play and I promised I'd come to see him this morning. Told he's a very practical chap.'

'Oh he is. He does all our DIY. Every bit. Come in. Come in. Do.'

'Thanks.' He meticulously wiped his feet. He knew Sheila would notice that and like him for it.

'Do sit down. I'll tell Ron you're here, he's

in the shed at the bottom of the garden.'

'You send him down there when you're fed up with him, do you?'

She was so flustered she didn't notice he was teasing. 'Oh no! Of course not. He's cleaning the mower. I won't be a moment. Coffee when I get back? It's not one of my mornings, but you're most welcome.'

'Why thank you, most kind.' He watched her open the french windows and trot down the garden. She lacked dress sense, she was too fat, she'd no *savoir faire* whatsoever, she had an almost pathetic desire to be liked, but there was something about her you couldn't help but be drawn to. An honesty and a simplicity he had to admire.

Sir Ron removed his garden shoes before he came in and Sheila opened up a copy of the *Daily Mirror*, placing it carefully in the easy chair before Ron sat down in it.

'You will excuse me, won't you? I'll leave you two to your men's talk while I make the coffee.' With a coy little nod of her head she disappeared from the sitting room.

'So, you're the Hugo Maude that's causing such a sensation.'

Hugo feigned surprise. 'Sensation?'

'Of course. Yes. They're all talking about you. Husbands as well as wives. There's a few husbands who are being told they're not

99

coming up to scratch, you see.'

'Oh dear. I hope I'm not causing any trouble.'

'All in good fun. Now what can I do for you?'

'Barry Jones is doing the scenery for the play, but really it's a two-handed job or even a three-handed one, and you were recommended as a very able assistant.'

'Me?'

'You. I do hope you'll say yes. We're running short on time, you see.'

'Well, now I don't see why not. I'd quite enjoy that and Barry's very easy to get on with. Yes, I will. Thank you for thinking of me.'

'Don't thank me, everyone agreed you'd be a good choice.'

'Right. I'm well pleased with the idea.'

'Barry and I had a long chat earlier today and he knows exactly what's needed. Mr Fitch has promised the wood and told Barry to buy whatever paints et cetera are needed, so it's plain sailing really. Just needs the time devoted to it and plenty of elbow grease.'

'Well, I've plenty of that. Turned this place inside out all by myself, you know. Took a while but I made it in the end. I'm well accustomed to public speaking but not acting, so backstage is all right by me.'

He appeared to Hugo to be flattered that he'd been asked and he wondered if the Bissetts weren't exactly accepted in Turnham Malpas.

Sheila came bustling in. 'Here we are, then. Coffee for three. I didn't get to the meeting, did you get plenty of helpers?'

'I did indeed. More than I needed. Do you know Mrs Peel?'

'Of course, she's the church organist. Very nice person she is, she's really blossomed since Peter came. You see, Mr Furbank that was the Rector before Peter, had no idea about music. But Peter is an organist himself, you know, so he knows how to get the best out of her.'

'I see. Well, she came up with the brilliant idea that we could have live music instead of canned for the overture and during the interval. She has a repertoire of the most unbelievably suitable music and she has a genuine nineteen twenties' dress and the piano's just been tuned, she tells me. So right where you expect a desert you find an oasis.' Sheila handed him his coffee and placed the sugar bowl and cream jug at his elbow on a small side table.

'Of course.'

Hugo helped himself to sugar. 'So wonderful

when gems like that fall into one's lap.'

'Indeed. I'm glad you got help like that. They're really very good in this village, but I expect it was your good looks and charm that carried the day.'

Hugo denied this by pursing his lips and waving a deprecating hand.

'Oh yes, it is, you can't fool me. I just wish there was something I was clever at that I could do to help.'

'But I believe there is. Flowers? Hey?'

Embarrassed, Sheila lowered her gaze. 'Someone's been telling tales out of school.'

'They have very justifiably too, I understand. Flower festivals and the like. Now, it means doing some research.'

'Research. Oh, I don't think I'm . . . '

'Oh yes, you are. Perfectly capable. The set is that of a country house in about 1921, not a large one but certainly an elegant one and I want flowers, two vases full, on stage to go on the grand piano.'

Sheila's eyebrows went up in amazement. 'A grand piano? Where are you going to get that from? In any case it would fill the stage and there'd be no room for the actors.'

'A baby grand, actually, from Mr Fitch's flat at the Big House.'

'My word, he certainly means business, doesn't he?'

'Oh yes. He does. No stone unturned. Back to the flowers. One vase a winter arrangement and the other a summer one. Now, how did they do flowers in country houses then? I know they weren't done like I saw them in church on Sunday, all thanks to you no doubt.' He reached across and patted her knee and she had to restrain herself from clasping his hand. 'And they certainly wouldn't be Japanese style. Ikebana, isn't it? So could you find out and arrange them for me? What do you say?'

'Well.' Sheila took a deep breath. 'Well, yes I'll have a try. Yes, I certainly will. Research, yes. Of course. I'm honoured that you thought of me.'

'To whom should I turn but to an expert.'

'Oh! Really! Hugo. You're too kind. How about the hall itself, shouldn't there be some in there?'

'Well, of course that would be wonderful if you have the time. Within reasonable limits Mr Fitch is paying all expenses, so keep your bills. The flowers in the hall must be in keeping. And very, very important, the vases themselves *must* look right too.'

'Oh yes, of course. I can see that. Authenticity. Research. Right. Well, I never expected this when I opened the door. How exciting! The ladies in the flower club will be most impressed. I shall ask you to sign my programme.'

'Well, there'll be an acknowledgement in there.'

Sheila, to whom an acknowledgement meant an announcement in the paper thanking people for their floral tributes at a funeral, looked puzzled.

'You know 'Flowers by Lady Sheila Bissett'.'

'Oh, right, I see.'

Hugo could tell how delighted she was and he was glad he'd asked her and glad she was on his side.

'Dr Harris is in the play, I hear.'

'Yes, she's playing the leading lady opposite me. Lovely lady to work with.'

'Oh, she is. I'm a great fan of hers. She's always so pleasant, so kind and she hasn't had it easy. No, not at all.'

'Really?' He knew he'd learn a lot if he played his cards right.

'No, she's had cancer recently but she seems to have got over that now. Then her parents were very badly injured in a road accident — touch and go for a while. Then she had all the trouble about the twins, no that was before the accident and the accident was before the cancer, yes that's right. It wasn't easy, but what a gesture taking his children on like she did for his sake. Wonderfully loving that was. Of course we all love the Rector, he's quite simply wonderful. One look from those blue eyes of his and we're all his slaves. I don't wonder she . . . '

'I know they're adopted, so they're actually *his*, not hers, are they?'

Suddenly Sheila knew she'd said too much, but he was looking at her with such a sympathetic expression on his face she knew he wouldn't use what she was going to tell him.

As she opened her mouth to begin the story, Ron, much to her annoyance reminded her it was getting late and they were meeting up with those friends at the service station on the bypass and they'd better be off and he still had to get washed and changed.

'Are we?' A strained look about his eyes convinced her she had to play along with him. 'Oh yes, of course, I'd completely forgotten. Oh dear. Will you excuse us, Hugo? Another time, maybe.'

'Of course. Off you go. Have a good time. See me when you can about the flowers and your ideas, and you, Ron, get in touch with Barry, will you?' He took Sheila's hand in his, raised it to his lips and kissed it lingeringly whilst keeping his eyes fixed on hers. A tremulous smile lit her face. 'Dear lady!'

105

Ron stood up. 'Of course. Yes, leave it with me.'

Hugo left disappointed that he hadn't heard the full story about Caroline. He knew that he definitely wouldn't hear it from her, it would be too painful for her to resurrect. So, it must have been Peter she was protecting when she wouldn't open up. Harriet, that was right. Harriet. She'd know.

But Harriet wouldn't co-operate. 'Ask Caroline, but don't expect an answer. And you're certainly not getting one from me.'

'Fine. Fine. I get the message.'

'You'd better and while we're on the subject, Caroline is off limits.'

He didn't reply.

'I mean it, Hugo. Off limits. Definitely a no go area. OK? Flirt with whom you like, I'll recommend a few if you wish, but not Caroline.'

'Flirt! What a word to use about me! I'm thoroughly demoralised by the prospect that I would *flirt*! Well, really. Me?' He helped himself to a scone Harriet had not long taken from the oven. 'Why so protective?'

'She's a dear friend and I won't have her hurt.'

'She's a grown woman with a mind of her own.'

'You're right. She is and she has. But she is

still *verboten*. I don't want to discuss it any more. I've got lunch to get, are you in?'

'Yes, and I'll lay the table for you as penance for upsetting you. In fact, I'll do it twice as double penance.'

Harriet gave him a quick kiss on his cheek. 'You're lovely, know that?'

Unashamedly he replied, 'Yes.'

They both fell about laughing, holding on to each other as they did so. Jimbo walked into the kitchen. 'May I share the joke?'

★ ★ ★

On Monday morning, having spent a rather chilly weekend with Jimbo looking glum most of the time, Hugo — partly to get out of the house and partly to have a chance to talk to Caroline on his own — decided to ask her if he could go round to the Rectory and run through her part with her in preparation for the rehearsal that night.

It was Peter who answered the phone. 'I'll get her for you. Just a moment. Darling! It's Hugo for you.'

'Oh right. Thanks.' She took hold of the receiver and said, 'Yes?'

'Good morning, Caroline.'

'Good morning.'

'Are you free sometime today?'

'When abouts?'

'Like now, for instance.'

'Yes, I am.'

'Could I come round and run through your part? Thought we could do some preparatory work, then tonight would flow more easily.'

'Very well.'

'In half an hour?'

'Fine. See you.' She put down the receiver and explained to Peter.

'I'll leave you to it, then. I'm off to Penny Fawcett, then I've some visiting to do, then I'm going into Culworth to take this article into the newspaper, and I'll call in at the hospital to see Lavender Gotobed, poor old thing.'

'Is she any better?'

'Not much. Bye, darling.' Peter put his arms round her and kissed her. 'Love you.'

'Love you. What about lunch?'

'I'll call back at the mini market before I leave and get it there.'

'Very well. Peter, I'm so looking forward to getting my teeth into this play, and thanks for helping me learn my lines last night.'

'It's a pleasure. I want you to do well, you see.'

'Thanks. I appreciate that.'

She stood at the front door to wave him off. The sun was shining on her, highlighting her dark curly hair and emphasising that happy look in her eyes which he hadn't brought about. It shone on her slender figure, and lit up the warm apricot-coloured dress she was wearing. God, how he loved her! He'd thought on his wedding day that he couldn't love her more than he did that day, but he did. Maybe love was self generating, the more one loved the greater the capacity for loving became. Peter raised a finger to his lips, kissed it and blew the kiss to her. He smiled at her delight but knew, in his heart, that the moment he drove away she would be thinking about Hugo Maude.

★　★　★

When Hugo rang the doorbell Caroline was on the telephone, so it was Sylvia who opened the door to him.

'Good morning, Mr . . . Hugo. Do come in. Dr Harris is expecting you. She said would I put you in the sitting room and would you like coffee?'

'Later perhaps, I've only just had breakfast.'

She left him seated in an easy chair. He hadn't been in many rectory sitting rooms, in fact come to think of it he hadn't been in any but somehow he knew there weren't many rectors relaxing in sitting rooms of this standard. The almost oriental design of the curtains picking up as they did the warm gold of the carpet. And the chairs! So comfortable. Nothing well worn and dowdy in this room. He wondered how the other rooms must look and how she'd furnished their bedroom.

On the mantelpiece were framed photographs of their children, but the photograph on the window sill was of their wedding. Hugo got to his feet and went to look at it. He picked it up and studied her closely. She hadn't worn a veil, simply a circlet of fresh flowers on her dark hair. Her dress was an ageless classic. Long narrow sleeves, a neckline just low enough to allow her to wear a double row of pearls which glowed against her creamy skin. Modest. Maidenly. Virginal. He studied Peter and was devastated by the look of joy in his face. Envy, monstrous envy filled Hugo's soul. To love like that! If Peter wasn't so damned good looking perhaps things wouldn't be so bad, but those good looks and Caroline and to be blessed with a love like that! How he envied him.

'Like it?'

He'd been aware a moment before of a perfume in the room. Now, at the sound of her voice, he knew it was Caroline's.

Hugo carefully placed the photograph back

on the window sill and turned to look at her.

'Hope you don't mind. Couldn't help but take a look. Got your script?'

'It's here.' She picked it up from the coffee table and went to sit on the sofa. He sat beside her with his script in his hand.

'I've already learned a lot of the lines, Peter's been helping me. This Marian character I'm playing, she's complex, isn't she?'

'Indeed. Tell me what you've learned about her.'

'Before the war, she was a dutiful wife. Usual thing, never had a job, married almost straight from school, the local boy everyone expected her to marry, had the prescribed two children, a boy and then a girl. The war came, he went into the army expecting her to be sitting tidily at home keeping the home fires burning and doing her bit by knitting balaclavas and mittens for the soldiers at the front. Well, she didn't. She got up off her backside, learned to drive, worked at the local big house which had been turned into a hospital for officers, became a nurse and saw more of the foul side of the war than most.'

'Yes, yes.'

'Then husband Charles comes home. He's not been physically wounded but emotionally and psychologically he's a wreck, but he manages to keep that particular problem well under wraps. Not even she has realised how badly damaged he is.'

'Excellent.'

'He is appalled at what she's been doing during the war and fully expects her to go back to doing nothing. Which she does, mainly because he is so adamant about it. I think there's a hint of cruelty in his attitude, and in addition it's almost as if he's afraid he might lose her if he doesn't keep her tied to the home. But she's so glad to have him back that she goes along with it. Then this man Leonard arrives. Am I getting it right? Is this how you see it?'

'It is.'

'He completely upsets the applecart. He upsets the husband and he upsets her. Stirs things up in her which she's never had stirred before. Husband Charles always insists on his conjugal rights but never quite gets it right. He's on a kind of 'Oh! It's Saturday, so it's our night' routine. So rather surprisingly, to her, she finds herself ready for anything, as you might say.'

Hugo sat back watching her as she outlined her ideas to him. He'd a powerful idea that her husband had a completely different approach from the husband in the play, and that she knew he knew and she guessed he was jealous. Which he was. She moved on to the effect the newcomer, Leonard, had had on the wife. What was she saying . . . 'So I can quite understand why she does what she does. Life with Leonard would be unpredictable. He's no job, just private money, and deeply in love with him though she is she can't cope with that so she opts for the safety of the husband and children. So sad Leonard gets killed the very night she tells him it's all over.'

'Do you think she's right?'

'To be glad he gets killed?'

'Yes.'

'It's never right to kill, no matter the provocation.'

'Do you think Charles kills him?'

'Oh! Definitely! Everything points to that.'

'It can't be comfortable, realising almost for certain her husband is a murderer.'

'Here, look, where she says to her friend Celia . . . ' Caroline leafed through the script till she came to the page she was looking for. 'Here it is. 'It was doomed from the beginning, I see that now and I shall pay the price for the rest of my life, because I have to live with it every day.'

'You've studied it all out, haven't you?'

'If I'm doing something then I do it right

and understanding what makes her tick is vital, surely?'

'Of course, of course. Let's do that scene where the chap first comes in. Act one, Scene two. Right. Off you go.'

'I haven't finished yet. Having an affair on the side was much more terrible then in 1920 than it would be today, wasn't it? You really do have to see it from their point of view to get the right message across.'

'Of course. That's the trouble with a lot of amateur productions, the cast don't have the width and depth of experience of life to get through to the essence of the part they're playing.'

Caroline, about to read her first line, looked up at him. 'I sincerely hope you're not suggesting that I've had experience of extra marital affairs and that's why I understand so well.'

Hugo who'd been lounging back on the sofa enjoying Caroline's company sat up straight. 'Oh no, of course not. With a man like Peter, what woman would want an affair? I'm sure you're quite satisfied on that score.' His slight hesitation before the word 'satisfied' angered her.

'Look here, I hope you're . . . Look, let's get on, please. Have you found the page?'

They read through and discussed various

points and only stopped when Sylvia said she was going to lunch and did Dr Harris want anything before she left.

Pulled back to reality by the request, Caroline had to think for a moment. 'No, nothing at all, thank you. See you later.'

'OK. Good afternoon to you, Mr Maude.'

'Hugo! Hugo!' His reprimand was spoken in such a pleasant way Sylvia had to smile.

'Yes, well, then, Hugo.'

'Good afternoon.'

★ ★ ★

Sylvia was clattering plates in the sink. 'Have you finished? Because I'm in a rush. I've got to get back, just in case. You were late, I've waited ages for you to come.'

Willie, who'd only had two bites of his sandwich, looked up, surprised. 'Come on, I haven't been in the house two minutes. What's the rush?'

'He's there.'

'Who is?'

'Who do you think. His lordship.'

'Oh, right.'

'I bet my bottom dollar he'll have stayed for lunch.'

'Put me a drop more milk in this tea, will yer? Look here, she's an upright, loving woman married to a lovely man. He's a priest, she's a doctor, she knows the position better than you and me. Stop worrying. She won't do anything wrong, believe me.'

'Won't she?'

'No, she won't. If he tries . . . '

'Which he will. I've seen that look he has in his eye before now.'

'Where have you seen it?' Willie picked up his cup.

'Dicky Tutt, for a start.'

Willie spluttered his tea over the cloth. He wiped his mouth, coughed a bit and then said, 'Honestly!' When he'd got over the choking fit Willie began to laugh. 'You're not suggesting there's going to be a real proper affair are you, like Dicky and Georgie?'

Faced with the question, Sylvia couldn't make herself voice her thoughts. If she said it, it might mean it would happen. 'No. not really. Well . . . '

'Give up, forget it. I know I'm right. You're worrying over nothing.'

Sylvia stood up. 'You finished?'

'I have now and I'll have indigestion all afternoon with hurrying.'

She cleared away, kissed him, reminded him to lock up after himself, and left him.

Their laughter reached her ears as she unlocked the front door. She called out, 'I'm back.'

They were sitting in the kitchen having lunch. A half-empty bottle of red wine on the table. An empty dish, which by the looks of it had held a cold beef salad and, waiting still to be eaten, two slices of her best fruit cake.

'You're soon back, Sylvia?'

'Lots of ironing to do. With not being in tomorrow I need to get on with it.'

'Of course. We'll take our cake into the sitting room. Bring the wine, Hugo, will you?'

Sylvia watched him follow her out. This kitchen belonged to the family. She thought about the times Dr Harris had sat in one rocking chair and she in the other giving the twins their bottles. She remembered when there'd been two high chairs round the table at lunchtime, with the Rector feeding one baby and Dr Harris the other one. What happy times they'd been. How much she'd enjoyed them. Lovely though he was, Hugo Maude didn't belong, he was dining-room company, not kitchen company. And wine at lunchtime! Now that was decadent. As she snapped open the ironing board Sylvia heard them laughing again. Caroline's laugh was joyous; happier than for some time. Well, at least that was a plus, she supposed.

7

Vera called in at the Store for a few vital necessities. Bread, milk, eggs, half a pound of bacon, some chocolate biscuits, a shaving stick and razor blades for Don. She was standing in front of the razor blade display trying to remember which kind Don used when she heard Mrs Jones' voice.

'There's ten parcels today, Linda. There's the list. Hurry up and we'll catch the lunchtime post.'

'Keep yer hair on! Shan't be a minute.' Linda finished sorting her postal orders, tidied the counter, put some paper clips back in her tray and tested the sponge she used for wetting her fingers when she was counting.

'Honestly! I haven't got all day! I've a costume to machine this afternoon when I get back. Beads to sew on as well. Hurry up!'

As Linda began weighing the parcels and writing down the cost on Mrs Jones' list Vera edged closer. Swallowing her pride because of her desperate need to help with the costumes she said, 'If you'd let me help I could be doing the beads. I've got a bit of 'oliday, time's getting on.'

'You! Not likely not after the way you spoke to me at the meeting. I wouldn't let you help, not for anything. I'd stay up all night first.'

'Would you indeed? You miserable old cow. I just hope Hugo doesn't like 'em and then you'll be in a fix.'

'Of course he'll like 'em. He's been with me every step of the way.'

'Oh! Very close, are yer? Hand in glove?'

'Don't be daft. We professional people have an understanding.'

Vera hooted with laughter. 'You professional people! I can remember the time when you were glad to clean at the pub when your boys was little. I don't call that professional.'

'So you think cleaning at a nursing home is a step up the ladder, do you?'

'Better than cleaning out stinking lavatories when they've all had too much to drink. And I don't stoop to nasty underhand tricks like you get up to, either.'

Mrs Jones grew belligerent at this accusation and looked ready to begin one of her famous tirades. Taking a deep breath she thundered, 'What do you mean, 'underhand tricks'?'

'Like that time when you reported Carrie Whatsit to the Show committee for buying a pot plant at the garden centre and kidding on it was home grown.'

'I never.'

'You did. Or that time when your Terry beat up the husband of that girl what works at the Jug and Bottle and you swore he'd been 'ome all night. Don't think we don't know what you get up to.'

'You've a mind like a sewer, you have.'

'You might think you're superior but yer not. You're a scumbag, that's what.' Vera took her shopping to the till where Bel totted it up and asked her for nine pounds twenty-five. Her hands were shaking so badly she couldn't unzip her purse.

'Here, let me do it for you. There we are. There's your change look, seventy-five pence.'

Vera nodded her thanks. The aftermath of the argument was having its effect and Vera was bereft of speech.

Bel whispered, 'Take no notice. She's not worth it. Been right on her high horse since she got that job.' She lifted the carrier off the counter and handed it to her. 'There y'go, love.'

Vera was about to leave when the door crashed open and Grandmama Charter-Plackett came in.

'There you are, Vera. You'd better get home quickly. I've just seen Greenwood Stubbs and your Rhett pulling up in the van and they're unloading crazy paving and bags of cement and carrying them through your house.'

Vera's shock at this piece of astounding news brought back her voice. 'Crazy paving? I haven't ordered crazy paving. What's he playing at?' She hurried out of the Store, raced across the Green and peeped over her fence. Rhett was stacking the pieces of stone as Greenwood was carrying them through.

'Rhett, what do yer think yer doing? We can't afford all that. We've no need for it. Take it back.'

'Shushhh! Come in and I'll explain.' Vera walked round to the front door and went in.

'Before he went away Mr Fitch said that all the rubbish that was lying about had to be cleared before he got back. He said it was all old stuff he'd never use and it was making the place look untidy. When I saw the pots and the table and chairs amongst it I thought, well, if he doesn't want it, I know who does. So here it is. Then I remembered we'd a load of crazy paving left over from the new paths Mr Fitch changed his mind about, and I thought he wouldn't miss the few bits that would make all the difference to our garden. Greenwood here said we could have it. So we've brought it and the old man won't be any the wiser, will he?'

'But what's it for?'

'I'm repairing all this old crazy paving here at the back and extending it for yer. Yer know, bringing it right up to the lawn, then there won't be that nasty bit of rough ground between. It'll look really good. Then yer'll have a patio to sit out on.'

Vera was wreathed in smiles. 'Oh, Rhett. What a lovely idea!'

'Greenwood's said I can have the old table and a couple of chairs, wrought iron they are. They're old and they need working on but they're yours when I've cleaned and painted 'em. They were going to the tip anyway. Nobody'll miss 'em, they've been at the back of the kitchen garden for years.'

'So I can have a cup of tea sitting out here on me patio. I shall feel like lady muck. Oh, Rhett! Wait till yer grandad hears about this. You are a love.' She flung her arms round him and gave him a great big kiss.

'Steady on.'

'But is it all right, yer know? It's not thieving or anything, is it?'

Greenwood came through with some more paving. 'Keep mum about it, that's all. What the old man don't know won't do him no harm. What we're bringing here is a drop in the ocean to what we've used up there. He'll never miss it.'

Vera almost skipped for joy. Someone was

at last doing something just for her, and the best of it was there was no price to pay because Rhett was doing it for love. Good old Rhett, worth his weight in gold.

★ ★ ★

Whilst he worked on the patio Rhett learned his part. Hugo had said it was a small one but it seemed big to him. He'd never acted in a play before and he'd no idea why he'd been chosen. At school he'd never had a chance, being in the bottom set of absolutely every subject you could name. Now he was older he regretted not having tried at school, but there really hadn't seemed any point in it, not him with a daft name like Rhett. With a name like that you were half way down the field from the start.

At the first rehearsal he'd stuttered and stammered, got embarrassed, dried up, moved into all the wrong places till by the end of the evening he'd decided to resign. Hugo, however, had given him a pep talk.

'Look here, I don't know what you're worrying about. You're not giving yourself a chance. By the end of four weeks you won't recognise yourself. Give it a go. Believe me, I'll coax it out of you. I've had professional actors do worse, and that's the truth.'

'You're pulling my leg.'

'I'm not! That's God's truth. Your voice is strong, which it needs to be seeing as we've no amplification, so that's half the battle. Remember, Caroline is your mother, treat her as if she is. On stage she's no longer Dr Harris, try to see her as your mum. Mmmmm?'

'I see. Yes, I see.'

'Have you a younger sister? No? When you're working, or whatever, think what it would be like to have a sister. Get to know Michelle, build a relationship, learn your parts together, and then you'll react better to her on stage. Right?'

Rhett nodded. 'It's the bits where I have to put my arm round Dr Harris and kiss her. It's blinking embarrassing, that is.'

Hugo shrugged his shoulders. 'That's because you see her as Dr Harris and not as your mother. That's where you're going wrong. Caroline? Have you a minute?'

Caroline came across to see what Hugo wanted.

'Yes?'

'Look here, Rhett is having problems seeing you as his mother.'

'Right.'

'We'll have a mini rehearsal right here and now.' He flicked through his copy of the

124

script. 'Here we are, look, page sixty-two. Half way down. Here's a chair, pretend that's the sofa. Go and stand behind her and say your lines. Sit on it, Caroline, that's it. Right, off you go, Rhett.'

Rhett stood behind her, put a hand on her shoulder and said his lines.

'*Why's Dad so angry about this chap Leonard? Seems all right to me.*'

'*You wouldn't understand, darling.*'

'*I'm not twelve you know, like Celia. I have got some idea about what goes on.*'

'*No, you haven't.*'

'*I do know things aren't right between you and Daddy.*'

'*Do you now? Even if it were true, which it isn't, it's none of your business.*'

'*It is if you're upset.*'

'*I'm not.*'

'*Very well, I know I'm right, but I'll have to take your word for it, I expect.*'

'*You do just that.*'

'*I just wish parents didn't lie.*'

'*I'm not. Goodnight, darling.*'

'*Goodnight, Mummy.*'

Hugo applauded. 'Well, done. Much better. But you're stiff. Look, this is how I would do it.'

He rested his forearms along the top of the chair and bent much closer than Rhett had.

125

As he reached the last line, instead of kissing the top of Caroline's head like Rhett had done he leant further forward and kissed her cheek.

'Like that. Kiss her cheek as she looks up at you. See? Try again.'

Rhett had done it again, been more relaxed and had kissed Caroline's cheek as Hugo had done.

'Much better, wasn't it? Didn't you think so?'

Rhett nodded. 'Yes. I've to forget Dr Harris is Dr Harris and then that does the trick.'

'Exactly. What did you think Caroline?'

'Big improvement.'

'Agreed! Right everybody. Three rehearsals next week. Monday, Wednesday, Friday. You're all doing fabulously. Monday Mrs Jones will be here with costumes. Well, some of them at least. No scripts by Wednesday. Everyone word perfect, please.' They all groaned. 'You can do it! Goodnight.'

As Caroline called out, 'Goodnight, everyone', Hugo materialised beside her.

'I'll walk you home.'

She laughed. 'Honestly, walk me home. It's only two doors away.'

'Nevertheless. You're doing me a good turn actually. I'm in the doghouse at Harriet's, so the longer I'm out of the house the better.'

'What have you been doing?'

'Nothing. Nothing at all, but Jimbo's upset. Bit stuffy is Jimbo, did you realise?'

They'd reached the Rectory door. The light came on and they stood in its spotlight.

'He's very protective of his family.'

'His wife, you mean. No trespassing.'

'I should think not.'

'Harriet and I go back a long way.'

'That's no excuse.'

'It isn't, is it? You can know someone five minutes and feel closer to them than to someone you've known for twenty years.'

She studied his face, wondering how sincere or how significant that remark was. He was handsome. Every feature in just the right proportion. It really wasn't fair for one man to have so many of the right ingredients. Not only that, he had the charm to match.

Hugo leaned forward and placed a soft kiss on her mouth. Then he took hold of her hand, raised it to his lips, and said, 'Fair lady!'

'Hugo!'

'Caroline!' His eyes roved over her face as he murmured, ''*All days are nights to see till I see thee. And nights bright days when dreams do show thee me.*''

The common sense part of her was angry with his dalliance, but there was something other in her which responded. She kissed his lips, patted his cheek, fumbled in her bag for her key, opened the door said 'Goodnight', and went in.

'I'm home! Where are you?'

'In bed.'

'I'm thirsty. Are you?'

'No thanks.'

'Won't be long.'

Caroline drank a glass of water and then went to check the children. As usual Beth had flung off her bedclothes and her nightgown was up round her waist. Caroline pulled the sheet up higher and thought about the innocence of this beloved child of hers. She stroked her face with a gentle finger and loved her deeply. There was nothing she would do to harm Beth. Nothing at all, and she must keep that foremost in her mind. That dratted Hugo. Quoting sonnets at her. Alex was fast asleep flat on his back, neatly covered up. She loved him just as much as she loved Beth. He was such a complete and utter darling. So like Peter. Damn that blasted Hugo.

★　★　★

'Had a good rehearsal?'

'Yes, thanks. Excellent. Rhett is really getting the hang of things.'

'Is he? He's changed then.'

'The thing is, Hugo can explain it so well. There's lots of actors I'm sure who know how to act, but getting it out of other people is beyond them. Like lecturers at college. Some were brilliant but their lectures were the pits. Hugo just has the gift.'

There was a short silence and then Peter said, 'Has he indeed?'

Caroline didn't reply. She walked naked to the bathroom. He heard the shower running and stopped the pretence of reading his book. It lay heavy on his legs. He knew he musn't trespass. This was her battle. He didn't know how to fight it on her behalf. Didn't know what to do to stop this runaway roller coaster. It was the light in her eyes, the spring in her step which frightened him. She may not know it, but Hugo was . . .

She came back in, wrapped in a towel and sat on the edge of the bed with her back to him. He always loved touching her skin when it was warm and damp and he couldn't stop himself from reaching across to feel her bare shoulder.

Caroline very slowly stood up, lingeringly rubbed herself dry, dropped the towel on the carpet, lifted the duvet and got into bed.

'Hugo can twist people round his little

129

finger, you know. Even old diehards like Mrs Jones are eating out of his hand. Is he acting *all* the time, do you think? Or is he really the lovable person he appears to be?'

'Only time will tell. It certainly means he gets his own way with everyone, doesn't it?'

'Not with Harriet. She has him under her thumb. She tells him off as though he were a child.'

There was a short silence and then Peter said, 'Perhaps he is. I would find it hard having him living in my house.'

'Jimbo does a little. Apparently Hugo had rather a chilly weekend.'

'I can't think Jimbo will tolerate any dalliance.'

His use of the word 'dalliance' startled Caroline. 'No, I can't think he will.'

'I'm going to sleep now. Goodnight and God bless you.' He turned on his side, made his pillow more comfortable and closed his eyes.

'And you.' Caroline was quiet for a while and then she said, 'No matter what, you are my soul mate. You do know that, don't you?'

But it seemed Peter was already asleep for there was no reply.

★ ★ ★

Next morning Caroline took the children to school and didn't return immediately. Knowing her propensity to find someone in need of help, Peter eventually left a note for her when she hadn't returned after an hour and he had to go out. It said, 'I wonder where you are? Got to leave, going into Culworth to the hospital to see Lavender Gotobed and then on to lunch at the Deanery. I've left the answer machine on. My love to you. P.'

She found it when she got back around twelve o'clock. She hadn't meant to be so long but as she'd emerged into Stocks Row on her way home from the school Hugo had come out of the Store.

'Caroline! Hi!'

'You're up early! I thought you never rose before eleven.'

'I don't usually. I think it's this country air, it's doing devilish things to my internal clock. You look all rosy and excited. Is it me who has brought this about? Flatter me! Tell me I'm right!'

'You're not.'

'How can you be so cruel? Does not your heart beat just a little faster when you see me? When you look into these dark dark orbs of mine, are you not in some kind of a fluster? Mmmmm?'

'No.'

'I'm losing my touch. Oh, God, I am! My charms are diminishing by the hour.'

'You are a fool, Hugo Maude.'

'Now that is a part I have never played: the jester. The lover, yes, but not the jester. Come walk with me.'

'Where to?'

'By gentle glade and gushing ghyll. Where is that quote from? I can't remember.' He put his head on one side and pleaded with her. 'Please?'

'Very well then, just for a while. If you're wanting a gentle glade we'll go down the footpath by Hipkin Gardens and into the wood.'

'To the woods!' He proclaimed it as though he were on stage. The mothers leaving the school couldn't avoid hearing him. Indeed, his voice carried so well that Caroline was convinced the entire village must have heard.

She was angry, and hissed, 'Be quiet. My reputation will be in ruins.'

'We shall be like Hansel and Gretel going to meet our fate together, hand in hand, in the woods.'

'I can't see the woodman.'

'Nevertheless he lurks, ready to blight our lives. I am filled with fear. Hold my hand.'

'I shan't.'

He whispered in her ear, 'Wait till we're out

of sight and then I shall claim you for mine own.'

He followed her down the footpath soberly enough but as soon as they were in the field he took her hand, kissed it and then held it firmly.

'Please, Hugo, let go.'

'Relax. I'm in need of comfort. I'm wondering if I've done the right thing by doing this play.'

'In what way?'

'A challenge before I'm ready for it. The real truth is I'm not sleeping at the moment. That's why I'm up so early. Must be my damned nerves playing up.'

'I'm sorry. Can you possibly hold out, do you think? Everyone's got so involved.'

'I know.'

'Perhaps steeling yourself to do it could be the best thing. Prove to yourself you really can still function. It's only a minor thing, isn't it? It's not as if there were thousands of pounds invested, like in a West End production.'

'Yes, you're right there.'

'If you only act at half cock it'll still be too good for a village play.'

'You underate yourselves. But that's what I can never do. Less than my best.'

'You're too hard on yourself.'

'Think so? Maybe I am. I sweat blood over my work. Did you know that?' Caroline shook her head. 'My life's blood ebbs away each time I go on stage.'

'That's why you're so good.'

'You think so?'

'The critics say so, and Peter says so too.'

'Ah! If Peter says so then it must be correct.' There was a hint of scorn in his voice and he looked at her with his expressive eyebrows raised.

She withdrew her hand from his clasp. 'I'm going back now.'

'Why? Too near the truth?'

'You're being insolent again, and far too intrusive.'

'I've guessed about the twins.'

'Have you indeed.'

'I know about the cancer.'

'Do you? And who's been letting the cat out of the bag? It wouldn't be Harriet, I'm sure.'

'Certainly not. She is without blame. No.' He gazed at the sky, wondering whether to tell her or not. 'It was Sheila Bissett.'

'I might have known.'

'But you do let him dominate you, don't you? His moral standards, his children, his life, his vocation. There's no end to your devotion.'

'There's nothing wrong with the principles Peter holds dear, and if it's what I choose.'

'Choose? Or has it been imposed?'

'My choice, because I love him so. He has supported me like no one else could. You couldn't have done what he's done for me, you're too much in need of support yourself all the time.'

They'd wandered into the wood and Hugo suggested that they sat down for a while. 'Here look, on this flat bit under the tree. You make me sound like a child and I wish you didn't. What are your children like?'

Lazily he helped her to sit down with her back against the tree and then he sat, with such elegance she noted, at right angles to her, leaned back, rested his head on her legs, and squinted up at her. 'The sun is coming through the trees and lighting your cheek bones in the most alluring manner. Is it love, do you think, that has made you look so beautiful? If so, would it were I who had inspired such love.'

'Hugo, for goodness sake, pull yourself together.'

'You're always so down to earth. Lighten up.'

'I shan't.' Caroline began to tell him about the children. She'd been talking for quite a while when she asked him if he regretted not having a child of his own. There was no reply, so she looked down at him and realised he'd fallen asleep. Poor man, it was true then that he hadn't slept well. She tentatively touched his hair, it was more silky than it looked, but very thick. His beautiful arching eyebrows tempted her to run a finger along them. No man had a right to look as devastating as he did. Nor so stunningly lovable.

She sat patiently waiting for him to wake.

★ ★ ★

It was their misfortune that Sheila Bissett had decided she needed to get healthier and had insisted on accompanying Ron when he took little Pompom out for his constitutional.

'You know, Sheila, Pompom isn't as young as he was. He can't go far.'

'Right into the wood and back isn't far, Ron. Do him good. I'm enjoying marching along. Hurry up, Pompom. There's a good boy.'

Ron sighed.

'Isn't it lovely this morning? So warm but so cool under the trees. Just the right place to be for a walk.'

'Right.'

'It's a pity more people don't get out and

about. It does you good, blows the cobwebs away. We have this lovely field and woods and you hardly ever see anyone using it. You could be murdered in here and no one would know. It's so secluded. It's more friendly though than Sykes Wood, don't you think? That always seems so gloomy. This one at least gets the sunlight.'

'It does.'

Sheila stepped along ahead of Ron because the footpath had narrowed, so it was she who came upon Hugo and Caroline first. By now they were both asleep. Caroline with her head resting against the trunk of the tree and one hand on Hugo's shoulder. Hugo lay just where he'd fallen asleep. Sheila was aghast. She turned round to face Ron and gesticulated to him to pick up Pompom. She saw him about to ask why, so she placed a finger against her lips and urged him to be silent.

The two of them crept past as softly as they could. Pompom snuffling to get down and Ron gripping his jaws tight shut to stop him yapping. They scurried down the path fearing to speak in case they woke the sleeping couple up.

When Sheila thought she was safely out of hearing she said in a loud stage whisper, 'Well, really. Did you ever? I can't believe it. What can they be thinking of?'

'Best thing we can do is say nothing. Pretend we didn't see them.'

'But we did and it's not right. It most definitely isn't. I think Peter ought to know.'

'You must promise me not to say a word.'

Sheila hurried along beside him, her mind boggling at what she'd seen. Mind you, he was gorgeous. She could understand . . . If she was younger she could quite fancy him herself.

'Ron, how are we going to get home? We can't walk past again, they might have woken up. You never know what might be going on.'

'For heaven's sake, as if.'

'They're only human. How are we going to get home, then?'

'We'll turn left off the path and go out onto Shepherds Hill and go home that way.'

'Oh right, of course. I can't believe it. Fast asleep in a wood. Like something out of a film. They looked so happy. So romantic!' They looked like people who are in love do, so . . . well, beautiful. To tell the truth if she really faced up to it she felt quite envious. She and Ron had never fallen asleep in a wood, never been so much at peace with one another. There came a feeling of regret to Sheila, a terrible sense of having missed out on life.

Ron grumbled, 'I can't see the village

calling it that, can you?'

'Romantic? No. What is she thinking of? I blame her for encouraging him. It's disgusting. It really is.'

'Mum's the word. Remember!'

But Sheila, already planning whom to tell first, never heard his warning.

8

Peter came back home around half past four. Instead of going into the kitchen and regaling Caroline with the details of his day he went straight to his study. The children called out to him but he took no notice of them.

Beth, full of sympathy for him, said, 'I'll go see to him Mummy, I expect he's had a bad day.'

'No don't, darling. Sometimes Daddy needs to be alone. Quiet, you know. Because he's from the Church, people tell him the most heart rending stories about their lives and he gets upset. He wishes he had a magic wand and could put it all right again for them. In a bit we'll go and dig him out.'

Alex said, 'I'm not going to be a Rector. I'm going to make lots and lots of money and buy you and Daddy a lovely house with a big garden miles and miles away from here, and then he won't have to listen to all these nasty stories.'

'That's extremely kind of you and I'm sure we'd both appreciate it. For the moment, though, that's what he does and he wouldn't want to be doing anything other.'

Beth declared, 'I do love my daddy. He could fight anybody, couldn't he? He's the biggest man in all the world.'

'He's not.' Alex stuck his tongue out at her. 'He is.'

Beginning to lose her patience, Caroline said, 'Get on with your jigsaws, please, there's good children. He is the best Daddy in all the world, he may not be the biggest but he is the best.'

But they didn't need to dig him out because he eventually came into the kitchen and stood watching the twins doing their jigsaws.

Beth shouted excitedly, 'Daddy! Look! I've nearly finished!'

Caroline, busy stirring a pan at the cooker, said, 'Hello, Peter. Had a bad day? Didn't it go well?' He was slow to answer, so she turned round to look at him. Instead of smiling at her, his eyes avoided her face and he quietly said, 'Bad day! I don't think it could have been worse.'

'Why, what's happened?'

Then he did look at her, and a dreadful sinking feeling began in her throat and found its way right to the pit of her stomach. Surely not. Please God, surely not. His unflinching gaze unnerved Caroline, and she dreaded what he would say next.

'You ask *me?*'

Alex shouted. 'Finished! I'm first. I'm first.'

'You're not, I am. Aren't I, Mummy? I finished just before Alex, didn't I? But I didn't shout.'

In a very controlled voice, with her eyes on Peter, Caroline said, 'I am not asking you, I am telling you to go play in the garden for a while. Chop. Chop. Quick now.'

Beth looked at her father and then at her mother and told Alex to go outside quickly.

'I don't want to.'

'You do. Come on.'

Alex looked at his mother and decided he would do as he was told. As the back door closed behind them Caroline asked, 'What is it, then?'

'I can hardly bear to tell you what the latest gossip is that's going round the village. It doesn't seem possible, but somewhere there must be a small element of truth in it.'

'You haven't been in the village today, so what can you possibly have heard?'

'Please, Caroline, don't prevaricate, we must have the truth between us at all costs. I can't believe it. In fact, I will not believe it because it cannot have happened as I have heard it, but I do need you to give me an explanation.'

Caroline, he noticed, was beginning to

142

tremble. 'It's about Hugo and I, isn't it?'

Peter left one of those cold silences which his parishioners, frequently to their cost, knew all about. He never took his eyes from her face.

Her voice came out jerkily and barely audible. 'I didn't intend going to bed tonight without telling you.'

'Is that so?'

'Yes, believe me.'

'So?'

'I met him as I came out of school. He was feeling unwell, he's not able to sleep at night, his nerves and such. So I took pity on him and agreed to walk with him. We went down the footpath and on to the spare land and then into the wood. He got tired, so we sat down under a tree and I leant against it and he laid down, he asked me to tell him about the children, and while I was doing so, he fell asleep. And then so did I.'

Peter almost snarled his reply. 'What about the children?'

'How old they were, what they got up to.'

'I see. Thank you.'

Aggrieved at the defensive situation she found herself in Caroline asked, 'Who the blazes saw us? No one went past that I know of.'

'Well, someone *did*.'

In a shaky voice Caroline asked him if he knew who'd seen her.

'Sheila Bissett.'

Caroline threw her arms up in despair. 'I might have known. I just might have known. It would have to be dear old Sheila, wouldn't it.'

'It scarcely matters *who* saw you. You *were* seen.'

'But I've told you the truth, what was the version you heard?'

He turned to leave. 'It's not repeatable. Obviously it was perhaps something like fourth hand or even fifth hand by the time it reached my ears. By then it had been embroidered beyond recognition. I don't mind telling you the person who told it to me quite relished the idea. They thought I *ought* to know what was 'going on'. But nothing on earth will make me repeat to you what I was told. *Nothing.*'

'That blasted woman! Damn and blast her.'

'Had you not gone with him, had you not fallen asleep, then you wouldn't be blasting her to kingdom come right now.'

'At least I should know what they're all saying about me.'

'Not from me you won't. There's a pan burning.'

Under her breath Caroline said, 'Damn and blast.'

'However, thank you for telling me the truth.'

'It's this Rector's wife bit, isn't it?' She emptied the blackened remains of the stewed apples down the waste disposal and viciously switched it on.

Speaking loudly over the noise, Peter said, 'No, at the moment it's what is between husband and wife. That's what it's about. What the parish thinks will be next on the agenda.'

Caroline threw the pan in the sink, turned the cold tap on so hard that the water flung itself into the pan and back out again all down the front of her dress. In desperation, Caroline fled.

★　★　★

She got to the rehearsal early, coinciding with the arrival of Sylvia who was anxious to be there in good time to get her kettles boiling in readiness for the calls for coffee she knew would arise as soon as everyone came.

'Hello, Dr Harris. You're early.'

'Hi, Sylvia. Yes, well I've got some lines to run through. I used to be able to remember lines so easily, but not now. Hugo wanted us word perfect tonight.' As she said his name her cheeks flushed at the thought that Sylvia

145

might well have heard the story going round the village, and she didn't want to lose Sylvia's good opinion of her. Although Peter believed every word she had said — she just knew he did because he was like that — she still felt his disapproval very severely. She knew he wouldn't ask Sheila Bissett not to repeat the story. That was pointless. The whole village would know by now, and Caroline certainly wasn't going to remonstrate with her. She wondered if Sylvia knew about the rumours and particularly whether she knew what Sheila Bissett had said was going on. She'd grasp the nettle, like her mother always said she should.

Following Sylvia into the kitchen, Caroline leant against the worktop, and asked her.

Sylvia took a moment to fill the first kettle and set it on the hob. As the gas flared into action she said, 'Oh, I've heard right enough. The Store was absolutely agog with the tale when I went in there this afternoon. Linda was really stirring it with a big spoon, and she had some very eager listeners.' She faced Caroline. 'Does the Rector know?'

'He does. But he's had the *truth* from me, not a load of lies and suppostions.'

'I'm glad they were lies. I'm very glad they were lies.' Looking sadly at her, Sylvia continued with, 'Just such a pity that people round about here are so happy to believe lies. That's where the damage is done.'

'What are they saying? Will you tell me?'

'I thought the Rector knew.'

'He does, but he won't tell me. Says he can't.'

'I'm not surprised, he must be very hurt.'

'Well?'

'They say . . . you were with Hugo . . . you know . . . you know, making love on the grass in the wood.' She turned away, her face red with the embarrassment of not wanting to put it into words, but knowing she must. 'There, you know now.'

'Oh God!'

'You had scarcely a stitch on, apparently.'

'Oh God! I could kill that woman. I could, so help me I could kill her.'

'Not entirely her fault, I expect it snowballed after she told it. That's what happens, you know.'

They heard the outer door open and voices in the main hall. It was most of the cast, including Hugo, all arriving at the same moment.

They heard his resonant voice calling out, 'Coffee, Sylvia, I'm dying for a cup.'

'Very well, Hugo, won't be two ticks.' Sylvia remarked quietly to Caroline, 'Go join the others and brazen it out.'

'Right.' She squared her shoulders and marched in, focusing her gaze on Harriet and heading straight for her.

Harriet greeted her with a pursed mouth and raised eyebrows.

Before they had exchanged a word Hugo came up and, putting his arm round her waist, planted a kiss on her cheek. 'How's my leading lady tonight? In full voice, I hope. We're doing a straight run through act one, OK? Know your lines?'

Caroline extricated herself from his grasp. 'Almost.'

'Almost? Almost, she says, with that enchanting smile on her face. She I shall forgive, but anyone else who doesn't know their lines will be hung drawn and quartered. Liz?' She nodded. 'Neville?' He nodded. Hugo asked each in turn and they gave him an affirmative.

'Thank God! Private tuition for you, Caroline my love, if you're not word perfect tonight! Right! Beginners please. My coffee! You're an angel.' Sylvia got an arm around her shoulders and a kiss for her effort. She thanked him nicely but shrugged him away.

'Act one, scene one. Pronto. Pronto. Barry! Less noise with the scenery, please. Props! Some chairs to represent the sofa. Liz, are you ready? Rhett? Michelle? Good, good.

Wagons roll. Hush, everyone.'

Rhett strolled on through the non existent door to the sitting room. He stood gazing out of the yet to be constructed french windows at what would be a back drop showing a lawn and well-tended gardens. He turned away and pretended to fiddle with the knobs of a radiogram.

'Stop! Rhett! You look as though you are walking about on the platform of a Church Hall.'

Surprised, Rhett replied, 'Well, I am, aren't I?'

Head in hands, Hugo moaned. 'Oh God! Oh God! Give me strength! No, you're not! You're in a drawing room, an elegant drawing room and you're the young man of the house thinking about going up to Oxford this autumn. You have the assurance — be it youthful, but you have it — that particular assurance peculiar to your class. You are monied!'

'Wish to God I was!'

'There you are, you see? You're still Rhett Wright, when you should be at this moment Julian Latimer with the world your oyster. Now come in again, and try harder.'

Harriet, standing close to Caroline, muttered, 'Well? I did warn you.'

'You've heard.'

149

'Couldn't help it. The world and his wife know, believe me. Jimbo's had the story ten times over today. Each time it got more lurid.'

'Nothing happened.'

'That's not what I heard.'

'Well, it didn't.'

'What does Peter think?'

'He knows it's all lies.'

'Next you'll be saying, 'We're just good friends.''

'We are.'

'Oh, come on, Caroline. You're fooling yourself, and I've always admired your commonsense.'

'I haven't lost it.'

'You have. Once the play is over he will leave here and we shan't see him for years.'

Caroline watched Rhett and Michelle together on stage while she prepared her answer. 'That won't bother me.'

'Three months from now someone might, just might mention Turnham Malpas to him and he'll say, 'Turnham what? Where's that?''

'Think so?'

'Know so. You're on.'

'Oh, I am. Sorry, Hugo.' Caroline fled into the wings and stepped briskly on stage. *'Sorry, darlings, I've got to go out; Celia is having a lunch to introduce the new man in her life to everyone, Leonard someone or* other. *I expect he'll be devastatingly boring, her men usually are, and I wish I didn't have to go, but I must. I promised. Doris will get you lunch if you need it. Have you anything planned for today?'*

She got through the evening needing only a few prompts. But it was hard going. The cold, uptight touch of Neville playing her husband left her unmoved. He was well cast because she always found him cold and uptight in real life. But each time Hugo touched her, declared his love for her, tried to seduce her, she wished it was for real. Harriet was right, she'd abandoned commonsense for this ridiculous idiocy and she couldn't put a stop to it.

By the time they reached the last line of the first act and Hugo had praised them to the skies for their efforts she was completely drained and in need of a stiff drink.

Hugo, in bouyant mood, called out, 'Right, everybody. You've done an excellent night's work and now we'll all retire to the Royal Oak and the drinks are on me.'

A cheer went up and they collected their belongings and rushed out in a frenzy of post-rehearsal chatter. Caroline made sure she walked alongside Harriet and Liz.

The pub was busy so they stood at the bar until a table became free. Caroline drained her gin and tonic as fast as she decently could and ordered another. Dicky served her and gave her a wink, which she ignored. As she paid him, a hand came out and pushed her money away. It was Hugo's. She could have recognised that elegant hand with its long tapering fingers and neatly clipped nails anywhere on earth.

'This is on me. Put your money away.'

'You can't pay for drinks for everyone all night.'

'I don't intend to, but I shall and will pay for yours. Here we are, Dicky. How's life?'

'Fair to middling, thanks.'

'Snap! Same for me. Fair to middling. Except I'm hoping this fair lady here will alter all that.'

Dicky grinned. 'You couldn't have made a better choice.'

Caroline spotted a table about to become free. 'Oh look, I'm going to sit over there.' Without waiting to see if he followed she went across, settling herself on a chair. In a trice Hugo was sitting beside her. He raised his glass to her and sipped from it. Looking at her over the rim, his eyes sparkled. 'Happy?'

'Not especially.'

'You turned in an excellent performance tonight. True feeling, not acting. Eh? Am I right?'

'You flatter yourself.'

'I feel you tremble at my touch.'

'For heaven's sake!'

'It's true, my love, and you know it.'

'I don't.'

'You're fooling yourself.'

'You're the second person to say that to me tonight.'

'I should guess the other was Harriet.'

'It was.'

'She knows me too well.'

'Is she right about you, though?'

He stared at Harriet still standing at the bar and then answered, 'Not always.' Hugo reached across the table and touched the hand holding her glass. 'Not this time.'

Caroline looked into his eyes, trying to judge the sincerity of what he was saying. His eyes left hers and looked behind her. His hand was withdrawn and she heard the last voice she wanted to hear at that moment.

'Darling, I thought I might find you here.'

She turned round to find Peter standing behind her. He was wearing a shirt she'd bought him only recently and his new linen trousers. He looked, as well he knew, a very appealing figure. Pure anger filled her to the brim but a lifetime of self-discipline enabled her to greet him civilly.

'Hello. What a surprise!' She pulled out a

chair for him and then as an afterthought said, 'The children! Who's sitting in?'

'Sylvia.'

A thousand thoughts raced through her head as she realised that they'd made an arrangement so he could watch over her. Damn them both, she thought. How dare they? Before Peter sat down he put a hand on her shoulder and kissed the top of her head. He drew his chair nearer to her and sat with his arm nonchalantly along the back of her chair.

'How did the rehearsal go?'

Hugo, unfussed by Peter's appearance, answered, 'Excellently well. I'm very thrilled with them all. Your wife is proving herself tiptop where acting is concerned.' He put a slight emphasis on 'acting' which angered Caroline even further.

Peter, well practised at shouldering difficult conversations, chatted away to Hugo leaving Caroline to compose herself. Inside she was fuming. These two men were treating her as though she were a brainless chattle to be bandied about at their convenience. Peter doing his caveman act, all he needed was the leg bone of a mammoth in his hand, and Hugo playing the charming dilettante. Each of them recognised the other's role but spoke about every subject under the sun other than the one which really lay between them.

It was when Peter began saying how much he'd enjoyed Hugo in *Macbeth* and Hugo had pretended to shudder at the mention of that dreaded word that she finally snapped.

'As the two of you appear to have lots to talk about I'll leave you to get on with it.' They both half rose in protest at her departure but she'd gone before they had a chance to speak.

On her way out she stopped to say goodnight to everyone and then coolly left, after a final wave to Harriet.

She greeted Sylvia with less than her usual courtesy. 'Hi there. Thanks for giving Peter a chance to come and have a drink with us. I've come home early because I'm tired.'

After Sylvia had left, Caroline checked the children were all right and then went to run a bath. She chose lavender bath oil to relax her and was just starting to simmer down when she heard Peter's key in the lock.

She listened as he checked the doors, shut windows, spoke to the cats, unlocked the cat flap and came slowly up the stairs. She'd imagined he'd come into the bathroom immediately but he didn't. Lying back in the hot scented water with her eyes shut, she contemplated where her feelings were leading her. Having arrived at the conclusion that she was infatuated with Hugo and it wasn't the real thing and she'd better get in charge of herself again quick fast, she became conscious of a movement close by and opened her eyes to find Peter in his pyjamas standing looking down at her.

Immediately the fury she had felt in the bar overcame her and she blurted out her anger. 'Satisfied, are you? You and Sylvia. That was a pathetic performance, Peter, and what's more it was beneath you and you know it. It was childish in the extreme.'

He knelt down beside the bath, laid his arms on the edge of it and rested his chin on them. 'I had to give the matter the stamp of my approval and it was the only way I could think of to get the message transmitted round the village that their soft-in-the-head Rector didn't believe a word of what they were saying.'

'Is that so.'

'Someone has to protect your reputation.'

'Oh, so that's what you were doing! And there I thought you were doing your caveman act.'

He trailed a hand in the water and she shifted her legs to avoid the possibility of him touching her.

'No. Though I can see it may have looked like it. But I don't want anyone looking at you as Hugo did tonight.'

'He has a massive ego and imagines every woman — excepting perhaps Harriet, who has his measure — will fall in love with him. He's probably quite right, most of them do.'

Peter flicked some water onto her shoulders and trailed his fingers over the wetness. 'He has no business to toy with your affections.'

'You make it sound as though I have no control over my own feelings. Well, I have.' She sat up, sploshing water over the edge of the bath and drenching his pyjama jacket. 'Sorry! I didn't mean to do that. Just leave it to me, will you? And don't ever again do what you did tonight. I am not a child. A jealous husband I don't need, because there's nothing to be jealous of.' Peter began touching her arm gently and persuasively. 'And you can take your hands off me, please, because I'm not having you going through the ritual of, as you see it, establishing your rights over me tonight. I am my own person and I won't have it.'

Peter sprang to his feet, angered by what she'd said. 'I have never done that. Ever. Not once. And well you know it. We have always been equal partners.'

The tremor in his voice appalled her. He was absolutely right. Damn and blast that

Hugo. He was driving her to say things which in her normal mind she never would. She would not allow Hugo to make her throw away the one thing most precious to her.

Caroline pulled out the plug, stood up and slowly unbuttoned Peter's jacket, saying, 'Put it in the airing cupboard to dry.' She thought, what stupid comments people who love each other make when they really mean to say 'I love you'. She waited for him to close the cupboard door before putting her arms around his neck. She said in a shaky voice, 'I'm so dreadfully sorry, I really don't know what's come over me. Please forgive me. Now I'm making you all wet again. Sorry.'

He helped her out of the bath, wrapped her in a towel and, holding each other close, they left the bathroom.

9

Vera carried the tray out onto the patio and placed it carefully on the wrought iron table. She checked to make sure she had everything she needed and then sat down to wait.

The geraniums were growing wonderfully well and already she could just see tips of pink showing in the buds. By next week they'd be ablaze. The pots Rhett had found were ideal. She patted the table top and admired the chair opposite her. It was painted white just like she saw in those posh gardening magazines at the nursing home. In fact, truth to tell, the whole of the patio with its pots of plants and the table and chairs could have been from one of them. Identical it was. And the crazy paving! He'd mended the worst bits and then extended it right up to the grass. Smashing, it looked. If she'd paid a thousand pounds, which she wouldn't have, it couldn't look better. Who needed a mansion to have a posh garden? There was no doubt about it, their Rhett had an eye for gardens.

She heard the door bell. 'That'll be her.'

Dottie Foskett had already opened the

door as Vera reached it.

'Thought you wasn't in, but you'd said half past three.'

'I was sitting out in the garden, it took me a minute. Go through. The kettle's already boiled, I won't be long.'

Dottie admired the garden while she waited. Their Rhett had turned out all right after all. Surprising in the circumstances, because she'd really thought he'd blown it with that witchcraft business the other year. Poor lad. What a start in life he'd had.

Vera came through with the teapot.

'New cups you've got then.'

'That's right. Got them from that china stall back o' Culworth market. I thought we needed something a bit different if we were joining the aristocracy.'

'Come on, Vera, you do give yourself airs.'

'I don't. Where could you find a nicer place to sit? There isn't a castle in the land with a lovelier patio than this.'

'They calls 'em terraces when they 'ave a castle.'

Vera pondered this for a moment and then agreed with her. 'You're right. Milk or lemon?'

'Milk, of course. Yer know they look God awful expensive to me. Are you sure they're not valuable?'

'Well, Greenwood Stubbs said they'd been laid about ever since he'd been there and nobody bothered with 'em so we got 'em. Pity for 'em to go to waste. Mr Fitch said they had to get rid of it all before he got back, so here we are.' Vera sipped her tea, put down her cup and asked, 'You weren't in the pub last night were you, Dottie?' Dottie, with a mouthful of buttered scone, shook her head. 'Rector came in, you know, and kissed her and that and sat beside her with his arm round her, talking to Hugo.'

'Bet you wished you were a fly on the wall when they got home.'

'No, I don't. I don't wish either of them any harm. They're a lovely couple. It's Hugo who's to blame.'

Dottie winked at her. 'Perhaps you should set your cap at him, take the heat off her.'

'Don't be daft. I can safely leave that to you.'

'Me!' Dottie made a show of being indignant. 'You've heard they're expecting another at Keepers Cottage?'

'Gilbert and Louise, yer mean. Yes, I have. Going great guns they are. Who'd have thought it, her being like she was.'

'The baby will only be eleven months when the next arrives.'

'Yer'd better have a word in her ear, then.

161

Tell her all yer know. She can't keep this pace up. I expect Louise'll be wanting you to do more hours. More tea, or another scone?'

Dottie eyed her closely through narrowed eyes. 'You're enjoying this, aren't yer?'

'Wouldn't you?'

'Suppose I would. That miserable flat I have's neither use nor ornament. Can't swing a cat.'

'Good job you haven't got one then!'

They chortled together over the tea cups and Dottie told her a few more pieces of scandal which mainly involved the antics of Kenny and Terry Jones and herself.

'Honestly, Dottie, you are a one. You're disgusting. It doesn't go with my nice china at all it doesn't, a tale like that.'

'Is that your bell?'

Vera listened. 'It is. They'll be waking Don up. All right, all right I'm coming.'

Standing on her doorstep were two big men in suits. Before they opened their mouths she knew in her bones that they were police officers.

'Mrs Wright? Mrs Vera Wright?'

Vera nodded. They flashed their identification cards and asked if they could come in.

She opened the door wider and showed them into her front room. She asked them if they'd like to sit down. What on earth were they doing here? Was it Brenda? Had something happened to Brenda? Don had always said she'd finish up in the canal with the company she kept.

'Is it my daughter? Brenda. Is she all right?'

The taller police officer shook his head. 'It's nothing to do with a daughter. From information we have received we believe that you have stolen goods on the premises.'

Vera was shocked. 'Stolen goods? I haven't got no stolen goods. Do you mean shop lifting? 'Cos I've not been doing that. I'm honest and hard working like me husband.'

'Where is he at the moment?'

'In bed. He's on nights.'

'Could you wake him for us, Mrs Wright?'

'Why should I? He's only been in bed an hour.'

Dottie appeared in the doorway.

'Well, we need to speak to him.'

Vera, fearing Don's temper if she woke him now, asked, 'Can't you tell me what it's about?'

'Can we look in your back garden?'

'I haven't got no stolen goods in the shed if that's what yer mean. Me, my Don and our Rhett, we're all hard working people and we don't steal, so there.'

'It's not the shed Mrs Wright, it's . . . ' he referred to his notebook, 'an antique wrought iron table, and two chairs, and a large quantity of crazy paving, two bags of cement and several highly-prized Victorian ornamental stone urns removed from the estate grounds in the last three weeks.'

Dottie gasped and reached out blindly for the nearest chair. 'Ohhh. Vera!'

Vera had gone white as a sheet. 'Oh no! Who's . . . ' She was going to say 'split on us' but she was astute enough, despite the shock, to know that would give the game away. 'Dottie, get our Don.' Dottie disappeared up the stairs on feeble legs, every step a mountain.

'Your grandson? Is he home yet?'

Vera glanced at the clock. 'Won't be 'ome for a while yet. He starts at half past six in the summer and sometimes works till it's almost dark. What do you want him for?'

'He's implicated in the theft.'

'He got permission.'

'From whom?'

Despite her fear, Vera couldn't name names. 'Oh, nobody. But he wasn't to blame.'

'Then who was?'

'I don't know.'

'You mean you won't say?'

'Something like that.'

Vera stared at Don as he arrived in the sitting room with his trousers hastily pulled on, and his rolls of bulging fat clearly visible in the gaps between the buttons of his pyjama jacket. Was she married to *this?* No wonder they'd never made progress.

'Mr Donald Wright?'

Don acknowledged he was with a nod of his head. As the officer revealed his reasons for being in the house Don grew more and more furious and when the officer finished speaking he vented his spleen on Vera. 'You and your fancy ideas! I might have known no good would come of it. La di da on the patio with yer cups of tea and yer gossip. It's her fault, officer. She encouraged him.'

'Could we see the garden, please?'

Vera led the way and Don and Dottie brought up the rear. They made notes about the number of stone urns, the half bag of cement in the corner by the shed awaiting disposal, and took particular interest in the table and two chairs. Then they counted the paving stones Rhett hadn't needed, then the new stones he'd obviously laid.

Vera found she had tears sliding down her cheeks. She scrubbed at them with a corner of a tissue lying dormant in her skirt pocket. Just as she'd clutched her dream it was being snatched away. Why was there never hope? Other people had it but not Vera Wright. Oh no! Not her. Bottom of the pile again.

'Would you mind telling me how you came to know about all this?' Vera waved her arm vaguely around the garden. 'You know, who told you?'

'It was reported to us by the owners.'

'I see. Oh, I see.'

'Now, these articles may not be removed from this garden until we have arranged to do it ourselves.'

'You're taking up the crazy paving, are you then?'

'Well, perhaps not, but we shall certainly be removing the urns and the garden furniture. Probably later this afternoon.'

'What if we pay for it all?'

'Sorry, but the owners want to prosecute.'

At the word prosecute, Vera knew it was all up with them. She sat down heavily on one of the wrought iron chairs but immediately recollected it wasn't hers to sit on any longer and leapt to her feet. 'Don, it could mean jail for yer.'

'Me? I'd nothing to do with it. It was all you. If there's anybody going to jail it'll be you not me. I can't afford to lose my job.'

'Neither can I, Don.' She went in the house, closely followed by Dottie, Don and the police officers.

'We'll say good afternoon to you, Mrs Wright, Mr Wright. Nothing is to be moved from here at all. We've made a note and we'll be back either later this afternoon or first thing tomorrow. Sorry about this, but we're only doing our duty. We could do nothing else but take action once it was reported.' They shut the door and left Dottie, Don and Vera alone. For the first time since Brenda had got herself into trouble with Rhett, Vera sat down and howled. Don took the opportunity to stomp off back to bed.

Dottie patted her arm, handed her a fresh tissue from the purple plastic handbag she was clutching, and said, 'Look here, why don't yer go up to the Big House and see Mr Fitch and offer to pay for the crazy paving and give him back the pots and that. Surely if he's not out of pocket with it he'll let you off.'

Vera stopped sobbing. 'That's an idea. I could do that, couldn't I?'

'Of course yer could. I'll come with yer, if yer like.'

Vera decided she'd do better on her own than with her flashy cousin. 'It's very kind but it's my problem and I'll go by meself. Where's Don?'

Dottie, who'd always had a certain amount of respect for the man of few words her cousin had married, said, 'He's gone back to bed. The rat.'

'He is, isn't he? A blasted rat. I've stuck

with him through thick and thin, but this time he's finally done it. Abandoning me like that. I'm going to get changed into something smart and I'm going up to the Big House and seeing what I can do about this. I'm damned if I'm going to prison.'

Dottie could almost hear trumpets sounding as Vera set off. She'd put on her pink suit from Brenda's wedding and carried with her her high-heeled shoes in a plastic carrier bag, having decided that her sandals would serve her better until she got within shouting distance of the Big House. She planned to change into them and leave her shopping bag under a bush while she went inside. 'Good luck, Vera. You'll win through.'

⋆ ⋆ ⋆

Vera went in through the main door. It had occurred to her that she ought to use the trade entrance but decided against it. She was here on business and she'd be at a disadvantage if she didn't use the main door.

Overawed by the dignity and beauty of the entrance hall, she hesitated, wondering where to go. A voice said, 'Good afternoon. Can I help you?'

It was a smart young thing behind a reception desk who had spoken.

'Mr Fitch. I want to see Mr Fitch.'

'Your name is . . . ?'

'Vera Wright. Is he in?'

'I'm sorry, Mr Fitch is in the States. He won't be back for a while. Can I help? Or the estate manager, Mr Mayer.'

Relieved at hearing a name she knew Vera said yes, she'd see Mr Mayer.

'Sit down and I'll page him.'

Neither of them had to wonder if he was coming because long before he hove into sight they heard his heavy breathing and felt the vibration of every step he took.

Vera hadn't seen Jeremy Mayer for some time and was amazed at how much fatter he had become. Even worse, his breathing was so loud. He reminded her of an old bulldog who used to come to visit one of the patients at the nursing home.

He grunted and panted and then said breathlessly, 'Vera! Come into my office.'

She followed him into an office filled by a large desk, several filing cabinets, book shelves and Jeremy. He lowered himself into his chair.

'I know what you've come to see me about.'

'You do?'

'Yes, and I'm sorry but we shall be prosecuting. Mr Fitch is very serious indeed

169

when it comes to staff stealing property.'

'But it was just lying about, and Mr Fitch had said he wanted it clearing away. No one had bothered with it all for years. It just doesn't seem fair.'

'Bothered with it or not it was, er, *is* estate property and is not to be removed.'

'If we return it all and pay for the crazy paving would that be all right? It wasn't done on purpose, kind of.'

'It didn't get into your garden all by itself, did it? When Mr Fitch finds out . . . '

'That's what I want to know, who was it split on us?'

Jeremy shut up like a clam. He fiddled with a pen, straightened papers which were lying haphazardly about his desk, coughed and said, 'I'm not at liberty to . . . Suffice to say I received information upon which I have acted on Mr Fitch's behalf.'

'Sounds like the bloody Gestapo to me. Does he have a torture chamber?'

Jeremy allowed himself half a smile. 'No, but we do have a very efficient information system.'

'Look. Could you speak on my behalf? Ask him to let us off. You know, not go to court. It wasn't done with any intent, not really. Just . . . '

'The matter is in the hands of the police

170

and that's that. I am acting under Mr Fitch's explicit instructions. Now, I'm a very busy man, if you'll excuse me.' He coughed and slipped a lozenge into his mouth.

'From what I hear that's just about all you do do, act under his instructions. A yes man, that's what you are. A yes man. He's got you right where he wants yer. Same as yer wife has yer, right where she wants yer.' As an afterthought she added, 'Except she doesn't want yer.'

Jeremy struggled to his feet. 'Madam, if you please.'

'We'll pay him for the crazy paving. He's getting everything back, everything. So if he's no worse off, do you think I might persuade . . .'

'I do not, Vera. It's more than my job's worth to cancel the charges.'

The word 'job' jolted Vera. 'And our Rhett. What about his job?'

'He finishes today.'

'You wouldn't do that to him! He was only trying to cheer me up. That's all. Just cheer me up. A good turn, that's all. And this is his reward. He'll be heartbroken.'

'He shouldn't have stolen, should he?'

'He didn't, he just kind of did a long term borrow.'

'There's nothing more to be said.' Jeremy

nodded in the direction of the door. 'Let yourself out.'

'Well, if you want to lose the best under gardener you've had in years then that's up to you. He's got his diploma, so I don't suppose he'll be out of a job for long.'

'No one will employ him if he has a criminal record.'

'Criminal record! You're prosecuting him as well?'

'Of course. You for receiving stolen goods and him for stealing. The estate has been driven into taking a stance on this. We lose thousands with all this pinching here and there, and it's got to stop.'

'Well, all I can say is damn your eyes. All this over a few stingy bits of crazy paving and he's a multi millionaire. We'll be ruined, but he'll go from strength to strength. It damned well isn't fair.'

Vera stormed out of Jeremy's office, sped down the drive as fast as she could and only remembered that night when she went to bed that her flat shoes were still under the bush at the Big House. Well, she thought, the dratted, dreary, boring things can stay there till they rot. Just like I'm going to rot.

★ ★ ★

The full implications of the situation didn't strike home until Vera went to the Royal Oak the following night. To her delight, Willie, Sylvia and Jimmy were at her favourite table and also Pat Jones, Duckett that was, waiting for her Barry to join her after the rehearsal.

'Vera!' Sylvia patted the seat beside her. 'Come and sit next to me. Willie, get Vera a drink.'

In obedience to Sylvia's request Willie stood up. 'What will yer have?'

'Arsenic?'

'Come on, it won't come to that.'

'Won't it? It's a police job yer know. In court. I could go to prison.'

Pat looked at her and said accusingly, 'It's all your Rhett's fault.'

Vera nodded. 'All he wanted to do was cheer me up 'cos I 'adn't got the job as wardrobe mistress. That Mrs Jones got there before me, as yer know. I know I was rude to her, but she cut me right out and I longed to do it.' A faraway look came in her eyes and Sylvia squeezed her hand. 'Poor lad, he's lost his job, yer know. Big fat Jeremy says even though he's got a diploma, with a criminal record he'll never get another job.'

Willie had come back with her drink and heard the last few words. As he put it down and pocketed his change he said, 'Yer mean

173

he's being prosecuted as well?'

Vera nodded. 'Me for receiving and 'im for stealing. Just a few old pots and a rusty table and chairs. It's not fair. He worked hours on 'em cleaning the rust off. So now old Fitch gets 'em back like new.' She took a sip of her lager and sat shaking her head in desperation.

Pat said angrily, 'And what about me?'

'What about you, you're not involved.'

'No, but my Dad is.'

'So?'

'When old Fitch gets back from the States Jeremy says they're going to decide whether or not Dad loses his job, too. After all, the gardens are his sole responsibility.'

'He'd never sack your dad! Greenwood Stubbs sacked! Never!'

'Don't you be too sure. We're shaking in our shoes, believe me.'

'But where would he be without him? The gardens! The glasshouses! He'd never find another to replace him, not like your dad.'

'Old Fitch is in no mood for being sentimental, he's on the warpath and we're being used as an example. They steal like mad from the estate. Fencing posts, top soil, tools, wood, paint, electric drills, you name it. They all think old Fitch is fair game. He knows it and he's out to stop it. So now he's got actual evidence of stealing and the balloon's going up.'

Slowly Vera thought through what Pat had said. 'It'd just be a fine, wouldn't it though?'

Pat shrugged her shoulders. Willie gloomily contemplated his ale. Sylvia grew cold with the thought which had just struck her. Pat and her dad would be sure to lose the house which went with the head gardener's job, in which case Pat and Barry, Greenwood and Dean and Michelle would be homeless. She decided to stay sympathetically silent.

Jimmy spoke up. 'I may not have led a blameless life, but I've never actually stolen anything. It strikes me that you're all feeling sorry for yourselves and thinking how unfair it all is, when in fact yer guilty.'

A stunned silence greeted his remarks, followed by an enraged babble of noise.

'Jimmy! You of all people.'

'Well, I never!'

'Whose side are you on?'

'Turned capitalist, 'ave yer, now yer in business for yourself?'

'You're a traitor, you are!'

Jimmy raised a hand to silence them all. 'Just a minute. Answer me this question. Leaving aside the fact that the stuff was all lying unused around the estate, who does it belong to? Not you, Vera. Not your Rhett.

175

Nor, Pat, does it belong to your dad even though he's head gardener. So who does it belong to?'

Reluctantly they all said, 'Mr Fitch.'

'Exactly. That's my point.'

Vera protested. 'But it was lying about doing nothing. He wanted rid of it, he said so. He wouldn't have missed it. What I want to know is who told him?'

They all agreed they didn't know. Vera smiled triumphantly. 'That's the point, he'd never have realised if someone hadn't told him. I've got to find out who it was.'

Jimmy groaned. 'Yer 'aven't got the point, 'ave yer. No matter who told him, yer still guilty of receiving stolen goods. Finding out who let on'll alter nothing.'

'I'd still like to know who it was, though.'

Sylvia didn't improve Vera's mood by saying, 'Anyone about that afternoon would have seen them unloading, you know. Anyone at all.'

Vera eyed Jimmy speculatively. 'It wasn't you, was it? Coming over all moral about theft just now, it makes me wonder.'

Jimmy snorted his anger. 'I wouldn't do a trick like that. I'm not that law abiding, I've no loyalty to that old Fitch, believe me. I'd rather see Ralph at the Big House, like he should be, than that old varmint.'

Pat said, 'And so would I. He wouldn't have minded Vera having a few stones and that, he'd have given them to her himself.'

Jimmy tapped the table with his forefinger, 'And that's why he isn't up there and old Fitch is. Men like Sir Ralph and those who went before him were too kind. They didn't watch the pennies, whereas old Fitch always has done and that's why he owns the Big House and old Ralph doesn't. Whatever yer say, Rhett, with your dad's connivance, stole that crazy paving and you're getting what yer deserve, hard though it may seem.'

Vera stood up. 'Well, all I can say is, Jimmy Glover, I shan't be drinking with you any more. I've always thought you were one of us, but I can see now you aren't and never have been. You're a traitor to your class, you are. A traitor. That's what.'

With what little dignity she had left after the battering of the last couple of days Vera left the bar, managing to hold on to her tears until she'd got through the door.

Sylvia filled the silence Vera left behind by saying, 'All this is Hugo Maude's fault. He's a lot to answer for.'

Willie asked, 'Yer mean *he* told old Jeremy?'

'Noooo! Of course not. If she'd got the job of wardrobe mistress, Rhett wouldn't have come up with the idea of cheering her up, would he? So at bottom, when all's said and done, it's Hugo that's caused it all.'

'Not only that from what I hear,' Jimmy said slyly.

Sylvia avoided Jimmy's eye and finished the last of her gin and tonic.

Pat asked, 'So what have you heard?'

Jimmy leant across the table and began to report the version of the tale he'd heard about Caroline and Hugo in the woods. He had just warmed to his story when the door opened and in came the entire cast of the play and the helpers. Barry came straight across to speak to Pat.

'Anyone ready for a refill? Be quick, I'm parched!'

They all agreed they were and he took their orders and eventually came back balancing a loaded tray. Barry sat down beside Pat, gave her a hearty kiss, shared out the drinks, toasted them all and downed half his glass at the first go.

'I needed that. By Jove, what a night we've had. Hugo's been losing his rag every five minutes.'

Sylvia laughed. 'He was firing on all cylinders when I left. He kept it up, did he?'

'I should say. He rants and raves and then next second he's as sweet as honey.' He shuffled closer to Pat, and whispered, 'Mind you, Dr Harris gets all the honey bit, it's the rest of us who get the ranting. That right, Sylvia?'

Sylvia gave a non-committal nod.

'In fact if I was Neville Neal I'd have resigned tonight. He couldn't get a word right.'

Pat asked 'Yer mean he hadn't learned his lines?'

'Learned his lines all right, just wasn't saying 'em like Hugo wanted him to. Give him his due, Neville stuck it out till he got it right.'

Pat recollected her responsibilities and asked, 'Barry, where's our Michelle? Who's taken her home?'

'Rhett.'

'Rhett? Oh, I see. Not our Dean?'

'No. Dean's over there, look, knocking 'em back. Michelle did real well tonight. Hugo's very pleased with her.'

Pat beamed. 'Well, I suppose that's something to cheer us up, there isn't much else, is there?' She looked across to where Hugo was standing beside Caroline toasting her not only with his drink but with his eyes. 'Dr Harris is skating on thin ice again by the looks of it.'

They watched Hugo put an arm around

179

her waist and keep it there.

Pat asked Sylvia if the Rector would be coming again tonight.

Sylvia shook her head. 'Can't do that twice, once but not twice. I've an idea he caught it in the neck about that.'

Willie asked what on earth was up with Dr Harris? Something funny had come over her and no mistake.

When they'd all finished watching Hugo lead Caroline to a separate table for two they all looked at Sylvia. 'Well?'

'I can't understand it actually. Her and the Rector, well yer don't need me to tell you how much they think about each other. Sounds soppy, but they are very, very much in love with one another, like as if they'd married only yesterday. He worships her and her him. Yet he can stand by and give her the freedom to mess about with him.' She jerked her thumb in Hugo's direction.

Barry observed, 'Seems funny to me. If Pat was carrying on like that I'd have blacked both his eyes for starters, and broken both his legs for the main course.'

Willie grunted. 'Well, they're educated, aren't they? Different class o' people from us. They see things differently.'

Barry snorted his disgust. 'I bet it's true they've been having it off. See him running his finger up her arm? Sexy that. They're only the same as the rest of us when it comes to hanky panky.'

Jimmy's eyes twinkled.

Willie looked embarrassed.

Pat gave Barry a nudge to shut him up.

Sylvia became incensed. 'Barry! Really! What a thing to say!'

Barry leaned over towards her and said quietly so as not to be overheard, 'Well, admit it, that's why you're so worried. That's what you're dreading's happened. I'm telling you by the looks of 'em it has. When the Rector finds out then believe me it'll be Coronation night and Bonfire Night fireworks rolled into one!'

Jimmy intervened by changing the subject to the chances of the Turnham Malpas cricket team this week, and how was Barry's batting lately.

But Hugo's finger was still following a vein on Caroline's arm, and she was still enjoying the sensation.

10

In bed that night after Peter had gone to sleep Caroline grew too restless to settle and went downstairs to make herself a drink. Sitting in her rocking chair beside the Aga she sipped her tea and thought about temptation. She looked at her arm, remembering the feeling of Hugo's finger tracing along her skin. God, he was tempting. There was that indefinable quality which attracted her to him. The way his hand clasped hers, those fingers so strong and yet so elegant. He was truly a man designed for women to adore. She realised Hugo knew he was desirable, whereas Peter never realised for one moment how attractive women found him. Hugo knew women fell for him. He was arrogant, self opinionated, egotistical, not at all the kind of person who in her right mind she would have liked, but at the same time he was gloriously fascinating. Damn him. The mature, experienced, commonsensical, well beloved Caroline had no need to crave for Peter's love; she had that always, forever. It was hers, whatever she did, whenever she needed it. But right now Peter's kind of unwavering love had become suffocating; she needed something different, something deeply exciting, before it was all too late. Some exquisite experience that would light her up whenever she thought about it in the years to come. In her heart of hearts the untried virginal Caroline of yesteryear lusted for Hugo. Coming as he did at this very moment in her life he was like the answer to a prayer.

Parallel to her thoughts about temptation and where it might lead ran her thoughts about her children. There was no way she could smash their lives to pieces, and that would be what she would do if she left Peter for Hugo. For Hugo? What was she thinking of? A life of racketing about, never knowing who he was with, what he was doing, never being sure he would come home at night. And the children. In all conscience could she take them from their blood parent? But they were hers, Peter told her so, time and again. They loved her as she loved them. Their dear hearts would break.

How sure could one be of a person like Hugo? One couldn't. Not so entirely as she could Peter. With Hugo she would have wonderful, glorious, delirious, hilarious times but when it came to the real challenge of life, when the chips were down then where would Hugo be?

Her mind wandered away from reality and she was back in the wood with Hugo's head resting on her legs and her fingers entwined in his dark silky hair. She remembered how she felt about him in the role of Leonard and particularly his attempt at seduction in the second act. With her cup she toasted him as the actor, the lover, the man and wished she was drinking some exotic, madly expensive wine instead of dull, everyday, comforting, mundane tea. Her thoughts were broken by a cry. Instantly, she raced for the stairs.

'All right, Beth, I'm coming! All right!'

After she'd soothed away Beth's nightmare Caroline returned to bed and lay on her side looking at Peter in the glow of her bedside light. She could see just the faintest of lines around his eyes, and a very slight hint of a white hair here and there above his ears. He had one hand tucked under his chin, the fingers half curled, and she examined his well manicured nails and recalled the sensitivity of the touch of his fingers. She leaned over him and breathed in the familiar scent of him mingling with the faint aroma of the soap he'd used before he came to bed, and risked waking him by touching his cheek with her fingers and then kissing him. But it wasn't only his physical attributes which impressed.

It was his courage, his all-adoring love and his steadfastness.

Unquestioning. Profound. Passionate. What more could a woman want?

Impatiently Caroline turned off the light and lay down again. Peter, feeling her presence even in sleep, reached out an arm and drew her close. How she wished he hadn't. At this moment she wasn't worthy of him.

★ ★ ★

The phone rang around half past nine the next morning. 'Turnham Malpas Rectory. Peter Harris speaking.'

'Oh! Good morning! Hope I'm not ringing too early.'

'Hugo! Good morning. What can I do for you?'

'It's Caroline really. Is she in?'

'She is indeed. I'll get her for you. Hold the line.' Peter went to the study door and called, 'Caroline! It's for you.' He picked up the receiver again and said, 'How are the rehearsals going?'

'Absolutely fine, thanks. Taking a bit of knocking into shape but very well really. Your dear wife is doing excellently. Really got into the part.'

185

'She's certainly enjoying herself, all due to you.'

There was a moment's hesitation and then Hugo replied, 'Good. I'm glad. How's life for you?'

'Couldn't be busier. Would you mind if I sat in on a rehearsal sometime? Just interested to see what goes on. Never seen a world class actor at work, you see.'

'Be delighted. Come any night you can get a sitter for those children of yours.'

Peter thought he detected a slight emphasis on the word 'yours'. 'Ah, here she is. It's Hugo, darling.' He made no move to leave the study so she could speak to him privately.

'Hello, Hugo! What can I do for you?'

Peter watched her listening to him: the restlessness, the barely disguised excitement, the slight huskiness of her voice. He turned back to the work on his desk.

'I'd love to. Yes, I really would. No, Peter's busy all day. I'd need to be back by three because of the children.' There came a pause as she listened to him. 'No, he cannot, he's working. See you about half past eleven then? OK. Bye.'

Peter watched the receiver being returned to its cradle, and waited.

'Darling, you don't mind if Hugo and I go out to lunch, do you? Just some things we need to talk over about the play. It's difficult when he's producing and acting at the same time, you see. There are important things he doesn't get a chance to tell me.'

Peter swung his chair round and faced her. 'Of course I don't mind. All I will say is be careful.'

'You're not suggesting he might seduce me over the lunch table, are you?'

Peter studied what his reply should be. 'That kind of comment is not fitting and well you know it. Of course I don't mean that.'

'Good, because there's no need for you to worry.'

'I'm not entirely blind to the effect he has on you. It's hardly surprising, even I can see he is a very attractive man.'

'Not to me he isn't.'

Peter sighed. 'You're fooling yourself, my darling girl.'

'Is this on the basis that the onlooker sees most of the game?'

'Something like that.'

'I'm not a complete fool.'

'I know. Indeed I do. Just a friendly warning, don't you know.'

'No, Peter, it isn't. You're doing what you always do, standing aside and allowing me to do whatever I want, pretending to be giving me my freedom but at bottom it's because you're so damn confident that your love for me will bring me to heel.'

'What would you prefer me to do? Go break his legs?'

Caroline gave him a slight smile. 'You could at that. At least it would be *something*.'

'Whatever, the warning still stands. *Be careful*. I don't want you hurt.'

'How about if I fancy being hurt? Fancy having a fling? Fancy doing my own thing? Fancy not doing the Rector's wife bit?'

'That's up to you. Do as you wish.' He swung his chair to face the desk and she took is as a dismissal. After she'd left the study, Peter tried to settle to his work, but on every page Hugo's face intruded on the words. He put a stop to the pretence of working and sat with his head in his hands thinking. He knew Caroline would realise the situation that was developing, she was too astute not to. What made it worse from his point of view was that she was going headlong into it with her eyes wide open. The play was merely the vehicle by which she gained access to the man. Damn and blast him. Why had he ever come?

★ ★ ★

The restaurant Hugo chose was one recommended by Jimbo. 'He says it's brilliant and

188

just right for a tête-à-tête luncheon.' He took a moment from watching the traffic to glance at her. 'Happy?'

'I am. It's years since I had a ride in an open car. They really are fun, aren't they?'

'They are. Fun, that's just what you need. Fun and lots of it.'

'You're right. I do. Being a doctor all the people you speak to you are people not at their best. It can be very draining. Then Peter has a similar kind of job in a way and between the two of us we have all the cares of the world on our shoulders. A bit of fun *is* just what I need.' Hugo pressed firmly on the accelerator as they turned onto the bypass and her hair began blowing about, bringing a stunning sense of freedom to her which she hadn't experienced in a long time.

'Did he mind?'

'Yes and no. He's like that.'

'Loves you very much, doesn't he?'

Caroline shouted back. 'He does. Too much sometimes.'

'Ah! I see. Cloying, is he?'

'Absolutely not. Well, just a little. What did you say this restaurant was called?'

'I didn't. Believe it or believe it not it's called The Lovers' Knot.'

Caroline laughed. 'That is just too obvious

for words. Are you sure it was Jimbo's suggestion?'

'Why? Does the word 'lover' have some significance for you and me?'

Quickly Caroline shook her head. 'Of course not, I don't know why I said it.'

Hugo smiled and pressed even harder on the accelerator. As the speedometer went up to a hundred he smiled even more broadly.

'It does for me. Have significance. I want you, Caroline.'

'Do you indeed.'

'Yes. I do.'

'Hard luck. How far is this place?'

'About twelve miles.'

'Twelve miles! Just for lunch? What are you thinking of?'

'I hug my thoughts to my breast, they are not for public declaration.'

'You are being ridiculous. I don't want to go twelve miles for lunch. Please turn round and we'll go to The George in Culworth. That's much nearer.'

'Too late.'

'That's what I shall be if you don't go back. I can't have the children coming home to an empty house, they would be devastated. In any case I'd never live it down if they had to sit on the doorstep waiting for me.'

'Tut tut. Your reputation in jeopardy again. Ring Peter and tell him you'll be late. He can be there.'

'No, he can't.'

'Yes, he can.'

'No, he can't.'

'This sounds more like Gilbert and Sullivan by the minute.'

'I mean it, Hugo. I want you to turn round and go back. There, look, half a mile there's a turn off.' This caused Hugo to speed even faster.

'You are upsetting me.'

'No, I am abducting you, my dear,' he said in the tones of a thoroughly ham actor, as he twirled the ends of his imaginary waxed moustache.

She had to laugh.

'That's wonderful, hearing you laugh like that.'

'You're right it is. I feel as though I've been deadly serious for far too long. Carry on.' She waved a carefree hand. 'Drive wherever you like. I don't care.'

At half past two she rang Sylvia on the hotel telephone to ask her to collect the children, but there was no reply. She rang the Rectory but there was no reply from there either. So she tried Harriet, then Muriel, and finally the school. Kate, the head teacher, promised to keep the children until someone came to collect them.

★ ★ ★

Hugo and Caroline arrived back at five o'clock. Hugo tooted the horn with a flourish as he pulled up outside the Rectory. 'There we are. Home at last. I have an apt quotation for this situation but it won't quite come to mind.'

'Good, because I haven't time to listen. Where's my bag? Oh, here under the seat.' As she brought her head up he kissed her ear. 'Hugo! For God's sake.'

'I know. Your reputation. Sorry.'

She didn't wait for him to open the door for her but got out, saying, 'Thanks for a wonderful day, it's been truly memorable. And the restaurant just as great as you promised.'

Hugo put his hand to his heart and murmured, 'I am desolate. My darling girl is leaving me.'

His unwitting use of a phrase of Peter's brought her back to earth with a crash. 'For God's sake just go.' As she fitted her key in the latch she heard Beth shouting. Relief flooded over her. Without even answering Hugo's wave she fled inside.

192

'Mummy!' Beth raced across the hall and flung her arms round her. 'You're back. Daddy came for us. We thought you'd got lost.'

'Not lost, darling, just busy talking to Hugo Maude about the play.' She bent down to kiss Beth and as she straightened up she realised Peter was standing in the kitchen doorway listening to her.

'You're back. At last,' he said.

'Of course. Did you think I wouldn't be back?'

'No, that wasn't what I was thinking at all.'

'We've had lunch.'

'You said.'

'Lovely place. Not somewhere to take children though, it's hideously expensive.'

'It would have to be. What's it called?'

Alex burst out of the sitting room where he'd been watching television. 'Mummy! Miss Pascoe let us play with her cats, Beano and Dandy. We had such fun.'

'Good. I'm sorry I'm late, I didn't realise the time.'

'Daddy came to find us.'

Caroline looked her thanks at Peter. 'Silly me. I shan't let it happen again.'

Peter said, 'I am glad. Just once is once too often, isn't it?'

The children disappeared. 'I did say it was just for lunch.'

'I know you did. What did you think I meant?'

She stood in front of the hall mirror and began dragging her comb through the tangles in her hair. 'He had the hood down on the car. It's ruined my hair.' Caroline tugged painfully at the knots.

'Here, let me have a try.' He took the comb from her and began gently combing her hair at the back. He caught her looking at his reflection in the mirror, and for a moment he looked straight back at her. Between two people who know each other intimately, a look can speak volumes. He was trying to assess how far things had gone that afternoon between her and Hugo; she appeared to be asking his forgiveness. But for what? Being late for the children?

Peter turned her round and began to comb the knots at the front. 'My word, you're brave, you're not even flinching.'

'Am I not?'

When he'd disentangled the last knot he straightened her hair and then, putting the comb down on the hall table, he took her face between his hands and kissed her mouth, a long slow massaging kiss. Then his arms slid round her and he held her close, but she wasn't part of it.

'My darling girl. I'm so glad you're home.'

'Have you started the meal?'

His arms released their hold on her. 'I have.'

'I'll carry on with it then.'

'You haven't told me where you went.'

Alex shouted from the sitting room. 'Daddy! It's that cartoon you like, be quick!'

Without looking at him Caroline answered, 'It'll keep.'

He watched her dash into the kitchen, leaving him no wiser. But surely she wouldn't have, would she? Not his beloved Caroline. He felt certain his instincts would have told him if she had. But then she wasn't herself at the moment. He damned Hugo yet again and went to watch the cartoon with the children.

11

Eating their supper seated around the table that night at the Garden House were Greenwood Stubbs, Pat, Barry, Dean and Michelle. They'd discussed what had happened during the day and had now got round to the subject of the theft.

Greenwood put down his fork, took a swig of his beer and commented, 'Well, Pat, from where I'm sitting things aren't looking too good. As I see it, Mr Fitch is bound to back old Jeremy's decision, and that means I'm out.'

Pat protested. 'But Dad . . . '

'No 'buts' about it, love, I'm for the chop. I think you haven't realised what that means.'

Pat scooped up the last of her pudding, licked the spoon and asked, 'What does it mean, then?'

'Barry and me's been having a talk and we've decided that I shall lose my job and with it this house. He won't employ me any longer, he won't be able to trust me, yer see. Teach me a lesson.'

'What!'

'House goes with the job, doesn't it? Let's

hope he gives us time to find somewhere.'

Pat was devastated. 'I never thought! Yer can't mean it? Does he, Barry?'

' 'Fraid so, love,' Barry replied: 'There's no way he'd allow me to have tenancy of this house. He'd need it for the new garden chap, it doesn't go with my kind of job. By the looks of it we'll be out sharpish.'

Michelle began to cry. 'I love this house. I love it. It isn't fair. I don't want to move.'

Pat lent her a handkerchief and Greenwood said, 'Come and sit on yer grandad's knee.' When Michelle had seated herself comfortably her grandad said, 'It's yer daft old grandad's fault and I'm sorry.'

Between sniffs, Michelle said, 'You were only being kind.'

Dean, who'd quietly been finishing his pudding while they'd been talking, remarked softly, 'It'll mean the end of that university scholarship old Fitch promised me.'

Pat burst into tears. 'Dean! I never thought. Oh, God! What shall we do? Barry!'

'Calm down, Pat. Anybody'd think we'd no money coming in. We have. You and me both. We'll see he gets to university, don't you fret. Don't give it another thought, Dean. I'll see yer all right. I shall be proud to have a son, even if he isn't my very own, at Oxford or wherever you go. Proud. That's what. We'll find the money somehow for whatever yer need.'

Greenwood apologised for the hundredth time.

'Just stop it will yer, Greenwood. You weren't to know. Let's face it, they do get stuff stolen day in day out and it is time they put a stop to it, and unfortunately it's you who's been caught out.'

'But it's not just me who's affected, is it? It's all of us. I'm that sorry, Dean, about yer scholarship. It's blooming rotten luck. Somehow we'll manage it, if I have to sweep the streets.'

Barry objected. 'There's no way you'll be sweeping the streets, you with your skills. No. I won't allow it. I reckon we'll manage fine.'

Michelle slipped off her grandad's knee and went to put an arm round Barry. 'You'll look after us all won't you, Barry?'

'Of course I shall. That's one good thing about me marrying yer mother, you've always got me at the back of you. I shan't let yer down.'

Michelle kissed his cheek. 'I knew you wouldn't. See Mum, you can stop crying now. You'd forgotten we've got Barry, hadn't you?'

'I 'ad, yer right. I'll take on more work with Charter-Plackett Enterprises, day and night if necessary and we shan't go short. How long before old Fitch gets back?'

Barry sipped his tea, put down his cup and looked to Greenwood for confirmation. 'They say Thursday after next, don't they, if nothing holds him up?'

Greenwood nodded. 'That's right. Thursday before the play on the Friday.'

'That gives us time, then.'

'Time for what?' Pat asked.

'Time to take action. Remember when old Fitch tried to steal the church silver that time? We all got together and showed him we wouldn't stand for it, didn't we? Well, how about a bit of action culminating on Thursday? He hates things going wrong. Likes it all moving along like a well oiled machine. Well, when he gets back it won't be a well oiled machine. It'll be chaos.'

Excited, they asked a million questions. Barry held up his hand to silence them. 'Be quiet! Right! I'll give it some thought and let you know. It can't be the central heating like last time, it's too hot for that to cause a problem at the moment. It could be the power, that'd ruin everything in the freezers.'

Pat interrupted. 'I don't want Jimbo getting hurt in this. It's all money to him is the freezers.'

'That's as may be. But I'll come up with something.'

Greenwood suggested he didn't have far to look. 'He's got that big directors' do day after he comes back. They're staying the weekend, country weekend and all that jazz. They've got seats booked for the play.'

Michelle looked horrified. 'You don't mean that, Grandad? Not Mr Fitch coming to see us?'

Grandad nodded. 'He's bringing the lot of 'em. Boasting, I expect, that we can attract such a big name as Hugo-the-big-I-am-Maude to the village. Fitch playing Lord of the Manor. I've flowers to provide for the bedrooms and that. Gardens to be looking spectacular and a tour of the glasshouses too. Me touching me cap to 'em all.' He imitated touching his forelock. 'He thinks!'

Barry clenched his fists and banged the table. 'That's it then. We'll sabotage that.'

Pat wagged a finger at him. 'Just a minute, I'm senior waitress that weekend. Friday dinner. Saturday lunch. Saturday dinner and Sunday lunch. Breakfasts as well. Blinking good money, it being the whole weekend. I don't fancy losing that. Not now.'

'Don't worry, love, I'll see you're all right.'

Michelle, excited by the thought of a bit of espionage, asked what Barry proposed to do. He tapped the side of his nose, 'Got to put my thinking cap on. Oh yes. If anyone comes up with any inspiration let me know. And not a word to anyone. This is our secret.' He pushed back his chair. 'Look at the time! Michelle, hurry up, you'll be late for rehearsal. And you, Dean.'

After they'd gone and Pat was clearing the table she asked her dad if he'd any idea who could have split on them.

'None at all. It's a mystery to me. Everyone in this village sees him and his belongings as fair game, they wouldn't mind us having a few bits of stone and some old wreck of a table and chairs, nor them old pots, some of 'em is cracked even. It's not someone getting back at me and Rhett, it's deeper than that.'

'Wish I blinking well knew who it was. I'd scratch their eyes out.'

'Don't fret, it'll all come out in the wash. Mark my words. Can I leave yer with all this?' He gestured to the washing up. 'I've had double the work without Rhett, it's nearly killed me today. The others are good lads and work hard but Rhett's taken a lot on his shoulders and we've really missed him.'

'Good lad, isn't he?'

'He is that. I'm going to try to get him a job in the Parks department. I still carry a bit of weight there.'

'Do you think there might be a chance that old Fitch will tell Jeremy he's a fool and cancel it all, and we'll be all right?'

'I doubt it. They stick together these folk. To save face he has to back him up, hasn't he?'

'I suppose so. It was me just hoping.'

'I know, love. I know. All our bright dreams gone. Thought Michelle would follow in my footsteps. We seemed so well set up, didn't we, all of us? Ah well. I can't say how sor . . . '

Pat squeezed his arm. 'Like Barry says, that's enough apologising. Go and watch yer telly. Go on, off yer go.'

★ ★ ★

When Pat went into the Store first thing the next day to check Jimbo's catering diary with her own she found herself catapulted into a furious argument.

Jimbo, increasingly agitated because the ambience he strove so hard to maintain was being destroyed, called out, 'Ladies! Ladies! Please.'

The main protagonists were the two Senior sisters, Mrs Jones, who was already wearing her smart mail order office tabard with Harriet's Country Cousin Farm Produce emblazoned across the front, Linda, playing her part from behind the post office grille, Georgie Fields from the

202

Royal Oak and Bel Tutt.

Valda Senior didn't heed Jimbo's request. 'When all's said and done, it's an unspoken agreement that if we can score off that old Fitch we do. Whoever it was who split on Vera deserves horsewhipping. We saw, but we didn't say a thing, did we, Thelma?' Her sister, with pursed lips, shook her head in agreement.

Georgie, small and pretty and looking as if an argument was the last thing she wanted, tapped on the post office counter and said through the grille to Linda, 'You ought to have more sense.'

Indignantly Linda answered, 'It wasn't me, I didn't tell. All I said was that they shouldn't expect to steal and then get away with it. That's all. I saw 'em unloading the stuff too but I didn't squeal. Not me.' She folded her arms as though to emphasise her innocence.

Bel Tutt pinged the till, gave Thelma Senior her change, and said, 'Well, if none of *us* has an inkling, who the blazes has?'

An uncomfortable silence followed this question which Pat filled with, 'By the looks of it Dad's going to lose his job, we're about to lose our house and Dean the university scholarship old Fitch promised him. If anybody would like to know, it's me.' She glared round. 'We're the ones suffering the most. Well, Vera is too and Rhett, but we could be losing the roof over our heads.'

Linda, coming out from behind the grille, said forcefully, 'In my opinion it's someone with a grudge against Vera. That's what's triggered it off. When they did it, they didn't see the consequences of it affecting you.'

'That's right. That could be it. So who's got a grudge against poor, harmless Vera?' Pat looked at each woman in turn, finally fixing her gaze on Mrs Jones, who flushed to the roots of her hair.

'Don't look at me. I've no grudge against anyone. Anyway, I've got work piling up.' She gave Pat a haughty stare and marched into the back of the Store.

Jimbo removed his boater, wiped his bald head with a handkerchief, replaced his headgear and said, 'Well now, having sorted that out perhaps we could get on with our shopping? Can I help anyone? Good offers on the meat counter today and tomorrow if anyone's interested?'

The two Senior sisters ambled out, Georgie paid for her shopping and left, Linda returned to her counter and Bel Tutt waited patiently behind the till.

Disgruntled by the argument Pat said sharply, 'I've really come in, Jimbo, to catch up on my dates. In the circumstances I'm willing to work whenever and wherever. Looks like we shall need the money.' She brought a fat red diary from her bag and opened it up.

'Come in the back. I need a break.' He took her into his office, took off his boater and reached for his diary from the top of the filing cabinet.

Before he had found the right page, Pat, making sure the door was properly closed first, said, 'Jimbo, did you notice that dear mother-in-law of mine didn't say she hadn't split? Just that she'd no grudge, that was all she said. Do yer think it might be her?'

'No idea, Pat, she's *your* mother-in-law. What's done's done. It's too late now. Just have to limit the damage as best you can.'

'I don't suppose you'd have a word, would yer? Just for me?' As an afterthought she added, 'and Dad, and our Dean.'

'With Jeremy?'

'No, not him. He's just a yes man. Well, yes, perhaps with him before it's too late. Well, no, I meant with Mr Fitch really. He's very partic'lar nowadays not to upset everybody, ever since he let Muriel Templeton persuade him to reinstate Sir Ralph as president of the cricket. If you could let him know on the quiet that the whole village is upset . . . '

'Well, they're certainly that. There's been no other topic of conversation in here but your bad luck and Vera's. Never known the village so worked up about anything.'

Pat frowned. 'That's what I'm worried about. They might take matters into their own hands. You know what they're like. I wouldn't want this director's weekend messed up.' Jimbo noticed that Pat looked as though she wished she hadn't said that.

He put his head to one side and looked at her. 'Do you know something I should know?'

Pat shook her head. 'No, no, nothing. No.'

'Because if this director's weekend is ruined I shall want to know who's at the bottom of it. It's important to me that the weekend goes well. They're all influential people with money to burn and it could mean an awful lot more business being put my way, which in turn lines your pockets as well as mine. We need to make a good impression, Pat. Right?!'

Pat nodded. 'Of course. About these dates.'

'Leave it for now. I'm expecting a rep any minute and I'm not in the mood. Why everyone has to choose my Store to air their disagreements I'll never know.'

Pat gave him a nudge. 'You know full well you like to be at the hub of all the gossip. You can't kid me.'

Jimbo grinned. 'You're right. I do.'

'It's good for business anyway.'

'Right again! See you, Pat.'

'See yer.' As she opened the door she turned back to ask, 'Will yer have a word?'

Jimbo nodded.

'Bye then.'

She left him staring out of the office window. What a mess. All because Rhett wanted to please his grandmother. Like a stone thrown into a pond, the ripples were far reaching. First Vera then Rhett and now the Joneses and Greenwood Stubbs. To save his own skin he'd better have a word. That fool Jeremy wouldn't listen, he knew that, but at least he could try.

He heard footsteps and found Harriet standing behind him.

He smiled at her. 'Darling! How's things?'

'Oh, fine, if only.'

'Mmmmm?'

Harriet ran her fingers through her hair in exasperation. 'It's Hugo. He's getting me very annoyed.'

'What's new?'

'I know I shouldn't have suggested he came to stay, but I did and we're landed with him. I told him that Caroline was off limits, but . . . '

'Mmmmm?'

'I'm amazed you haven't heard. He took her out to lunch yesterday and went all the way to The Lovers' Knot, which you so kindly recommended, and it made her late collecting the children.'

'That must be the best part of a twenty-five mile round trip! For lunch! He is a fool. I didn't mean him to go there. Just mentioned it in passing.'

'What worries me is Caroline agreeing to it. He's absolutely captivated her, you know. I warned her about him and I thought she'd heed it.'

'Keep out of it. Peter will solve it, I'm sure.'

'Will he, thought? You know how much Peter's into personal-freedom-in-marriage-our-love-is-strong-enough and all that.'

'One can't help liking Hugo, that's the trouble.'

Harriet sighed. 'I know.'

Jimbo looked hard at her. 'Harriet! Harriet!'

'Don't worry, not me.'

'Like me to have a word?'

'If you like. Diplomatically, of course. I can't stand atmosphere at home.'

'I could always ask him to sling his hook.'

'No, we've all worked so hard on this play, and not just us, but Anne Parkin with the advertising and ticket sales, and the props and things. No, we can't put the play in jeopardy. Be tactful, that's all I ask.'

'Tactful? What about?'

They both turned at the sound of Hugo's voice. 'I came to see if I could make lunch for you, Harriet dearest, and you too Jimbo if you can spare the time from your — ' he waved an expressive hand round the office, 'emporium.'

He was wearing the briefest of white shorts with a tight fitting white tee shirt. The tan of his shapely legs was emphasised by the short white socks and white leather slip-ons he wore. He smiled at them both and said, 'Well?'

Jimbo cleared his throat. 'Look here, Hugo . . .'

'May I take a seat, it sounds like a dressing down is on the agenda.' With perfect poise he placed himself on a stool beside the filing cabinet.

'You're right it is. Harriet and I are very, very fond of Caroline and we are not prepared to stand on the touch-line without blowing the whistle once or twice. She is off limits. *Verboten*. Forbidden. Not available for . . .'

'Yes?' Hugo's eyes sparkled with fun.

'Damn it, man, you're too charming by half, and you know it. Please, leave her alone.'

'Or . . . ?'

'You'll have me to answer to, to say nothing of Peter. He may be a man of the cloth but he is extremely fit and I wouldn't give much for your chances if he really blew his top. And, believe me, he can't be far from it.'

'You don't have to worry about Peter. He allows Caroline to do exactly as she wishes. He loves her so much, you see.'

'Is that so? I wouldn't bank on it. However, if you wish to remain in my good books, and Harriet's, you'd better cool it.'

Hugo looked humble. Just how much of his humility was genuine and how much an act Harriet wasn't quite sure, but she listened carefully to what he said next. 'For the first time in my life I'm in love. Don't spread that abroad, I don't want anyone to know.'

A deathly silence greeted his statement. Then Harriet broke it by laughing loudly. 'You! In love? You don't know the meaning of the word except where it relates to yourself. Come on, Hugo, pull the other one.'

Hugo got up and, with tears glistening in his eyes, he said, 'That's my trouble, you see, no one believes I have genuine feelings. Lunch it is, then. For three.'

When Harriet saw the lunch table she wondered if there was anything left in the fridge at all. He really had made an effort.

He'd even poached some wine from Jimbo's secret store.

'Well, that's wonderful, Hugo. We shan't need another meal for a fortnight. Thank you so much.' Harriet kissed his cheek and he heartily kissed her back.

Jimbo stood in the doorway admiring the table. 'Thanks greatly. I usually have an out of date pork pie or left over sandwich in the office. It's really a treat to come home to this. Thanks.'

'Not at all. Your hospitality has been above and beyond, I had to do something in return.'

Jimbo smiled a little grimly. It hadn't cost Hugo a penny. Then he remembered not to be mercenary and thanked him again for all the trouble he'd taken. 'It makes no difference to what I said earlier. In love or not, you cool it. Right?'

'I heard.'

★ ★ ★

Jimbo left Bel and Harriet in charge at the Store and dashed up to the Big House straight after lunch. As he pulled up in front of the house the gravel spurted beneath his wheels and he narrowly missed one of the students taking a chance for a quick smoke between lectures. He called out cheerfully,

211

'Sorry!' The student waved his acknowledge-ment of Jimbo's apology.

Jimbo strode into the hall. 'Good after-noon! How is my favourite girl this afternoon? Firing on all cylinders? As usual?'

The receptionist beamed her pleasure at his arrival. 'Jimbo! You darling man. Lovely to see you. Favourite girl indeed! Mr Fitch isn't . . . '

'I know, it's Jeremy I need to see.'

'He's in his office, do go straight through.'

'OK.' Jimbo made off in the direction of Jeremy's office but stopped before he'd left the hall. 'You don't know anything about this prosecution, do you?'

In a stage whisper she answered, 'Only that he's hell bent on going through with it. I wouldn't like to be in his shoes when Mr Fitch finds out he's lost his head gardener and a first rate under gardener and from what I hear his estate carpenter too, because Barry's been in and threatened to resign. Tread carefully!'

Jimbo nodded. 'Indeed. Right, thanks.'

Jeremy hastily threw the wrapper of a Mars bar into his waste bin as Jimbo entered his office.

'Good afternoon to you. Got a minute?'

'For you, Jimbo, yes. How can I help? Catering problem is it? This directors' weekend causing probs, eh?'

'No. May I sit down?'

'Of course.'

Jimbo seated himself in one of the plush chairs and, leaning forward confidentially, asked, 'When is Mr Fitch back?'

Jimbo thought he detected Jeremy giving a slight shudder at his question. 'Thursday.'

'I see. Glad to have him back at the helm?'

'What's that got to do with you?'

'Nothing, except . . . '

'Yes?'

'Have you got your bags packed in readiness?'

'In readiness for what?' His huge bulk shifted uneasily.

'Leaving. You and Venetia.'

Jeremy suddenly got the drift of Jimbo's questions and began to bluster. 'If you've come to persuade me to change my mind about prosecuting the lot of 'em, you're barking up the wrong tree. Mr Fitch knows full well the village takes every advantage of him they can, and he said before he went away, 'From now on anyone caught red-handed will be prosecuted, no matter what the consequences.' So all I'm doing is carrying out his instructions.'

'But it's so damaging! He may think it not worth the candle. Everything returned, the crazy paving paid for and no one, least of all Mr Fitch, will be any the wiser. Withdraw the charge. Honour restored on both sides.'

Jeremy's hand strayed towards the bottom drawer where he kept his supply of chocolate. He drew it back and said angrily, 'Someone has to be made an example of. What would you do if one of your staff was taking food home? Eh?'

'Sack 'em. But then kitchen hands are soon replaced, a talented gardener isn't. You haven't understood what it means, have you? A whole family out in the street. That'll look good in the paper. Mr Fitch will love that. Oh yes.' Jimbo paused for a moment to compose the most damaging headline he could but Jeremy got in first.

'It's none of your damned business. If you've nothing better to do, I have, so just leave.'

'I've rattled your cage though, haven't I?'

Jeremy pressed his hands on the desk and heaved himself to his feet. He stabbed a thick finger in Jimbo's direction. 'Your influence extends as far as that green baize door in the dining room and no further, so get back to your kitchens and leave me to attend to more important affairs.'

Amused, Jimbo stood up and, sounding rather more like an avenging angel than the entrepreneur he was, he said in sepulchural tones, 'Be warned! The oracle has spoken. Your end is nigh.' He left the room and quietly closed the door behind him. Grinning all over his face he waved to the receptionist and said, 'I've upset him. Take care.'

'Damn you for a nuisance, I'll have no peace all afternoon.'

Cheerfully Jimbo called, 'Sorry!' and left. He took the opportunity to call in at the kitchens to check that this rather important slice of his empire was in full swing. The staff were glad to see him and he enjoyed a ten minute chat with the chef about the arrangements for the directors' weekend.

Before getting into his car he went out through the back door of the kitchens to inspect the bins and check that they were being kept well disinfected. He'd planted bushes around the bin area to shield them from the bedroom windows at the back of the house and as he approached he sniffed the air and decided that despite the hot weather they were clean. What he hadn't expected to find beyond the bushes was Hugo's red sports car. He had half a mind to find out what Hugo was up to, but shrugged his shoulders and decided to mind his own business. A sneaking suspicion made him look up at the

215

windows of the flat Venetia and Jeremy occupied. A curtain flicked back into place and he thought he caught a glimpse of Hugo's face as he quickly retreated from the window.

12

Caroline had been watching television while Peter had been at his Parochial Church Council meeting. As soon as she heard him coming in she called out, 'Peter, I didn't tell you. I've got six months' work at the practice coming up. Four days a week. Isn't that brilliant? They rang this morning and I accepted and then it went completely out of my head. The other woman doctor is pregnant and they need a stand-in.'

Peter bent over and kissed her. 'That's wonderful, truly wonderful and I'm very pleased.'

'Are you?'

'Oh, yes.'

Caroline frowned at him, suspecting some ulterior motive behind his delight till she remembered he wasn't made like that. 'You don't normally rejoice when I work, what's brought about the change?'

'I rejoice on the basis that what's good for you is good for us all.'

'I have the distinct feeling I'm being patronised.'

Peter shook his head. 'Absolutely not, as if I would.'

Caroline looked closely at his face as he leant over her. It was deadpan. He looked down at her and his eyes lit up with laughter.

Caroline returned his kiss and patted the seat beside her. 'Sit here. I need your advice.'

'About . . . ?'

'I'm getting terribly worried about this play. What if I turn out to be a complete fool on the stage and ruin it for everybody. When I agreed to do it I was so full of myself I could have done it single-handed, but now I'm not so sure.'

'Hugo will see you through it.'

'Yes, he will. Of course he will. He's a brilliant actor, you know.'

'He is?'

'Oh yes, you can feel him rising to the occasion. He kind of puts on a mantle, you can visibly see him do it and he's no longer Hugo Maude, he's whoever he's playing. What a gift.'

'Indeed.'

'It's the most enormous privilege to work with him. He pulls everyone into his enthusiasm, draws them in, whisks them along. As a team leader he's amazing, he has them all eating out of his hand. The rehearsal tonight went wonderfully well. We are incredibly lucky, you know, to have him here. We're all well blessed.'

'I shall have to come to a rehearsal to see this great man at work.'

Caroline gave him a sharp look but his expression was completely innocent. 'Even Rhett, despite his troubles, is coming along splendidly. I watched him in the scene where he talks to his father about me and my new boyfriend and he almost had me in tears. It was very moving. Such a sensitive performance, all due to Hugo's coaching. You can't imagine Rhett being like that, can you?'

'No, you can't. It's surprising what talents people have.'

'It is. I do love it, all the rehearsing and such. It makes me quite skittish, kind of like a young foal in a field all excitement and jollity, capering about through life. Our lives — yours and mine — are so serious, aren't they? Always helping the lame dogs and such. There's not much time for laughter, is there?'

Peter thought for a moment before he answered. 'You're right, there isn't. But I can't change it. Not *my* life, at any rate.'

'Oh, I know, and I wouldn't ask you to in a million years. You're not in a job where you can decide to have a career change mid-stream, I know that. Yours is a vocation. And I fully accept that and always will. But I do think we should find time to laugh more. Don't you?'

'I shall give that matter my earnest consideration.'

'There you are, you see, all seriousness again. You should let up more often.'

'What's brought all this philosophising about?'

Impatiently, Caroline shook her head. 'Nothing. Nothing at all.'

She was silent for a while and then said, as though he were always at the front of both their minds, 'He's a little boy lost, you know. Needs a wife who's a mother as well.'

Peter didn't need to ask whom she meant. 'Like most men.'

'Only more so. The slightest thing can hurt him intensely. That's why he's such a good actor, so emotional. He's very touchy feely.'

'Oh! I'm sure he is.' He ran a lazy finger along her arm and as she watched it she wondered why nowadays he didn't ignite her like Hugo did with just the same gesture. Peter stood up offering her his hand. 'I'm ready for bed. Coming?'

'In a while.'

'I rather thought . . . ' Peter shrugged his shoulders. 'Never mind.'

'Not tonight.'

★ ★ ★

220

Peter decided to fulfill his promise and make it possible for himself to attend the next rehearsal. Willie volunteered to sit in. 'Be glad to, sir, no trouble at all.'

'I shan't stay all evening, I don't think, but it's just a chance to see a great actor at work.'

'Oh quite. Yes, sir, you do right. Good idea. I'll tell them children a goodnight story and they'll be off to sleep in a trice.'

'About dragons as usual?'

'Oh yes, dragons is my speciality.'

'They make a big impression.'

'My dragons do! About quarter past seven, then?'

'That's right. Caroline likes the children to be asleep by eight at the latest.'

'You go and enjoy yourself, nothing like seeing at first hand.'

Peter wore his most relaxed looking shirt and shorts and wandered off in the steaming heat to the Church Hall. It was in darkness and the cast were standing on the stage listening to Hugo.

' . . . Four more rehearsals. Four more tries. Four more before lift off. You're doing brilliantly. Wonderfully. Fantastically well. I'm most impressed. But . . . that is no reason to give up trying to improve your performance. No one is ever perfect, least of all me . . . '

This last was greeted by hoots of derision.

Hugo held up a hand for silence, 'No, I mean it. If ever you get satisfied with yourself then it's curtains. Kaput. Finito.' He ran a finger across his throat. 'You're dead. So . . . all the stops out tonight and we're going straight through the whole of the first act. No interruptions. Remember! Never stop improving on your last performance. Remember how we felt our pace dragged a bit at the end? Don't let it happen tonight. We want the audience to be disappointed and not relieved that the interval has come. OK?'

They all nodded. 'Beginners, please.'

Peter seated himself on a chair at the very back in the shadows. He'd told Caroline he was coming but hadn't reminded her just before she'd set off for the hall. He rather hoped she'd forgotten.

They were good. There was no doubt about that. Talent such as he had never suspected from Liz and Rhett, from Michelle and Neville and from Harriet as the badly betrayed lover of Hugo.

There was a whisk of the curtains and a hushed minute of silence to denote the passing of time and then act one, scene two began. It was Hugo, now looking somehow like a nineteen twenties man about town, coming to return Caroline's umbrella. He hadn't got costume on, simply a pair of jeans and a tee shirt, but he looked what he was, a lounge lizard with a heart.

Peter listened to their dialogue. He admired Hugo's voice. Then it was Caroline's turn to speak. It was quite astounding to him how her voice had changed. At once languid and seductive, at once an ice maiden and a temptress. This Hugo had far more going for him than Peter had ever imagined. He sat fascinated. Every member of the cast was transformed. Even young Michelle was a changed person. When she cried there were genuine tears running down her cheeks.

Act one, scene two ended with a telephone conversation between Caroline and Hugo. Peter recognised restlessness, the need for excitement, the yearning in her voice and in her body language, she did it so well that although one couldn't hear Hugo's replies one knew exactly what he would be saying.

He couldn't help himself; he applauded.

Sylvia clapped too, and so did Barry, Ron and Dean. They couldn't help themselves either. Barry climbed onto the stage and gave Michelle a big kiss. 'Wasn't she marvellous, Hugo? Absolutely great. I'm that proud.' Michelle blushed and Rhett took her hand. 'And you Rhett, very powerful.'

Peter moved towards the stage. 'I'm exceedingly impressed. It was just wonderful.'

He reached up and signalled to Caroline to jump down off the stage into his arms. He hugged her and whispered, 'Fantastic! I'm so proud. So very proud.'

'I'd forgotten you were coming. Are you just flattering me?'

Vehemently he answered, 'I'm not. You were excellent.'

'Thanks.'

Above the hubbub Hugo called, 'Right, that's it for tonight. See you next rehearsal, full scenery, full props. Goodnight! And thanks.'

They all retired to the Royal Oak except for Rhett and Michelle. The bar was moderately busy for a weekday night. Sitting like a peacock amongst a flock of sparrows sat Venetia Mayer, alone in a corner from which she had a full view of the whole bar. She wore her purple outfit, with matching slouch socks, trainers and headband. She didn't seem to have noticed that crushed velvet had been out of fashion for quite a few years now. Her hair, abundant as always, was blacker than ever, and her eye make-up would have been obvious to a blind man.

She waved vigorously to Peter and Caroline who headed the rush for the bar. They returned her wave and, having collected their drinks, went to sit at her table.

'May we, or are you expecting someone?' Venetia didn't answer, but simply invited them to sit by patting the seat alongside her and smiling.

Peter recollected he hadn't seen Jeremy for a while so he asked Venetia how he was.

'Jeremy? He's fine.'

'I heard you'd put him on a diet.'

Disinterestedly she answered, 'I did, but he wouldn't agree to it. It's a waste of time talking to him.'

'I see, that's a pity.'

Venetia wasn't making coy passes at Peter as she had done often in the past, instead she was scanning the crowd at the bar. He noted her satisfaction when she spotted whoever it was she'd come to see.

'You'll enjoy the play when you see it, Venetia. Hugo's done a wonderful job, everyone's quite excellent.' She wasn't listening, she was watching someone. He saw her face light up again and in a moment Hugo was sitting beside Caroline and opposite Venetia. There was a recognisable togetherness between Caroline and Hugo, the result of working on the play in such close harmony. Peter saw it and wondered if Venetia had too. He turned to say some platitude to her and saw the flinty look in her eyes. They were rapidly flicking between Hugo and Caroline, and for a moment he couldn't understand her anger, and then he did. It was the anger of a jealous woman.

Venetia, grimly keeping a hold on her temper said, between gritted teeth, 'Good rehearsal?'

Hugo asked Caroline to give her opinion. 'Excellent. It's all coming together quite brilliantly. Isn't it, Peter?'

'It certainly is. I was very impressed. You and Hugo here together are a dynamic duo.' Caroline and Hugo laughed. 'You should have joined the cast, Venetia. You could have had some fun.'

'Could I indeed? Well, well. Not my scene, as you might say.'

The four of them chatted together about many inconsequential things until Peter looked at his watch. 'I'll have to go, I promised Willie I wouldn't be late. You stay, darling, if you wish.'

'No, I'll come too. I've had a long day and I need my beauty sleep.' Caroline picked up her bag and squeezed out of her seat. Hugo stood up.

He took her hand and kissed her fingers. 'Sleep perhaps, but not beauty sleep, my love.' He held her hand a moment longer than he needed to and Caroline was forced to pull it free.

'Goodnight to you, flatterer!'

'Cross my heart and hope to die, I always speak the truth to my leading lady.'

Peter laughed at his flirting. 'No wonder all the girls idolise you, Hugo. You're too charming for words.'

Hugo turned to look at Peter. 'I mean it. It's true. You're a lucky man, though perhaps you don't know it.'

'I do, I do. I'm just unaccustomed to hearing other men say it, that's all.'

'Other men?' Hugo put a delicate hand to his brow. 'Other men? Shame on you. Shame. Me! Other men! I am unique! Quite unique!'

He pretended to feel faint and slumped back onto his chair, dramatically prostrate. He withdrew a handkerchief from his pocket and mopped his brow.

Peter smiled while at the same time admiring Hugo's almost flawless physical beauty. 'You're right, you are unique, no one but you could have collapsed in such a stylish manner! Goodnight to you, and thanks, everlasting thanks for producing the play. It's going to prove to be truly memorable. Goodnight, Venetia.'

Her lips, tight as tight, only just allowed, 'Goodnight' to escape.

Caroline called out her goodbyes to everyone and closed the door behind them.

As soon as they were out of hearing she said, 'What on earth is the matter with Venetia, she hadn't a word for the cat. Have we upset her?'

'Not us, no. Watching him just now the word 'beauty' came to mind. Not a word I would readily use when referring to a man, but he has such classical beauty. For a split second I did wonder . . . '

'Have you got your key? Wonder what?'

As he reached to put his key in the lock, Peter said offhandedly, 'Is he straight?'

Angrily Caroline said, 'Of course he is. But what would it matter if he weren't?'

Peter pushed open the door. 'It wouldn't matter one jot, would it now?' He looked intensely at her face in the muted light of the hall and saw briefly in it a kind of naked passion, which she quickly veiled.

'No, it wouldn't matter. What *does* matter is his talent and his great generosity in making the play possible. We'll never have another chance like this, and we should take it with both hands and not dig for motives or stances or anything at all. Just take our opportunity eagerly.'

'Of course. Willie! We're back! Everything all right?'

Willie appeared in the sitting-room doorway and, looking directly at Peter, said, 'Yes. Everything all right with you?'

Peter forced a firm reply. 'Oh yes. Absolutely hunky-dory.' Leaving Caroline to say their thanks and goodnights he took the stairs two at a time and went directly to bed.

★　★　★

Caroline's enthusiastic support for Hugo would have been seriously diminished had she witnessed the conversation Harriet had with him the following day. Hearing him thumping about upstairs she went up and, looking into the tiny boxroom next to his own room, she saw he was dragging his cases out.

'Excuse me for asking, Hugo, but what exactly are you doing?'

Breathlessly he replied, 'Packing.'

'Packing? Might one ask why?'

He straightened up, pushed his hair from his forehead and announced, 'My agent, that was him on the phone. I simply can't turn it down.'

A very nasty, insidious dread invaded Harriet's brain. 'Explain yourself.'

Hugo perched himself on one of his cases. 'He wants to see me immediately. I've got the chance of Hamlet at Stratford. I've never played Hamlet, would you believe, never. That prize, that glittering, fabulous prize is within my grasp. Agreed I'm second choice, because Sir John is scheduled. But he's had a heart attack, so they've rung me. It should have been me to begin with, but Johnny's got a thing going with the director so that's how he got the job. Well, now he's got his just desserts.' Hugo shrugged his shoulders then dramatically clenched his fist and stared at it. 'I simply cannot turn it down. I've got to go.'

Harriet went from icy despair to total fury in the space of a moment. 'You slimy toad. You foul, thoughtless, self-centred pig. How *dare* you? How dare you sit there and say that to me? Now, I really know exactly what you are. Shallow. Vain. Mean. Jimbo's right, there's only one person in the whole world as far as you're concerned and that's Hugo St John Maude. You're an overrated, arrogant, egotistical, self seeking, swollen headed exhibitionist. How could you do this to us?'

She stormed downstairs and rang the Store. 'I don't care where he is or what he's doing, he is to come home immediately.' She listened for a moment and then shouted, 'This instant, whether he likes it or not and I don't care if he's signing the contract for Buckingham Palace garden parties, he's to come home *now*. You tell him from *me*.' She slammed down the receiver and paced up and down the hall, her anger intensifying as the moments passed.

Hugo came slowly down the stairs. 'Look, I know doing this makes me *persona non grata* . . . '

'That's true! There isn't a quote in Shakespeare or anywhere else more apt, more apropos . . . I should have had my head examined for asking you here. Never, never again as long as you live will I ever . . . '

The front door burst open and Jimbo hurtled into the hall.

'My God! What is it? What the hell's happened?'

Harriet turned on him. 'You may well ask.' She pointed a shaking finger at Hugo who was sitting on the bottom step. 'That . . . snake in the grass is leaving.'

'Leaving? What's he done? I'll kill 'im first and ask questions afterwards, shall I?' Jimbo's face flushed an ugly red.

Harriet shook her head. Arms akimbo she said scornfully, 'Tell Jimbo, then. Go on, tell him.'

Hugo, in a short speech full of self justification, told him why he was leaving.

Jimbo could scarcely contain his anger. In a cold fury, the like of which Hugo had never seen before, ashen-faced and visibly shaking with temper, Jimbo clenched and unclenched his fists, his lips set in a thin mean line. 'You misbegotten, arrogant, base, self-seeking low life. How can you leave everyone in the lurch like this? Have you any idea how much people are banking on you? You've come here, stirred us all up, agreed to produce the play, only a week to go and you do this to us all?' Jimbo strode over to Hugo and, grasping the front of his shirt, hauled him to his feet. 'I've a good mind to ruin your good looks once and for all. Then see where you'd stand as Hamlet. You'd be more fit for a second rate Richard the Third when I'd finished with you. You're despicable!' He unceremoniously released his hold on Hugo's shirt front and maliciously watched him clutch the newel post to keep his balance.

Hugo gathered about him the remnants of his self respect; physical violence always terrified him. 'That's rich, that is. I'm supposed to give up the opportunity of a lifetime for a *village* play? Come on! Be fair!'

Jimbo, his anger spent, stood surveying him silently. Harriet burst into tears. 'I feel so responsible! It was me who asked you in the first place.' Jimbo lent her his handkerchief.

'I know who could take my place. Peter! With that amazing voice of his, he'd be wonderful. Better still, he'd be freed of all his angst.'

Harriet hurriedly wiped her eyes and said, 'Angst? What exactly do you mean by that?'

Hugo shook his head. 'Oh! Nothing.'

'Explain yourself. Have you really given him cause for angst like they all say?' Jimbo took a step towards Hugo. 'I warned you!'

Striking a pose Hugo mockingly answered, 'Me? The cause of it all? Me? Of course not. As if I would. But when all's said and done, I'm going.' He turned to go back upstairs.

Harriet remarked, 'You're feeling up to it, then?'

'Oh, yes.'

'So staying here has done some good then?'

Hugo paused halfway up the stairs. 'Certainly it has.'

'You owe us all something then?'

'You could say so.'

'Well, repay your debt by staying and doing the play for us. There's no way Peter can take up the part at such short notice, he isn't an actor.'

From the top of the stairs Hugo looked down at her. 'Oh, but he *is*! His oratory from the pulpit and his behaviour towards me, especially, prove otherwise. He's doing an excellent job of being the supportive husband, the broad minded cleric, the gentle Christian, when underneath he'd like to beat me to a pulp and drag Caroline back to his cave. Believe me. Can't talk now, got to pack.'

Jimbo discovered he was still wearing his

boater. He took it off and smoothed his hand over his bald head. 'Come here.' He folded his arms around Harriet and rocked her slowly. 'There, there. Don't fret. We'll have to cancel. It's unfortunate but we shall. Old Fitch will be bitterly disappointed. He'll go ballistic in fact, but he can't do anything about it.'

'Oh, Jimbo, they'll *all* be so disappointed. I know *I* am. It's heartbreaking.'

'You've known for years what he's like. I'm surprised he's lasted this long.'

'I shall never, never ask him here again. This is the end of a beautiful friendship.'

'Oh, good.'

'Jimbo, you are a baby!'

He gave her a tight squeeze. 'I know, but I'm nice with it.'

'For heaven's sakes! At least you're *reliable*.' She wiped her eyes. 'There. I'll make a start on ringing everyone up. I can't bear it. I just can't. It's all my fault, I should never have encouraged him.'

Jimbo tapped the side of his nose. 'I have an idea. Don't ring yet.' He left the house.

★   ★   ★

The Store had been full of customers when Harriet had rung Jimbo, so the news that

234

something serious was afoot at the Charter-Plackett's had become the sole topic of conversation in his absence.

Linda, who'd answered the phone, avowed she knew nothing of what the trouble was, except that Jimbo had got the contract for catering for the garden parties at Buckingham Palace. That was all she knew, but wasn't it exciting, they might all get an invite if they played their cards right.

Bel knew nothing either, except she was doubtful about the contract Linda mentioned.

Mrs Jones, who'd been concentrating hard on her mail orders which seemed to flow in ever faster, reluctantly confessed she knew nothing, except that by the tone of the conversation Linda had repeated to her it sounded as though Hugo Maude might have a lot to answer for.

Miss Senior, the woolly hat she wore summer and winter madly askew with the excitement, raised an eyebrow. 'You don't think he's been . . . you know . . . making lewd suggestions to Harriet? You know what actors are like. First one and then another.' She rather relished the idea, and put her head on one side and winked knowingly.

Venetia Mayer was on red alert, her ears felt as though they'd grown to twice their size, and jealousy was getting the better of her.

One of the weekenders said, 'I wouldn't like to be in Hugo's shoes if he has. I reckon that Jimbo has a nasty temper when it comes to a showdown.'

Linda agreed. 'He was very nasty to me once, gave me my notice. Very sarcastic he was. Mind you, he soon took me back when he found he couldn't manage without me.'

Bel said bluntly, 'Don't overestimate your value to him, Linda. He's clever enough to learn your job in half a day.'

'Huh! Half a day? I should cocoa. It's taken me years to get it under my belt.'

Bel looked askance at her and Linda retired behind the grille, hurt and indignant.

Reluctantly Miss Senior left the Store but the little brass bell on the door had hardly settled into silence before she was back in again. 'The Rector's just gone across to Jimbo's, and Jimbo's coming here. Watch out!' Determined to hear all the news, Miss Senior pretended to be having difficulty choosing a birthday card.

The door bell jangled furiously as Jimbo slammed the door shut behind him. He surveyed the scene. Not a limb moved, not an eye met his. He smiled to himself, raised his boater, said, 'Good morning, everyone', straightened some peaches which had been tumbled into the apples by a careless customer, poured himself a coffee from the machine and, to their extreme annoyance, stepped quietly through into the back.

★ ★ ★

Peter had listened to Jimbo's impassioned pleas and at first had declined to offer his services.

'Look here, Peter, it's no good me trying. I've already had him by the throat . . . well, not literally, but nearly. We go back a long way he and I, so he's taking advantage of our friendship and I'm not having any effect. Please.'

Peter was staring out of the study window and didn't reply.

'Go over there, cassock and cross, the whole job and do your good Christian bit. It'll work, I know it will. Please?'

Still Peter didn't answer him. Jimbo stood waiting. Eventually Jimbo said, 'I'll be off, then. We feel so bad about it, Harriet and I. We're completely to blame, you see. If we'd had any sense we'd have remembered his selfishness and never encouraged him to do the play in the first place. Thanks anyway.' He waited a moment wondering whether to say what he had in his mind, and decided it needed saying. 'Man to man, I can fully understand you not wanting him to stay.' He opened the study door and closed it quietly after him, just as it clicked shut he heard Peter calling him back.

'Jimbo! Does Caroline know?'

'I shouldn't think so, he's only just had the phone call. Unless . . . '

'No one's rung here.' Peter continued staring out of the window.

Jimbo felt himself dismissed. 'I'll be off then.'

'I'll come with you.' Peter went to the hall cupboard, took out his cassock and put it on. His cross he took from the pocket, placed the chain around his neck and tucked the cross itself into his leather belt. 'There, will that do?'

'Excellent. He'll love the drama of it, he's really into costume. Ooops, sorry! That didn't come out quite right, I didn't mean your cassock is a costume in the theatrical sense. I didn't tell you he fancied you taking over his role.'

'Did he.' Peter called up the stairs, 'Caroline, I've just got a visit to make, shan't be long.'

Faintly they heard Caroline call, 'OK. See you soon.'

Peter explained, 'Tidying the attic.'

Jimbo nodded.

They had parted company by the pond, Jimbo heading back to the Store and Peter to see Hugo. He was standing by the wardrobe taking clothes off hangers and laying them on the bed. Peter tapped on the door. 'Can I come in?'

Hugo was startled by Peter's arrival. For a moment he'd remained silent, recollecting what Jimbo had said about Peter's fitness and dreading any physical confrontation. Peter filled the doorway, his head bent to avoid the lintel, silent. Hugo had eventually said jokingly, 'Jimbo's brought in the heavy cavalry, has he?'

'What's this about you deserting your post?'

'To be shot for cowardice in the face of . . . ?'

'No. For greed.'

'Certainly not, the money matters not one jot.'

'There are different kinds of greed.'

'I know of only one.'

'That's sad.'

'Sad? There's nothing sad about me. I'm on the threshold of . . . '

'No, you're not, you're beyond the threshold now.'

Hugo preened himself, for he adored praise. 'Yes, you're right I am.'

'You're so well established you could almost call any tune and they would dance to it, and well you know it.' Peter moved some of the clothes and sat down on the bed. Hugo dumped them on the chair and sat beside him.

'That's right. I could.'

'Then, Mr Hugo Maude, why are you leaving in such a hurry?'

Hugo didn't answer.

'Well?'

'Got to go. Arrangements to which I have to agree. These theatrical people screw you for the last drop of blood, believe me. There's no holds barred where contracts are concerned. Yes, must go.'

Peter raised a sceptical eyebrow. 'It's not because you've suddenly realised that you'll be taking part in a village play which will bring you no prestige whatsoever, which will not further your career, will not enhance your reputation and, if it got into the press, would make you look like someone who's finally flipped his lid? That couldn't be it, could it?'

Hugo shook his head indignantly.

Peter sighed. 'Come now. The truth, just this once. Look inside yourself and speak to me with complete honesty. It won't go outside these walls.' Still Peter got no reply. 'You see you can afford to do this thing. Someone still climbing the ladder couldn't, but the great Hugo Maude could and if he faces up to it he'll know he can. The press will be here like a shot once they know. I think, done right, it could be a superb publicity stunt.'

'How?'

'By explaining your motives for doing it. Be honest. Come right out with it all. Let them see the real Hugo Maude that's behind the actor.'

'Think so?'

'Oh yes. Tell them about your close shave with a nervous breakdown, the exhaustion of acting to such high expectations every time you're on stage, et cetera, et cetera. Such courageous honesty would be the headlines in every newspaper this side of the Atlantic and beyond.'

'You think so?'

'Yes. Go up to London today. See whom you must and then come back tomorrow. Jimbo has a fax, and e-mail, you can be in touch all the time. What a gesture on your part. You never know, the play could get to the West End! You in the leading role, and with that story behind it, it would be a glorious success.'

Hugo's face lit up at the prospect. 'It would, wouldn't it? There's a bit of an air of *Brief Encounter* about it, isn't there? That kind of pure love. Yes, it might, it really might. Especially with the right publicity. *Dark Rapture*. Brilliant title!'

'When do you expect rehearsals to start?'

The anticipation fell from his face and ambition took its place. 'Three, four weeks' time, but there's all sorts of preliminary meetings and things. I can't miss them.'

'You'll only miss the first week, and you must.'

'Who says?'

'I do. They'll wait for you. Man of your stature.'

'I'd rather hoped you'd step into my shoes and let me go with a clear conscience.'

'Absolutely not. You and she have the right chemistry. Everyone can see that. The combination is quite explosive, and it's not just in the play.' Peter stood up and went to look out of the window.

Hugo gave a sharp intake of breath. 'Knowing that, you've come here to beg me to stay? Most men would press me to go and good riddance.'

'Yes, of course they would. But I'm not most men. Sometimes these things have to run their course. It's no good asking me to act. I'd be no good playing the part of her lover anyway. I love her too much for that, you see. The thought of even a fictional lover like Leonard feels like slow strangulation.'

Hugo studied Peter's back view, for the moment lost for words. After a short silence he said softly, 'You've made me feel very humble. You just have no idea how much I envy you for the privilege you have of loving like you do, so unselfishly, so profoundly. I think if I loved, it would be a jealous love, an all consuming love which in the end would eat up both the giver and the receiver.'

Peter turned back from the window and looked Hugo straight in the eye. 'It doesn't feel like a privilege at the moment.'

'I can see that.' The need for an apology became paramount. 'I'm very sorry.'

'Are you?'

'Yes, I am.' Hugo shook off his moment of perception and said, 'I'll go and I'll be back tomorrow, that's my promise to you. They'll have to dance to my tune as you so rightly say.'

'Crisis over then?'

Hugo nodded. 'I'll be here to do the play come hell or high water.'

'This is just between us?'

'Yes. Not a word shall I disclose.'

'Nor me.' Peter looked at him. 'You'll never

regret doing this for the village, it has that kind of effect. Only good can come of it.'

★ ★ ★

When he returned to the Rectory he climbed the stairs looking for Caroline. He found her still in the attic, sitting on a small stool surrounded by their mementos.

'Darling! Come and sit here and look at these with me. I keep finding fascinating things, things I'd forgotten all about. I'll never get tidied up at this rate.' She paused to clear a space for him to sit down and then realised how tired he looked. 'What's the matter? You look drained. Has something dreadful happened?'

Peter had no intention of revealing anything to her of his conversation with Hugo, so he simply remarked, 'I've been persuading Hugo not to desert us. What have you found?'

She looked up amazed. 'Why? Where was he going?'

'To London and then Stratford to do Hamlet.'

Caroline demanded all the details. To his response she alternated between delight at his opportunity and shock at his cavalier treatment of their play.

'You've *definitely* persuaded him to stay, then?'

'No rehearsal tonight, but he'll be back tomorrow.'

Caroline shuffled uncomfortably on her stool, torn between rushing over to see Hugo and not wishing Peter to realise how much she cared. 'Are you *certain* he'll come back?'

'As sure as I can be.'

'I can't quite believe it.'

'It's true.'

'How could he desert us all?'

'Well, he isn't, not now.'

'Thank you, Peter.' Caroline clasped his hand in hers. 'I know you don't . . . appreciate him, but I do and I'm sure you had far more chance of persuading him than I could ever have had.'

Peter blurted out, 'I think you are deliberately understating your influence on him.'

Caroline paused to think about what he had said, realising that this was a turning point in the whole matter between the two of them. 'I don't want to hurt you.'

'But you have already, haven't you?'

The harsh note in his voice frightened her, and she bent her head to avoid his eyes, muttering almost inaudibly, 'Peter, one. Caroline, nil.'

'Don't joke, please. I'm finding all this extremely hard to bear.'

'I'm sorry to be causing you pain. I don't quite know why it's happening. Once the play is over . . . '

'Then what? *Status quo*?'

'I don't even know that. Everything is all mixed up. I love both you and . . . '

'Say it.'

Deliberately slowly and quietly, as though crystalising her feelings for the first time, she said, 'I love you and am bewilderingly bewitched by Hugo all at the same time. I know he's candy floss and you're permanent and such a wonderful support to me, and most of all that you adore me and I should have gratitude for your love always . . . '

Peter snatched his hand from her grasp. 'Please! Not *gratitude*! I can't bear that.'

' . . . yet I can't shake off this fascination for him.' She paused and then added sadly, 'Sometimes the candy floss of life is very tempting.'

Peter painfully digested what she had told him and then, as a further challenge to her, declared, 'He wanted me to step in and play Leonard.'

Caroline was appalled. Looking into his bleak face she protested, 'Oh no, that would never do.'

'That's what I told him.'

'I couldn't, not in front of . . . '

Peter placed a finger on her lips to silence her, took her hand in his, kissed the palm and then pressed her hand against his cheek. 'Neither could I. Come what may, I shall still be here, like I promised on our wedding day, unto eternity and beyond. Now let's enjoy looking at what you've found.'

As he picked up the first photograph the door bell rang. He stood up abruptly. 'You answer it, I'm not in. The car's in the garage, they'll never be any the wiser.'

Caroline lurched downstairs, distressed and bewildered, and answered the door. Standing on the step looking contrite was Hugo.

His eyes looked her over, noting her old cotton shorts and the sleeveless tee shirt she wore and then came back to her face. She looked worn, like the shorts, and bleached white like the shirt. What had she been through to make her look like this? Was his leaving the cause of it?

'Peter must have told you, then?'

'What?'

'That I'm off to London.'

'Oh! Yes.'

'I'll be back tomorrow. Hamlet. I've had an offer to play Hamlet and I can't turn it down. Can I come in?'

Caroline opened the door wider. 'Of course, be my guest.'

'You don't seem surprised.'

'I'm delighted, absolutely delighted. Very, very, pleased for you. I shall expect a ticket.'

Hugo took her hand and held it against his cheek saying, 'Of course. And for Peter and Jimbo and Harriet too.'

'Thank you, I'll look forward to that very much indeed.'

There was a slight tremor in her voice and Hugo raised his eyebrows. 'Yes? Miss me?'

'Of course. *Dark Rapture* is all right then, even so?'

'Of course. I couldn't let you down, not my Caroline.'

'Thank you. It will make it all the more exciting, won't it?'

Still holding her hand, Hugo said, 'Darling!' The whole of her being clamoured for the thrill of his touch. He drew her into the study and kicked the door shut behind them with his heel. In a gesture reminiscent of Leonard in the play, he put his hand at the nape of her neck and drew her towards him. 'Darling Caroline!' The longed for kiss was deeper and more meaningful than they had ever experienced before. Her blood was pounding in her throat, her knees weak, and her body craved him. When they'd finished

Hugo took in a deep breath and stepped back, releasing her as though he was almost afraid of the emotions he had stirred in her.

'Must go. Long way to drive. See you when I get back. Sorry about that just now, couldn't help myself.'

'Don't apologise. It was me as much as you.'

Gratefully Hugo asked, 'Was it?'

'Oh yes. Safe journey, and I'll be waiting your return, and want to hear all your news.'

'Thank you. That makes it very certain I shall be back, knowing you're waiting.' He kissed her forehead and squeezed her hand tightly. Fumbling behind him for the handle he opened the door, bunched his fingers, kissed them twice and left.

Caroline sat in Peter's chair, leant her elbows on his desk and wept.

13

'Well, then, Pat, 'ave yer heard yet when yer dad's case is coming up? Shouldn't be long now.'

'Not yet, it hangs over yer like a big black cloud, I wish they'd speed things up and get it out of the way. I'll thank you not to mention it, I'm trying hard to forget.'

Jimmy offered to get her another drink.

'Thanks, might as well. It's when yer on yer uppers you know who yer friends are.'

'I thought you'd stopped speaking to me after that row we 'ad about thieving. I was only trying to be fair.'

Pat half smiled. 'I know yer were Jimmy, but it didn't half hurt.' She paused. 'Old Fitch is back soon.'

'Is he indeed? Then yer should be hearing something. Be interesting to know who has the greater pull, yer dad or Jeremy. I reckon old Fitch could manage without Jeremy easier than he could without yer dad and Rhett and your Barry.'

Pat's head came up with a jerk. 'Without Barry? Is he getting the sack as well then?'

'Oh! I've let the cat out of the bag. Sorry.'

He didn't say any more, but busied himself instead with collecting Pat's glass.

Pat laid a hand on her glass to stop him. 'Just a minute, why should Barry lose his job?'

'Didn't yer know, he's threatened to give his notice in if yer dad gets the order of the boot. Just trying to put some pressure on Jeremy, yer see.'

Pat stood up. 'The fool. The absolute fool. The blessed idiot. As if we're not in a bad enough state as it is. We'll all be on the social if we don't watch it. I'm going round to the Church Hall to give him a piece of my mind. Rehearsal or no rehearsal, he's going to get it in the neck.'

'Don't bother. There isn't one.'

'Isn't one? Then where's Barry gone to, and Michelle?'

'I understand that Hugo's done a runner.'

Pat sat down again. 'A runner?'

'Gone up to London, got the offer of Hamlet at Stratford and he's hopped it.'

Vera slapped her glass down on the table. 'Evening all. What's up Pat, just had yer purse pinched? Cheers.' She raised her glass to her friend.

'Hugo's done a runner. The play's off.'

Vera began to laugh. At first it was a slow chuckle then it turned into a gasping staccato

251

laugh, then a rip-roaring guffaw.

Pat couldn't laugh with her. 'To be honest, Vera, I don't know what's so funny. They've all put such effort in, it simply isn't fair of him. In fact I'm downright disappointed in him. It's mean and thoughtless 'opping off like that.' Pat nudged Vera with a sharp elbow. 'Just stop it, will yer, they're all looking.'

Vera endeavoured to pull herself together. She mopped her eyes, coughed to clear her throat and said loudly, 'That's one in the eye for Mrs Jones, anyway. That'll have taken the wind out of her sails and not half, serves her right after the way she treated me. I haven't laughed so much in years.'

'You might find it funny but no one else does.'

'I know, but all them costumes she's made. What a laugh.'

Jimmy stood up to get Pat another drink. 'Don't mind admitting he'll cut a fine figure in them tights and that on the stage. He'll make a handsome Prince of Denmark.'

Vera scoffed at him. 'Hark at 'im! Gone all classical, 'ave yer? Surprising what an effect that Hugo's had on this village.'

'It is,' Pat agreed and counted off on her fingers the people he'd most affected. 'Us probably being made homeless into the bargain. Your Don willing to let yer go to prison, who'd have thought that of him, 'im without a word for the cat. The rector in a right state over 'im. Dr Harris coming over all peculiar about 'im. Our Dean losing his scholarship, there's no doubt about that. You, Vera, in a stew about prison. The list is endless. Sooner he goes the better, I think.'

Vera sprang to his defence. 'Oh, I don't know. He's lovely. I could buy a ticket for Stratford just for the pleasure of seeing 'im in tights. He'll strip something gorgeous, I bet. Yer can forgive a man like 'im an awful lot. All them lovely costumes, too.' Vera stared into the distance thinking about her life and where it was going, and about Don. If only . . .

As though able to read her thoughts, Pat said, 'Well, begging your Don's pardon, he hasn't exactly a figure to die for, has he? Not meaning anything disrespectful like, but seeing as we're letting our hair down, he's not like my Barry.'

'But then your Barry's at least ten years younger. Though, come to think of it, even ten years ago Don didn't look like him. No, it could almost be said I've made a big mistake with Don. There's something to be said for living with someone, isn't there?'

'Oh, I don't know about that. Look at your Brenda, for a start. I wouldn't just have lived with Barry, I've got my children to think of. I want to keep their respect. It's not decent when you've got kids.'

'It must be lovely going 'ome to a handsome man, though.' Vera traced a pattern on the table with her finger and then asked, 'What was yer first husband like?'

'Useless. He did us all a good turn when he died. Lifting his elbow too often was his problem.'

'Can't say that about Don, that is one thing he doesn't do. I just wish he'd brighten up, though. Sparkle a bit, yer know. Your Barry's got plenty of sparkle, hasn't he?'

Barry arrived in time to answer before Pat could get a word in. 'He has, Vera, enough and to spare! What can I do for you, Vera?'

Vera giggled. 'Oh! Hark at him! Nothing, thanks, I'm off. Back to the ironing. I just wish he'd wear something exciting. I've been ironing his baggy underpants for over thirty years. Just like him they've got bigger and baggier as the years 'ave gone by. Ah well.'

Vera left Barry and Pat on their own; Jimmy was caught up in an argument at the bar.

Pat stroked Barry's arm. 'I'm so lucky. Poor Vera. Which reminds me, where's our Michelle? And if you knew there was no rehearsal, why did the two of you set off together as if there was?'

'There's something I have to tell you. Don't fly off the handle will yer?'

'How do I know if I will or not?'

'You don't, but don't anyway. Michelle has gone to the cinema in Culworth with Rhett. I took 'em in the car.'

'You let her?'

Barry nodded.

'What were yer thinking of?'

'Two young people enjoying each other's company. She's got to grow up sometime and Rhett's promised to take care of her.'

'Has he indeed. I shall have something to say to her when she gets back. Cinema indeed, with a boy Rhett's age.'

'No, you won't Pat, you'll ask her how she enjoyed herself and what the film was like, and that's all.'

'She's my daughter and I'll . . . '

'She's mine too, now I've adopted her. I've vetted the film and talked to her about going out with Rhett, and I've told him she's precious and there's to be no hanky panky.'

'So that's something else we can lay at Hugo's door.'

'What's he got to do with it?'

'If he hadn't come Rhett and our Michelle would never have got it together.' Pat calmed down until she remembered the other bone

255

she had to pick with her husband. 'So what's this about putting your job in jeopardy by threatening to resign over Dad?'

Barry looked uncomfortable. 'Just a try to help your dad, but it didn't work. So it's plan B now.'

'Look, Barry, this weekend is important to Jimbo, if it goes wrong there'll be *none* of us in work, and then where will we be?'

'Leave it all to me, my darlin'. Barry's in charge.'

With a slightly sarcastic note in her voice, Pat replied, 'Is he? Oh, well then. I understand the gorgeous lover boy has done a bunk.'

'Back tomorrow.'

Pat raised her eyebrows in surprise. 'That right?'

'The Rector got him to see sense.'

'Thank heavens for that. Our Michelle would have been heartbroken if he'd cancelled it. She thinks the sun shines out of his . . . you know what.'

'She's not the only one.'

'Yer mean Dr Harris.'

'I do. If I'd been the Rector I'd have let him go without a word. Glad to see the back of him.'

Pat giggled. 'Couldn't see you as a Rector! Heaven 'elp us!'

Barry laughed his agreement. 'Nor you as the Rector's wife! I've got Rhett and Michelle to collect. Coming with me?'

'Yes, I will.'

★ ★ ★

The first act in Barry's campaign to have the court action dropped was to head a delegation to the estate office. In Pat's opinion this was a pointless exercise, but Barry insisted that it was what they should do first of all. He checked with the secretary to make sure Jeremy would be in and assembled Greenwood, Rhett and Vera at the Big House as the stable clock struck two.

They'd agreed to see Jeremy in their working clothes and gave all the appearance of earnest people of the soil. As Greenwood said, a bit of kowtowing never did anyone any harm so long as they *knew* they were doing it, though he drew the line at touching his cap.

Jeremy had enjoyed a large, fattening lunch in the dining room at the small table reserved for senior management, and was contemplating a Mars bar to round it off when the secretary rang through to say that he had visitors. Reluctantly the chocolate was returned to the bottom drawer of his desk and he put on a welcoming smile. It swiftly left his face when he saw whom his visitors were.

'Yes?' he asked abruptly.

Barry, chosen to make the initial speech, took half a pace forward and cleared his throat.

'Good afternoon, Mr Mayer. I am well aware that you have already spoken to all of us in turn concerning this matter of the crazy paving and such, but we are making this last appeal to you before the court case and asking you to withdraw the charges . . . ' Jeremy attempted to interrupt, but Barry held up a commanding hand. 'Let me finish, please. Even a condemned man has a right to be heard. Everything has been returned to the estate and Vera, as you know, is more than willing to pay for the paving and the cement which was used for her patio. We feel sure that Mr Fitch . . . ' at the mention of his employer's name, Barry swore he saw Jeremy shiver 'does not want to put himself in bad odour with the village yet again. In the past he's trifled with people's opinions to his cost and a further confrontation would do him no good at all. Therefore in *his* interest we have come to suggest — only suggest at *this* stage, you understand — that in Mr Fitch's interest and your own you inform the police that the charges are dropped. Mr Fitch need know nothing at all about it.' Barry stepped back and waited.

During the speech Jeremy Mayer had fiddled with his pen, straightened his tie, gone red, gone white, begun to sweat and then reassembled his confidence. After a short pause he declared, 'Mr Fitch is behind me in this. I have his full support. We are sick and tired of the thieving that goes on.' He thumped the desk with his fist as the assembly began to protest. 'No, don't deny it. He is intent on putting a stop to it. I had my instructions before he left and I'm carrying them out to the letter. I will *not* be moved. You're not the only ones who've been to try to change my mind, and I haven't and I shan't.'

Vera piped up with, 'Who's been to see you besides us, then?'

'Jimbo Charter-Plackett and . . . '

'Yes?'

'The Rector.'

Greenwood was shocked. 'You mean the Rector's been and you still haven't changed your mind? That's a first. He can charm a monkey out of a tree, he can. You must be rotten through and through not to do as he asked.'

Angry, Jeremy spluttered, 'I have my orders.'

Barry, also angry, replied, 'Your trouble is you're scared, running scared of old Fitch. Well, if that's how matters stand and you're not going to shift then we know what to do next.'

Heaving himself to his feet, Jeremy, furious that Barry had found his Achilles' heel, shouted, 'I will not be moved on this! The case goes ahead no matter what. When Mr Fitch gets back you'll see, he'll back me to the hilt. Now, please leave.'

'Oh, we will. But you've not heard the last of this, believe me. We've other moves up our sleeves. One way or another, we shall win.'

The four of them left the office and didn't speak until they were out on the gravel car park.

His eyes blazing with missionary zeal, Barry said forcibly, 'Well then, it's stage two. We've got him shaking in his shoes, believe me. Old Fitch gets back next Thursday, dress rehearsal night. His weekend party arrives Friday and it's the first night of the play — bit awkward, that, so it'll have to be early teatime. Do we know what time they're expected?'

Greenwood said he didn't, not exactly, but the domestic staff and the secretary would know and he'd find out for sure.

'Right then, we'll all be in touch. I'll muster

the troops. You, Rhett, know what you've to do, seeing as you're not working. I'll get you the materials. Wood, nails, et cetera. Right?'

Rhett grinned and shook his head. 'Tut tut! I don't know, pinching from the estate. It's criminal it is.'

They all laughed. Barry offered Rhett and Vera a lift and they roared off down the drive in Barry's old red van. Greenwood watched them go and wondered where it would all end. He couldn't remember a job where he'd been happier. All those years with the Culworth Parks Department when he'd laboured away at the daily grind and thought he was fulfilled, but the satisfaction of working at Turnham House! Now *that* was something. His own master, a lovely home, his glasshouses, his flowers, the vegetables! Row upon row, bursting with life and beauty. And not just the gardens themselves but the people he worked with, too; loyal and hard working and happy. What a team. But, by the looks of it, it was all going to be snatched away. Life just wasn't fair. He turned on his heel and walked across the gravel back to his work. As he reached what he considered to be his very own part of the estate he paused to enjoy the sight of the bright splash of colour made by the Busy Lizzies flowering abundantly along the foot of the mellow terracotta red walls of his kitchen garden and his heart grew heavy.

Damn that Jeremy for his shortsightedness. Damn him!

★   ★   ★

Jeremy did feel damned. Damned if he did and damned if he didn't. But Mr Fitch's wrath was his worst fear. A pack of village people with scarcely a brain between them couldn't compare with the kind of wrath Mr Fitch was capable of. One scathing look from his employer and he, Jeremy Mayer, was reduced to jelly.

He reached down into the desk's bottom drawer and rustled about in the rubbish for a Mars bar. As he sank his teeth into it he relished for the third time that day the thought that a Mars bar always met his expectations: each and every one more faithful, more reliable than any lover could ever be. In the midst of his pleasure, without so much as a knock, the door opened and in walked Venetia.

He was too late to hide the chocolate bar from her. His joy turned instantly into a sin.

'Jeremy!'

'I know. I know.' He cleared his mouth as best he could and said, 'I need this, I've just had a drubbing from the estate lot.'

'What's new?' Venetia wandered across to the window and idly looked out across the gardens.

'You seem at a loose end,' he observed.

'Do I?'

'Lover boy done a bunk, has he?'

Startled by his outspokeness, Venetia rounded on him and brutally inquired. 'So? What's it to you?'

He cringed at her reply, he couldn't help himself. Whenever he saw her trim bottom, her slender, taut figure, her neat rounded bosom, her cloud of dark hair — even if it was darker than nature intended — it was his own Venetia who, despite everything she ever did, he couldn't stop loving in his own spaniel-like way.

He laid the Mars bar down on his desk without noticing that a trail of caramel had fallen on a letter he was about to sign. Head down, looking at his clenched hands, he muttered, 'It hurts.'

'Hurts?' Venetia stood opposite him and leant her hands on the desk. 'Hurts? Since when have you 'hurt' about anything? Tell me that!'

'I might not protest, but it hurts all the same. How do you think it makes me feel?'

'You haven't got any feelings.'

'That's what you think.'

'You haven't been near me for years. When I think of the great times we had together, but not now . . . Eh! not now.'

Helplessly Jeremy gestured at his body . . . 'I can't, can I, like this.'

Venetia swept the remains of the Mars bar from the desk, and by chance it landed in the wastepaper basket. 'Stop eating these, then. I've tried to stop you, but you won't. It's disgusting.'

Jeremy bent down to rescue his treat but it was sticking to a tissue he'd used to clean his computer screen and was lost to him.

Venetia, savage in her desperation, shouted, 'If only you'd try.'

'What's the point? It's like a nail in my coffin every time you . . . '

'Some nail. Some coffin. That's where you'll be if this snacking doesn't stop.'

Jeremy looked up at her. 'Fine Christian you're turning out to be. Lip service on Sundays and on Friday night at the youth club, but where's your religion now? If Peter knew what you get up to he'd be appalled.'

This statement brought Venetia up short and silenced her. It was the truth, as well as the shock of Jeremy speaking out. Not often troubled by her conscience, now long dormant, this last comment struck home. She swallowed hard. 'You're sticking the knife in and no mistake.'

'You stick it in me all the time with what you get up to . . . '

'But you've never said. Never complained. I thought you didn't care, didn't even realise.'

'But I've known, I've always known. I'm not completely stupid. I've loved you from the first day I met you, but it's hard to cling to that when you throw it in my face time after time. And another thing, I've always known that's why we got this job here, because of you and *him*. Don't you think it sticks in my craw having *him* lording it over me?'

'Craddock's not been interested in me since before . . . not since before he thought he would be getting married and then didn't.'

'I know, but the thought is always there in my head.'

'I didn't realise you knew all this.'

'Too wrapped up in yourself, that's why.'

Venetia stared at him as though he were a stranger. They'd been together for nine years now but she realised she barely knew him any more. So he'd known all along despite her being, as she thought, discreet. If Peter ever found out . . . She'd die. Literally die.

'What did that lot want?' she asked.

'Me to drop the case.'

'Why don't you?'

'Fitch would find out, somehow, and then where would we go? I'm in a cleft stick, me, a cleft stick.'

She slumped into the nearest chair and threw her head back so that her hair fell down the back of it. She closed her eyes. Immediately her conscience burst into life and she felt uncomfortable, disturbed. Leaping out of the chair, she said, 'I'm going into the village, shan't be long.'

She went to the church and sat in the little war memorial chapel where she knew Peter prayed every day. Venetia hoped that perhaps some of his crystal clear integrity might rub off on her if she sat there long enough. She waited an hour and came out feeling cleaner and purer than she had done for a long time, and vowed to behave better. None the less the moment she walked through the lich gate and out into the road her first thought as she slotted her key in the car's ignition was, 'He'll be back tonight.'

★ ★ ★

And he was. Bright, breezy and full of himself, Hugo burst into the rehearsal like a revitalised firebrand. With outstretched arms and beckoning hands he called out, 'I'm back! I'm back! Gather round.'

Everyone, props, stage manager, actors, lighting, music, hangers on, rushed to him, full of questions, eager to welcome him back and ready to listen open-mouthed to his news. His eyes found Caroline first and foremost and he told most of the story as though she were the only person in the hall.

'So I said to the director, I have a project in hand very dear to my heart and nothing short of an earthquake will drag me from it. So, old chap, you'll have to wait, I said. Yes, I know the RSC usually takes precedence, but this time it's the Turnham Malpas Amateur Dramatic Society that comes first. 'The what?' he said. I told him, one day you'll speak that name with awe, for they're going to make a name for themselves! They are the dear, dear people to whom I owe a massive debt and they have first priority. So here I am, back in the bosom of my dear friends, in top form and so . . . ' he paused as though searching for the right words and then his voice dropped to a soft whisper as he said, 'deeply, deeply glad to be amongst my friends.' Hugo sprang up on to the stage, faced them all and called out, 'To work, I say! To work!' His rallying cry was answered by a cheer.

'Act one, scene one?' Someone shouted

from the back of the crowd.

'Exactly! Beginners, please!'

They'd never done it better than that night. Every move, every gesture, every word was perfect. Hugo was beside himself with delight and, after the curtains closed, he kissed everyone with whom he came in contact.

'To the Royal Oak! Anyone with the time to spare. Drinks on me, celebrate your success and mine! Come with me!' He took Caroline's hand and led the way. Everyone followed: an excited, exhausted, exhilerated band of players on a high because of Hugo's praise and their own success. They burst into the saloon bar like a whirlwind, setting it alight with their enthusiasm and energy. Dicky and Alan worked like slaves to get them served and amidst a lot of laughter and leg pulling they finally settled at tables.

By an unspoken agreement they always left Hugo and Caroline to sit by themselves once the initial serving of drinks was over. He took her to a small table beside the open hearth and, lifting his glass, saluted her. 'Glad to have me back?'

'Oh, yes. I did begin to wonder if we'd lost you for ever.'

His dark eyes glowed as he said, 'With you here, nothing could keep me away.' He drank his vodka in one go and flung the glass into the fireplace. The sound of shattering glass caused everyone to look their way in astonishment. Hugo was nonplussed.

'Another Vodka, Georgie, and I'll pay for the glass!'

'It wasn't Peter, then, who persuaded you to come back? It was me?'

Hugo hesitated for a moment before he answered, allowing Georgie to place a second glass in front of him, saying quietly, 'Don't make a habit of it, will you? It might catch on.'

His mind intensely occupied in finding a reply to Caroline's question, Hugo didn't answer. Then he looked up, gave Georgie one of his stunning smiles and said, 'No, I won't. Sorry.'

Turning back to Caroline he asked her if she knew everything Peter and he had said.

'Of course not. Just that he persuaded you to come back.'

'I see. Caroline! What can I say. You're married to a remarkable man. I have the greatest respect for him. In fact, I'm truly humbled by him and there are not many people who can do that to me. I'm jealous of him, too.'

'You are?'

'He has *you*, hasn't he?'

Quietly the answer came back, 'Has he?'

Hugo looked up and waited for Caroline to raise her eyes and look at him. 'Hasn't he?'

She took a sip of her drink, neatly replaced the glass on the beer mat in front of her and said, 'At this moment in time I don't really know.'

'You mean there's *hope* for me? For you and I?'

'I didn't say that.'

'You hinted.'

Caroline's hand let go of her glass and gently touched his fingers. 'I did, didn't I.'

They were so absorbed in looking at each other, in their desire to read each other's real meaning, that neither of them had noticed Harriet standing beside their table.

'You two! Georgie's called 'time'. Those who want to are retiring to our house. Are you coming? Caroline?'

Her voice was inescapably full of meaning. This was Harriet telling Hugo to call a halt, and warning Caroline to watch her step.

Caroline said she wasn't, thanks, she'd get home. Hugo ignored Harriet and said to Caroline, 'Please come.'

'No. I have things to do before I go to bed. Anyway, I'm tired. Good night.'

Hugo leant forward to kiss her cheek but she avoided him and quickly left.

Tight-lipped, Harriet whispered forcefully,

'You're damned selfish, that's what you are, through and through. Now git! If it wasn't for the play I'd get Jimbo to throw you out tonight. You have the morals of an alley cat.'

Equally quietly Hugo answered 'It's none of your business, darling. I love her, you see.'

'That doesn't give you the right to . . . '

'It does.'

'Being in love doesn't give one the freedom to do as one wishes with other people's lives.'

'You're taking this far too seriously.'

Angrier with him than she could ever remember being, Harriet pushed him out of the door and into the street. Facing him in the dark she asked, 'Are you behaving like this for your own amusement, then? Because if you are you're even lower than I could ever have imagined.'

The sounds of the others hammering on her front door came to her as she waited for his reply. 'Of course not. No. I am in love. And so is she.'

'She won't be when I tell her what I know about what you're up to. You're despicable.'

Jimbo called, 'Are you two coming in, then, or shall I close the door?'

Hugo's eyebrows shot up in surprise. 'You know? I didn't realise.'

'I do. Every breath you take is monitored by this village. You're a newcomer, you see, so

271

they all keep an eye on you. If I tell her it will break her heart. I can't do that.'

'Well, don't. I'll deal with it.'

'It's your massive ego, Hugo. You can't cope without the adulation, can you? You're a child in a man's body. Sad really, when you've so much going for you.' Harriet stormed into her house leaving him standing out in the road. Within minutes she caught the sound of the throaty roar of his sports car zooming away, and fervently prayed he wasn't going for good.

14

'Don! Don! Are you up? Don! I'm back!' Vera flung off her cardigan and went to the foot of the stairs. 'Don!'

She heard the sound of the bathroom door being unlocked. 'Hold on! I'm coming down.'

Impatiently she filled the kettle, they'd have a celebration cup of tea, something stronger tonight in the pub. Wait till she told them all. At last, Vera Wright was on the up and up. She was so excited her hands trembled as she put out the cups, filled the milk jug, warmed the pot and brewed the tea. Don came down just before she finally erupted with the excitement of her news.

'Don! . . . '

'You're late, I'm wanting my tea.'

'You won't when you hear my news.'

Don dropped himself down onto a kitchen chair. 'Well?'

'You know the nursing home's been bought out?'

Don nodded. 'So?'

'Well, they're making sweeping changes. Bringing the nursing home right bang up to scratch. Obeying all the rules and that. More staff, higher fees, naturally, but a much better service, ensuite bathrooms, you name it. All them social workers who've been poking about for months can go back into their burrows now, 'cos we're going to be one hundred per cent politically correct. No flies on us!'

'So?'

Vera drew in a deep breath. 'So-o-o-o, now this is the exciting bit, so listen carefully . . . they've invited me to be assistant housekeeper!'

Don perked up at this. 'More money, then?'

'Well, kind of.'

He tapped the table, 'Now see here, promotion means more responsibility and that means more money. You're not doing it if there's no more money in it. I'm not having you exploited. They've had enough out of you over the years and it's time to call a halt.'

'Be quiet and listen. They've suggested and I haven't accepted yet 'cos you've to give the go ahead, I can't do it without you.'

'Me? What's it to do with me?'

Vera took another deep breath. 'I can have the position of assistant housekeeper so long as I'm willing to go live there. We'll have this beautiful flat, really beautiful flat, fully furnished, heating and lighting free.'

'There must be a catch.'

'Well, there is. Well, not a catch but . . . I'm to be the backup person on the premises during the night. So if there's an emergency they've always got someone on hand besides the night nursing staff. To help, like. A body, paid to be there. The flat, oh! Don, it's beautiful. Lovely furniture, newly decorated, lovely bathroom, a beautiful living room looking out over the side garden, and two *huge* bedrooms, so our Rhett's all right, he can come with us.' Vera sipped her tea with a faraway expression on her face. She could just see herself entertaining people on her day off. That carpet in the living room! The kitchen with all that lovely equipment! She looked round her old cottage, the cottage she'd been waiting years for Don to bring up to scratch and thought, 'Goodbye, you horrible dump. Goodbye.'

'They want us to move in first of the month. Just think, Don, it'll be nearer to work for you. Cut five miles at least off the journey. They might even have casual work for you, and if our Rhett doesn't get a job they might have him as gardener 'cos the grounds are 'extensive', as they say in the brochure. Isn't it wonderful? Vera Wright no longer at the bottom of the pile!' She nudged his hand where it lay inert on the table, because he

275

hadn't shown any enthusiasm. 'Well?'

He'd drunk his tea and now pushed his cup towards her intimating he needed a refill.

'And what would you do with this place, then?' He jerked his head and looked around the kitchen of the home he'd been born in and had never left.

'I've been thinking about that all the way back on the bus. Clean it up and rent it out, then when I get the order of the boot we can turn out the tenant and bob's yer uncle, we're back home with lots of lovely rent money in the bank. Well?'

'We're not going.'

The kitchen was filled by the heavy silence which lay between them. It was broken when Don slurped his tea, unconcerned by Vera's deep and puzzled frown. Finally, she found her voice. 'Not go? Not go?'

'*We're not going*,' he repeated with emphasis. 'I've lived here all my life and this is where I'm staying. I leave here feet first in a box.'

'But the money! To say nothing of the chance of a lifetime!'

'Money isn't everything.'

'You could have fooled me.'

'Say what yer like, I'm not going.'

'What if I say I am?'

Don calmly replaced his cup in its saucer

276

and repeated, 'We're not going. I've said. So that's that. You can tell 'em tomorrow when yer go. Our Rhett said he'd be back soon, he'll be wanting his bloody tea, just like me, so get cracking, girl. It's no good looking at me like that, we're not going.'

All her years of struggle hammered one by one into her brain with the aggression of a pile driver. The insistent thud shattered any restraint she might have had in the past and she knew once and for all that she'd never climb out of the mire to the upland plains which were her just reward if he'd always be there to drag her back. Vera rose to her feet filled with hatred.

Don nodded his head at her and through a mist she heard him say, 'In any case, they won't want yer when they know you've got a criminal record, they won't want someone who's done porridge, will they? Stands to . . . '

Standing on the top of the cooker was one of the cast iron pans Vera had inherited from Don's mother and never had the money to replace. She picked it up and hit him on the head with it. He sat looking at her, quite still and not speaking. Her temper boiled over even further at his lack of reaction, and she hit him again. He fell slowly sideways as blood oozed from the top of his head in a great trickle. There was a single grunt and then no more except for the thud of his body as it fell between his chair and the cooker. Vera put on her cardigan, picked up her bag and marched out of the house.

Where she was going she didn't know, but somehow the Store felt like a haven and she knew Jimbo would know what to do. He'd advise her. He was a businessman. He'd tell her how to go about renting the cottage out. She marched down Church Lane towards Stocks Row, breathing rapidly, still blind with rage. As she turned the corner she heard the jangle of the bell on the door of the Store and by chance it was Mrs Jones who came out. Vera's temper boiled over again and, like a flash of lightning, she suddenly knew it was her who'd blown the gaffe to the estate about her garden pots and her lovely table and chairs, all because of the wardrobe mistress business. Unaware of Vera's rage-inspired revelation Mrs Jones set off to go down Shepherds Hill, a loaded carrier bag in her hand. From behind she received a stunning blow from Vera's bag which caught her on the side of her head. She staggered, retrieved herself and twisted round to see who'd attacked her.

Vera, purple-faced, screamed at the top of her voice, 'You bitch, it was you, wasn't it?

You told 'em, didn't yer? It'll be the end of me but I don't care. I'll go down fighting.' She grabbed Mrs Jones by the throat and began shaking her so that Mrs Jones' head swung back and forth violently. All the time Vera was shouting, 'You bitch! You bitch!'

At last, Mrs Jones struggled free of Vera's grasp, stumbled over her fallen shopping and tried desperately to escape by running back into the Store. Her way was impeded by Linda, Jimbo, Bel and a customer who'd rushed out into Stocks Row when they heard the shouting. Vera caught up with Mrs Jones and began hitting, punching and scratching her, anything to get her own back. Linda couldn't stop saying, 'Oh! Oh! Oh!' at the top of her voice, but Bel waded in and grabbed Vera, while Jimbo stood in front of Mrs Jones to protect her.

Vera, still screaming, fought like a wild cat to escape Bel, but the sheer weight of Bel's body prevented her. Finally Vera capitulated and began to groan, 'Oh! God! Oh! God! Oh! God!'

Jimbo and Bel took Vera inside, followed by Linda holding on to Mrs Jones who was trembling and so white they thought she was going to faint.

'Linda! First aid box, small brandy for these two. Come now, Vera, sit here and calm down. Mrs Jones, you too, sit yourself down. My goodness me, what a hullabaloo! What were you thinking of? Bel, ring Harriet. No, better still, ring the Rectory. Get Dr Harris. Tell her it's urgent. Quick sharp, please.'

Linda arrived with three brandies, one for each of the two antagonists and one for herself. She tossed it down, went weak at the knees, pulled out a stool and plumped herself down on it. 'Oh, Mr Charter-Plackett! I feel terrible. What's it all about?' she asked.

'Sip it, Vera. Steady now.' Jimbo, still supporting Vera, looked over to Mrs Jones, who was tossing back her brandy as though it was cola. 'Mrs Jones, steady with it, please. Do you know what's caused this?'

Mrs Jones shook her head. 'No more than you.' She took out her handkerchief and mopped her lips.

Vera, encouraged by the warmth the brandy was bringing her, said, 'She does know. It was her told Jeremy Mayer about my pots and that, just to get her own back.'

Mrs Jones opened her mouth to deny it but catching Jimbo's baleful eye she closed it again without a word.

Vera finished her brandy and gave the paper cup to Jimbo saying, 'It was her, I can see it now, to get back at me about them costumes. Well, she got more than she

280

bargained for, didn't yer? Yer own son and his wife perhaps made homeless. Serves yer right. No wonder yer wouldn't confess.'

Linda, catching a whiff of scandal and emboldened by her brandy, said, 'No, really? Is this true Mrs Jones? Was it you?'

Mrs Jones didn't reply, but Jimbo looked sorrowfully at her and said, 'Better to get it out now and apologise before it's all too late.'

'Before it's too late?' Vera stood up, wobbled a bit, and then sat down again. 'It's already too late. The damage that old cow's done . . . and now she's most likely lost me a blinking good opportunity to kick myself into a lifestyle above and beyond what I've got now.'

'The brandy's gone to her head. What on earth is she talking about?' Mrs Jones sniffed derisively. 'Lifestyle! What lifestyle can she ever expect?'

Caroline arrived in breathless haste. 'What's happened? Bel said there'd been an accident.' She looked from one woman to the next, then at Jimbo.

'We thought Mrs Jones was going to faint and Vera's not feeling too perky. There's been a disagreement, you see, between the two of them.'

'I see.' She looked more closely at Mrs

Jones. 'You're going to have a lovely black eye.'

'Am I? That's all your fault, Vera. Hitting me like that.'

But Vera had suddenly gone very quiet. The blood had drained from her face and she was nervously plucking at her cardigan sleeve. Caroline bent over her, her arm around her shoulders. 'All right, Vera? Is there anything I can do for you? Get Don, perhaps? Walk you home, maybe?'

'I'd come to ask Mr Charter-Plackett how to go about renting out my cottage. That's all.'

'Are you moving, then? I didn't know.'

'No one did.' Abruptly she stood up, clutched her handbag to her chest and made a move to leave. 'I'll go to our Dottie's. She'll sort me out.'

'But that's in Little Derehams. There's not another bus now till nearly six o'clock.'

'I'll walk. Do me good, some fresh air.'

Jimbo raised his eyebrows at Caroline, who shook her head. 'Dr Harris says you're not fit to walk all that way. I'll take you in the car.'

Vera tried to smile at him, but it wouldn't quite come. 'Will you? Then we'll talk about renting out the cottage on the way. Got to get it straight for tomorrow.'

'Of course. I'll just have a word with Bel.'

He winked at Caroline and left the office.

When Jimbo and Vera had gone, Linda went to pick up Mrs Jones' shopping and Caroline sat down facing Mrs Jones and asked her what it was all about.

There was a moment of indecision, then she said, 'It's all my fault. I'm the one who split to Jeremy Mayer about the garden stuff. I never let on, someone must have told her it was me. She's quite right. I should never have done it. I didn't think about the consequences, you know, about it affecting our Barry and that.'

'All over the costumes?'

Mrs Jones nodded. 'That's right. Then when it all blew up in my face I couldn't, just couldn't let on. Our Barry was so upset for the kids and that. I couldn't have faced him, just when life was going really well for 'im. My own grandchildren, 'omeless.' She dabbed her eyes with her handkerchief but it made her wince. 'But she just attacked me, didn't even speak, just hit out at me. Such a shock.'

'It must have been. You'll need to apologise, best to come out in the open, you know. Your eye's looking worse by the minute.'

'Never mind, I'll get my herbal stuff out, I've cured more bruises for my three boys

283

than I've had hot dinners. I'll just go see if Linda's rescued all my shopping.'

'We'll both go, then. Vera did seem odd though, didn't she?'

Before Mrs Jones could reply they heard a commotion in the Store and Rhett shouting, 'Quick, Bel, ring for an ambulance — the call box is out of order. It's Grandad, he's fallen and split his head open. There's blood all over the place.'

Rhett wouldn't go inside the cottage again, said he couldn't bear all that blood, he'd wait outside in Church Lane and direct the ambulance when it came and would Dr Harris do what she could? Instinct told Caroline that something more than a bad fall had taken place at Vera's cottage: Vera's confused behaviour at the Store, and two cups and saucers on the table with the teapot still quite hot. Don, who never touched alcohol and hadn't ailed a thing all his life, falling off a chair? He was unconscious on the floor, looking for all the world as though he'd fallen and hit his head on the corner of the cooker as he went down. Lying on the floor in the pool of blood was a heavy pan. He must have clutched it as he tried to save himself, or knocked it off the cooker with his arm, perhaps. She moved it away to make a space so that she could examine him.

After making sure she'd done all she could for Don, and despite realising she might be interfering with evidence, Caroline quickly washed up one cup and saucer and put them away in the cupboard, rinsed the bloodstains from the saucepan and replaced it on the cooker.

It took twenty-five minutes for the ambulance to arrive.

'Dr Harris! How's things? Those two nippers of yours all right, are they? Good. Good. What have we here?'

'This is Don Wright. It would appear that he's fallen and hit his head on the corner of the cooker. He's not spoken since I got here, he's out for the count and no mistake.'

The ambulance man gently removed the clean towel Caroline had put on Don's head and examined the damage. 'Cor, he's bleeding like a stuck pig.'

'Well, you know head injuries.'

'I do. Certainly looks as if that's what's happened. Poor old fella.' He bent down to sniff Don's breath. 'Not been drinking, 'as he?'

Caroline shook her head. 'Only tea,' she gestured towards the teapot, 'he doesn't drink alcohol. Well known for it.'

'Wife, has he?'

'Yes. She's at her cousin's. I'll let her know,

leave that with me.'

They expertly fixed a thick dressing to Don's head to absorb the blood and carried him off to casualty, leaving Caroline feeling guilty and distressed. She'd interfered where she shouldn't. She shouldn't have done it. Rhett had gone with his grandad, so she locked up the cottage with the key Rhett had given her and went back to the Rectory to telephone Dottie with the news about Don.

★ ★ ★

'I'll drive her in, Dottie, if she would like.' Caroline waited while Dottie explained her offer to Vera. But Vera wouldn't go.

'I'm sorry, Dr Harris, she doesn't want to go.' Dottie's voice dropped to a whisper. 'She's behaving real odd, I don't know what's the matter with her. Funny like, something about a fight with Terry Jones' mother, and she won't answer proper about Don. Insists on going to work tomorrow, says she's got business to attend to and can't have a day off.'

'Look, Dottie, I'll ring casualty and find out what's going on, and let you know. I'll make some excuse about Vera being ill in bed. OK? I'll be in touch. Take care.'

Don came home after three days and had

only Rhett to look after him because Vera refused to go home.

The general consensus was that Don had dropped asleep at the table and fallen off his chair. In the Store, heads close together by the tinned soups, they nodded wisely and agreed, 'All that night work, can't be good for a living soul that can't, must upset yer body clock and it's caught up with him at last.'

'Drink isn't to blame like it could be with some.'

'Our Kev knows the ambulance chap who came for him, he said he hadn't been drinking and he should know.'

'Poor Vera. Taken real bad she is. Still 'asn't come home from their Dottie's. Going to work, though, she can't be that bad.'

'She'll be having a bit livelier time there than she's had for years with that Don!'

'What I can't understand is where Vera was. I saw her get off the bus when I was coming out of here — I'd been to collect one of Mrs Charter-Plackett's birthday cakes for my old man — and I called out, 'Hello, Vera', she seemed real excited about something. So where was she between getting off the bus and beating up old Mrs Jones? Nobody's answered that one, have they?'

'One of life's unsolved mysteries, that is.' The gossip topped the list for days and even surpassed the talk about the play and the troubles Hugo Maude had brought upon the village.

15

Vera, disgusted by her cousin Dottie's nocturnal comings and goings and spurred on by her need to get her belongings together, eventually returned home after work. She stepped off the lunchtime bus, two plastic carrier bags she'd borrowed from Dottie in her hand. She cursed her bad luck as she saw Mrs Jones coming out of the Store. Vera turned on her heel and set off for home but Mrs Jones called after her.

'Vera! Just a minute! Hold on!'

Reluctantly she turned back.

'Vera! I'm sorry. Very, very sorry for what I did. Shouldn't have tried to get back at yer. I never should. My Vince is blazing.'

Vera studied over the apology, turning it over in her mind, pondering on the effort it must have cost Mrs Jones to make it, her being a proud woman. 'Not 'alf as sorry as me. However, I shall accept it. I owe you one too for going for you the other day. Perhaps you've learned a lesson from it. Barry and Pat don't deserve all this trouble, yer know.'

'I know they don't. I've been up and told 'em. Greenwood had a lot to say.'

'I bet.'

Mrs Jones had put down her bag and was twisting her hands together, looking down at them as though transfixed by their movement. 'I did wonder . . . I 'ave to admit I'm getting nervous about the play. I don't suppose . . . I mean, would you be free to . . . '

'Yes?'

Taking a deep breath she said, 'I could really do with another pair of hands on the night, well Friday *and* Saturday. Back up, kind of. Would you . . . ?'

Masking her triumph as best she could, Vera replied graciously. 'Why, of course . . . Greta . . . I'd be delighted to help. It's more than one body can do, isn't it?'

Mrs Jones, smarting under Vera's use of her Christian name, agreed. No one ever called her by her Christian name except for Vince. 'It is, it gets very fraught.'

'I shall be moving into my new flat on Thursday but I'll make it somehow.'

Mrs Jones' eyebrows shot up in surprise. 'Your new flat? What new flat?'

'I've got the job of assistant housekeeper at the nursing home and a flat goes with it. When I've got straight you'll have to come one afternoon for a cup of tea and have a look round it.'

'My word, Vera, that's a turn up for the book and not half. What does Don think? He must be pleased.'

'He isn't coming with me. Staying where he is, is Don.'

Shock registered in every bone in Mrs Jones' body. 'Not going? You mean you're *leaving* him? Vera! After all these years. Yer can't be!'

Vera studied this question for a moment and then said, 'I suppose I am. Yes, I am leaving him. Yer right. In one way you did me a good turn refusing to let me help yer and then splitting on us. It made me take stock. Sometimes it does yer good to take stock, yer know. What time shall I be there?'

'Where? Oh, the play. Come to the dress rehearsal Thursday, if you can manage it, that is, I wouldn't want to put you out. Six o'clock. Learn the ropes. Well, I never.' She strode away down Jacks Lane shaking her head.

Vera became aware that the boost to her morale which her triumph over Mrs Jones had given her was steadily evaporating the closer she got to home. She prayed that Rhett would be in, he'd be glad to see her even if Don wasn't. His reaction to her return to collect her things was a definite unknown quantity. Would he remember it was she who knocked him unconscious? Would he remember about the flat?

She didn't need to use her key, the door stood open in the afternoon heat. Don was sitting at the kitchen table on the very same chair, the same teapot and cup and saucer in front of him, a newly opened carton of milk to hand. It was as though the whole incident had never happened. She glanced at the cooker and saw the pan stood on the top as before. It was just as it was. Every blessed thing in the same place, even Don. Nothing had changed. Her heart jerked. Had she been given a chance to retrieve herself, time having taken a queer turn? Had it all been a dream? Then through the gloom she saw the massive bruising on Don's forehead, the shaved scalp and the stitched cut. So it was true, then.

'You're back.'

She put down her bags. 'I am. Any tea left?'

Don picked up the pot and weighed it in his hand. 'Enough for another one. Get yerself a cup.'

She sat at the table with him and poured herself some tea. It was stewed but for now it would do. In her mind's eye she imagined herself in the kitchen in the flat. All light and airy, the sun filtering through those lovely blinds framed by the matching curtains, all quiet and peaceful and glorious.

'How's things, then?'

She sipped her tea. 'Fine! Fine!' Didn't he know what she'd done? The stupid pillock. The stupid, dull, boring, useless, hopeless *pillock*.

Don sat without speaking and then burst out with, 'I've not been shopping. There's nothing in for tea.'

'I see.'

'I'll have to be off about seven. They want extra hours. Still, the money will be handy.'

'It will.'

'Rhett'll be back soon. Been out for a job interview, he has.'

'Right.'

His small brown eyes covertly watched her from beneath his thatch of grey disordered hair. 'Well, then, are yer going shopping?'

'When I'm good and ready.'

Don's eyes focused on hers. They looked steadily at one another, saying nothing but meaning a lot. She realised he wasn't going to mention what she'd done. He was going to ignore it. Shelve it. Pretend nothing had happened. Like always. Don't mention it and it'll go away, and Vera will carry on slaving in this tip like she's always done.

'I take over the flat on Thursday. Jimmy's giving me a lift with all my things. Are you coming?'

'I'm going nowhere, and neither are you.'

'I am. Don't say I didn't ask.' She stood up to put her cup in the sink, pouring away most of the stewed tea. There'd be no more stewed tea from now on. Rhett came in.

'Gran! You're back! Feeling better?' Vera nodded. 'Grandad tell you I've been for an interview for that garden job? Job's mine if I want it. Said I'd let them know.'

Vera smiled at him. 'That's good, I'm pleased, really pleased.' She paused. 'Rhett, I'm moving to the new flat, Thursday. Like I've said, there's a bedroom for you, and you're more than welcome. What do you say?'

Rhett nodded his head in his grandad's direction and raised his eyebrows.

'Grandad's staying here.'

'You're going without 'im?'

Vera thought about her answer. 'I am. Come with me tomorrow on the bus and have a look see. You'll love it.'

'I will. It's very tempting.' He looked round the depressing shambles that was his gran's kitchen. 'A real fresh start.'

'Oh, it is. Mrs Jones has climbed down and asked me to help with the costumes. I tell yer, there's a whole new life beginning for your gran right here and now. I'm off upstairs to sort some things out ready for moving. Here, take this ten pound note and go to the Store and get us something for our tea. There's nothing in. Get something we can just bung in the oven.'

Amazed by his gran's sudden generosity Rhett departed, his mind ranging over the selection of frozen meals Jimbo always kept in his freezer for emergencies.

Don sat impassively studying the design on the old teapot, his life being decided for him over his head.

As Vera went towards the stairs he said loudly, 'It'll be a different tale when they hear about your conviction. I'll tell 'em about what yer did to me, too, that'll put the frighteners on 'em. They'll be thinking yer might do it to one of them old bats yer talk so much about.'

Vera turned back and bent her head close to his unwashed, unshaven face. Her eyes only inches from his, through clenched teeth and with a steely purpose the like of which she had never known she possessed, she uttered a desperate threat. 'You'll keep your bloody trap shut, Don Wright. 'Cos if you utter one single word about anything at all to anyone I'll do for you once and for all. That blinking cut-throat razor of your grandad's with the genuine ivory handle yer keep prattling on about will suddenly find itself, after years of idleness, being put to good use.'

She drew her finger across her throat. 'Get my meaning? Nothing and nobody's getting in my way. OK? Know why? Because something'll turn up and put things right for me, because now is Vera's moment. Not anyone else's . . . Vera's. See? And if I don't take life by the throat right now, it'll be the end of me.' Her trembling legs carried her upstairs on the first step to freedom.

★ ★ ★

Not only Vera's legs were trembling. Jeremy Mayer's were too. Mr Fitch, having returned from abroad in the early hours and waking from a snatched and miserable sleep feeling totally disorientated, had come into his office wanting to catch up on the latest news about the estate.

'This damned jet lag plays havoc with me. What time is it?'

'Three o'clock.'

'It feels like ten o'clock. Where's my coffee?'

'I'll order some.' Jeremy pressed the number for the kitchen on his telephone, anything at all to delay telling him the crucial news about the court case. When he'd put down the receiver he shuffled his papers about, cleared his throat, shot his cuffs . . .

'Well? I'm waiting. What's the news? Bring me up to date.'

'The new crazy paving path is finished, and looks very good. It was a commendable idea of yours, sir. Greenwood Stubbs has brought in the flowers for the main rooms in readiness for tomorrow, and the girl's arranging them. The training staff want to have a conference with you, some new ideas they've got, think you ought to give your approval. I've had Jimbo in and confirmed the menus for the weekend, so he's all set. The fencing is almost done. Home Farm is having staff problems, two cowmen ill, but they're coping. The tickets are here for the play on Saturday night. First two rows centre. Everyone you invited has confirmed. Apart from that, nothing really.'

The girl came in from the kitchens with coffee for Mr Fitch. A nicely laid tray with silver coffee pot, cream and sugar and biscuits, just how he liked it. Jeremy thanked his lucky stars that Jimbo had well trained staff.

The girl carefully handed Mr Fitch his coffee and then said, 'Don't know if you need to know this, Mr Mayer, but the banners have arrived.'

His head shot up. 'Banners?'

'Yes, Barry's just fixing them up. Thought

you might need to know.' There was a smirk on her face which boded no good.

Mr Fitch stopped sipping his coffee. 'Banners? What kind of banners. I didn't order banners.' He waited for Jeremy's explanation.

'I don't know what they're about, Mr Fitch. I'd better go see. Obviously there's been some mistake. You finish your coffee.' He lumbered to his feet and stumbled out of the office, his heart leaden in his chest.

Strung from the first floor windows were pieces of sheeting with lettering, huge lettering from one end to the other. He didn't read them because he couldn't: his eyes had clouded over as a result of the tremendous explosion of temper he experienced at the sight of them. There was a mysterious pounding in his chest and his ears throbbed. Sweat began to run down his face, the hair on his neck grew wet, his knees, already trembling, began to shake. Had he been able to see himself he would have seen that his whole body was shaking. Fear had him in its grip.

He roared at Greenwood Stubbs who was standing giving directions to someone in an upstairs window. 'Stubbs!'

Nonchalantly, Greenwood swung round and innocently answered, 'Yes?'

'Remove those at once! At once, I say! At once!' By now his face was beetroot red.

Greenwood's response was to laugh. 'Not likely! We've got to draw attention to the injustice of this prosecution you've brought. It's not fair and you know it.'

'Prosecution? What prosecution?' Mr Fitch had come out to the front, cup in hand, he turned round and saw the banners. 'What the hell's going on? Mayer! Inside. Greenwood, take those banners down this instant.'

Greenwood Stubbs ignored him and carried on giving directions to the person at the upstairs window.

'Do you hear me? I pay your wages, so I'm the one who calls the tune round here and I insist you remove them.'

'Not for much longer you aren't. Or so Mr Mayer gives me to understand.'

The coffee cup began to rattle against the saucer as Mr Fitch took on board what Greenwood had said. 'Mayer! In!' Jeremy stumbled after him, his heart pounding as never before.

Mr Fitch led the way to his own office, seated himself behind his desk, put down his cup and saucer, and waited.

Jeremy began to settle himself in the nearest chair, but a withering glance from Mr Fitch persuaded him it wouldn't be a very good idea in the circumstances, so he stood like a small boy in the headmaster's office.

Summoning all his strength Jeremy began, 'Before you went away three weeks ago you stated quite categorically that the next time any member of staff, either outdoor or in, was caught stealing from the estate they were to be prosecuted. The full works, police, the lot.'

'I did.'

'Therefore when I got information regarding the disappearance of a quantity of crazy paving, an Edwardian wrought iron table and two chairs, and several Victorian garden pots of considerable value, I apprehended the guilty party and they are being prosecuted. The case comes up on Monday and I am giving evidence.' Relieved to see an element of agreement in Mr Fitch's face he began to lower himself into a chair.

'Just a minute!'

Jeremy straightened himself up. 'Yes?'

'Who exactly is involved?'

Jeremy counted them off on his fingers, then while he waited for Mr Fitch to speak he got out his handkerchief and wiped the sweat from his forehead.

'Have you interviewed these people?'

'Of course. I've seen Vera and . . . '

'What did she have to say?'

'She said she would return everything and

pay for the crazy paving and the cement if I would drop the prosecution, but I said no, I was under your strict instructions . . . '

'And Rhett?'

'Well, he said something about his grandmother needing cheering up and . . . '

'And Greenwood?'

'Stubbs agreed he'd used Jones' van for an hour to transport all the stuff, and that he'd been a party to the theft.'

'Knowing this village like I do, has anyone been up to speak on their behalf?'

Jeremy began to feel uncomfortable all over again. A sneaking suspicion that Mr Fitch was not entirely pleased with him began to permeate his subconscious, and he started to bluster.

'Now see here, Mr Fitch, I was only carrying out your orders. You said quite categorically that . . . '

Mr Fitch tapped the desk with his pen to stop the tirade and bellowed. 'Who?'

'The Rector.'

'You sat here in this chair and . . . '

Jeremy, clutching at straws, protested, 'Not that chair, my chair.'

'It bloody well doesn't matter which chair, what matters is you don't know when to let things go. I've spent years now building up a relationship with these people — why, I'm not quite sure, but it's something I know I have to do — and in one fell swoop you've destroyed all my work. When the Rector came you could have given in very gracefully indeed, made him think it was him who'd changed your mind and honour would have been satisfied, not just with him but the entire village. They set great store by that Rector. Come to think of it so do I. That would have been the end of the matter.'

'But you said . . . '

'Never mind what I bloody well said, you fool. It'll look fine, won't it? Every newspaper in the county will be running the headline about greedy landlords and home-less workers.'

'Homeless?'

'Yes, if Greenwood's found guilty I've nowhere to go but to sack the man. I can't employ someone who's been proved to be an accessory to theft from the estate. Think of the example to the others. The house goes with the job, the whole family would have to vacate it. The best gardener any estate could hope to have, and the best carpenter . . . '

'Barry Jones is an idle layabout. If I didn't keep hounding him . . . '

Mr Fitch rose to his feet. 'That's your job, to keep him on his toes! He's a craftsman and there's not many of those about. To say nothing of Greenwood. I can't afford to lose him. There's no man alive who would keep those glasshouses in such tiptop condition for the money I pay him. He's a brilliant asset I can ill afford to lose. No, he's not the one to go, it's more likely to be you who goes. You're expendable.' He leaned across the desk as he fired this salvo and Jeremy could see the whites of his light blue eyes and the slight flush on each of his thin pale cheeks. His snow-white hair appeared to crackle with anger.

'Me? What have I done?' The pitch of Jeremy's voice rose higher and higher. 'All I ever do is what you want, every decision, every letter I dictate is at your bidding . . . what more can I do?'

'For a start you can cancel that court hearing,' Mr Fitch snapped.

'If I do that I'll have no credibility left.'

'You have no credibility and never have had, that's why I need to tell you every move you make. You . . . bloody, blithering idiot.'

Jeremy opened his mouth to protest at Mr Fitch's ungentlemanly language but no words would come.

'You couldn't organise a chimpanzees' tea party, I should never have given you the job in the first place.'

Their voices were now so loud that there

had grown quite a gathering of students and staff in the hall wondering whether or not they should intervene. The office door was partly open so they couldn't help but hear every word. Someone had gone to fetch Venetia and she'd appeared downstairs to witness the dispute for herself.

'I . . . I . . . I . . . ' Jeremy clutched at his shirt collar and tried to drag it away from his throat, but his fingers had no more mobility than a bunch of carrots. He couldn't breathe and the sweat poured in rivers down his putty coloured face.

It was Venetia who rushed in first as soon as Jeremy began choking. The choking ceased, he gave three deep rattling breaths, then fell over backwards to the floor with the most tremendous crash and lay quite still.

'Oh, God! He's dead! He's dead!' Venetia knelt on the floor beside him, fitfully pounding his chest and then breathing into his mouth.

Mr Fitch went white and dropped like a stone back into his chair.

★ ★ ★

Later that evening Mr Fitch sat down at Pat's kitchen table. Pat, worried beyond belief by his unexpected arrival, inquired whether or not he would prefer to sit somewhere more comfortable.

'No, thank you, Pat, this is fine.'

'It's terrible news about Mr Mayer, isn't it? Have you heard any more? Is that what you've come to tell me?'

Mr Fitch studied his hands while he answered quietly, 'It's touch and go I'm afraid.'

'He's a bit of a chump but you can't help feel sorry for him with that Venetia . . . It can't be easy her being like she is.'

Mr Fitch didn't bother to ascertain whether or not Pat was scoring a point against him. 'Where is everyone?'

'Barry, Dean and Michelle are at the dress rehearsal and Dad's upstairs in his room watching telly.'

'Of course, yes, the dress rehearsal. Get him to come down, will you Pat? If he wouldn't mind.'

Greenwood Stubbs came downstairs and stood in front of Mr Fitch. 'Well, then, sir, what have you come for?'

'Sit down, man. Sit down. Tomorrow morning I am going personally to the court in Culworth and doing whatever is necessary to withdraw the prosecution against you. You must clearly understand that I do not approve of stealing, most especially from myself. If I had been asked, then I would more than likely have said yes, Vera could have all that stuff, but I wasn't and Mr Mayer acted on my instructions. He is completely exonerated on that score. I know I said I wanted all that rubbish clearing away, but, well, I didn't realise it was antique stuff — not being well up in that area. But taking it and using it and pinching the crazy paving isn't quite the same thing, is it? Don't let it happen again Greenwood, will you? Wait and ask *me* first. Right?'

'Very well, Mr Fitch. I much appreciate your understanding . . . '

Pat, hope rising in her chest, asked, 'Does that mean we shan't have to leave? Does it?'

'Of course it does.'

'Thank you very much, Mr Fitch.'

Making up an excuse for his change of heart he answered, 'No, thank the Rector. If he hadn't been on your side, neither would I.' Mr Fitch stood up and looked around Pat's cheerful kitchen, admiring the sunny yellow walls and the bright flowers on the sill. 'You've made a lovely home here, Pat. Lovely.'

'Thank you, we love this house. You've just no idea how grateful I am. It would have broken my heart if . . . ' Pat smiled at him nervously.

'Well, there's no need for you to worry. I know a good man when I see one and your father's one of those. Now . . . ' he rose to his feet, 'I'm off to Vera's to tell her the good news.'

'Oh! But did you know Vera's moved to the nursing home in Penny Fawcett? She's got promotion and a flat goes with it. She moved in today. Oh no, I've just thought. She's helping at the dress rehearsal. She'll be at the Church Hall.'

'I'll see her there, then.'

Greenwood reached out to shake hands. 'Thank you, Mr Fitch. Thank you very much. I can't say how grateful I am.'

'Not at all, not at all. The least I can do. Can't lose hard-working skilled people like you, Greenwood. Don't worry about Dean's scholarship. If he gets in, the money will be in place like I promised. I'll be off, then, to see Vera.'

★　★　★

Mr Fitch stood at the back of the hall while he accustomed his eyes to the darkness. The stage was brightly lit, the body of the hall empty except for Barry, Sir Ronald and Willie Biggs who were conferring quietly in the far corner away from the stage. Barry was pointing something out to the other two concerning the stage, it involved a lot of arm waving and apparently denial on Willie's part. Mr Fitch became absorbed in the argument. He smiled to himself. It wasn't just big business, then, which caused serious disagreement. It happened in two-bit places like Turnham Malpas over a two-bit play. When he heard the powerful persuasive tones of Hugo Maude his attention was drawn to the stage.

The set was splendid. Far and away better than he could ever have expected. His baby grand piano had pride of place, with a bright Indian patterned, heavily-fringed silky cloth draped over it. His eye was drawn to a vase of flowers so totally in keeping with the nineteen twenties set he could hardly believe it. Seated at the piano was . . . who was it? It was Caroline Harris! She wore a beautiful evening dress, light and beaded, and a jewelled band round her forehead. She was transformed; the sensible, caring Caroline he knew had been replaced by a siren out of the top drawer, no less. Her hands trailed along the keys, picking out snatches of tunes and then she began to play. Or was she? No, there in a corner was Mrs Peel, the organist, doing the real playing. How clever.

'*My dearest! That's the tune they played*

for us in the restaurant!'

Hugo crossed the stage and stood behind her, his hands on her shoulders, his lips raining kisses on her head, tiny trembling kisses. His hands roved over her shoulders and arms. She looked up at him and, seeing him upside down, said, '*Dearest, you look quite strange this way up. I've never seen you like this before.*'

Hugo captured her hands and raised them above her head so he could kiss them. '*Beloved!*'

She clasped her hands behind his head and drew it down so they were cheek to cheek. His hands began roving over her, down to her hips and back up along her arms until he unfastened her hands from behind his neck. He pulled her to her feet, pushed the piano stool away and they stood locked together, kissing.

In the dark Mr Fitch found himself blushing: not because the acting was bad but because it was so good. Too good. He was stunned. Moved might be a better word to describe how he felt. He noticed the three arguing in the corner had stopped to watch, and no wonder.

He looked again at the stage and now Neville Neal of all people had entered. The other two had broken apart on his arrival and were looking genuinely appalled. That was nothing to what that cold fish Neville Neal had unexpectedly become capable of. It really was as though he'd caught his own wife in the arms of another man. For a moment Mr Fitch was confused, mixing reality with the play. He shook himself. By Jove! It was going to be a real corker, was this. Those chaps he had coming to see it on Saturday night would be mighty impressed. He had a further shock when he heard Caroline, well not Caroline in truth but . . . She was giving her husband what for in no uncertain terms. 'Your constant, unwavering, everlasting love is sickening.' She pointed to Hugo. 'He's given me more excitement in two months than you have given me in twenty years. I never knew how thrilling loving could be till I met Leonard. Your feeble faithfulness, your self-righteous loyalty, your clinging to something which is no longer there! I'm weary of it. Weary! Do you hear me?'

Mr Fitch was spellbound.

'Will you never realise that I am not the person you left behind in 1914? You've come back to a new me. I've changed utterly and completely. That's what the war has done to me. Changed me for ever. But it doesn't seem to have changed you. You still have the same expectations of me.'

Neville Neal shook his head and wept.

Mr Fitch cleared his throat. It was all too realistic for words. He became convinced it was all true. Then he pulled himself together and remembered it was only a play. But what a play! Caroline was clinging to Hugo, her dress half off her shoulder, Hugo's arm around her waist, knee to knee, hip to hip, standing there watching Neville.

Then Rhett Wright came on stage. A transformed Rhett. A handsome, debonair, well dressed Rhett. And him only a gardener. What had happened to everyone? He couldn't wait to say nonchalantly to his guests, 'Oh, yes, that's one of my under gardeners. Talented lot, aren't they?'

Rhett and Neville left the stage. Caroline and Hugo kissed passionately and the curtains closed.

Mr Fitch crept out before anyone could see him. Vera would have to wait. He lit a cigarette, and stood outside looking at the stars and going over in his mind the tremendous excitement of the last few minutes. This only a village play and he'd financed it! Just showed what money could do. He walked down the path to the road to get in his car. Mr Fitch was well aware he was insensitive to other peoples' feelings and the incident with Jeremy that afternoon had proved that all over again, but right at this moment, excited by the play, he had a flash of insight and thought about how Peter would feel when he saw it. The light was on in Peter's study. He wondered if Peter knew what was going on? The Rector's wife acting her knickers off in a dodgy play in the Church Hall. Such good acting you thought it was real! Heaven's above. It wasn't, was it? Were they really having an affair? Surely not. They couldn't be. Or could they? He'd better warn Peter. The poor man. They couldn't cancel it now, it was all too late, but he'd better know, better be forewarned.

Peter answered the door. 'Why, good evening, Mr Fitch, how nice to see you. Do come in.' He led the way into the sitting room and invited Mr Fitch to sit down. Mr Fitch was glad Peter was in mufti, it made it easier somehow to talk man to man.

'I'm sorry, I know it's late but I had to come. I've just been watching a snatch of the play.' Mr Fitch cleared his throat. 'Have you seen it, by any chance?'

The light casual note in his voice amused Peter. 'I have.'

'Oh, right. I thought it a bit . . . *risqué* for a Church Hall.'

'In this day and age . . . ' Peter shrugged his shoulders and smiled.

'Oh yes, I know. But Caroline, your wife, she's certainly putting her heart and soul into her part.'

'Unexpected talent!'

'Indeed. This Hugo Maude. What d'you make of him?'

'Full of charm, too much for his own good.' Peter laughed. 'But a brilliant actor. He's bringing out the best in the most unexpected people.'

Mr Fitch nodded his head. 'Oh! I agree. Rhett Wright, for instance. Whenever I see him he's got his boot behind a spade. Now, suddenly ... well, it's quite unbelievable. And Neville Neal, crying real tears on the stage? Always such a cold fish. That Hugo must have something special if he can get him to do that!'

'Exactly, he has got 'something'.'

Mr Fitch took out a cigarette case and asked for approval.

'Of course, somewhere we have an ashtray.' He searched along the book shelves and found one. 'Here we are.'

'Thanks. Thirty years ago that play wouldn't have been staged in a Church Hall and, what's more, the Rector's wife wouldn't have been playing that part.' His voice had taken on a harder tone and Peter waited for the rest of what he had to say. 'Always admired you and the doctor. Wonderful couple, an example to us all. Married life isn't what it was though, is it? All this living together and divorce. Where do you stand on this divorce question?'

'For myself, marriage is for life. But for others I can see there are times when if it is a living hell, then . . . ' Peter shrugged his shoulders.

'For life. No matter what?'

'No matter what.'

'I admire you for that. This Hugo Maude, ladies' man, is he?'

'Oh yes. They all love him.'

'I expect Caroline admires him?'

'She does. He's taught her a lot.'

Mr Fitch's eyebrows shot up. 'Has he indeed. None of my business, but . . . ' He stood up to go. 'This is a warning from a friendly bystander. He needs watching. You do realise that?' He looked up at Peter who'd stood too. 'Not got your scruples you see, the man hasn't, I should imagine. Besides which, the village is bound to be talking.'

'True. Leave him to me. I know what I'm doing.'

'Shouldn't be telling the Rector what to do, you're far wiser than I about such matters. But I just had to say something, that's really why I've called. Take some advice from an older man with plenty of experience.' He looked into the distance as though weighing his words very carefully indeed. 'That man is endangering your happiness, believe me. Don't leave it too late to take action. By the way the prosecution's off. Well, it will be when I've had my say. Never known anything so ridiculous.'

'I'm glad, so very glad. I couldn't manage to persuade Jeremy to drop it. Thank you. How is he? Have you heard?'

Mr Fitch looked anywhere but at Peter.

'Very, very ill. I wouldn't say this to anyone but you, and I hope it won't go further than this room, but I'm feeling guilty about the chap. I was so blazing mad at the way he'd handled it all, but really the poor fellow was only carrying out my orders. Pay peanuts, you see, and you get monkeys. Must go. Jet lag. Remember what I said about you know who! Goodnight to you.'

★ ★ ★

It was almost one o'clock when Caroline came home. Peter, ready for bed, was in his study reading. He carefully inserted his bookmark in his place, put the book on his desk and went into the hall to greet her.

Caroline looked shattered. Her hair was

tousled, her stage make-up smudged, her clothes thrown on rather than worn and her eyes avoided his. She dumped her bag of things on the hall floor, saying, 'Don't say a word. I'm going straight to bed. I know I'm late, I know I should have let you know. I'm exhausted and, what's more, I don't think I can face tomorrow. Goodnight.'

She stood with her hand on the newel post, one foot on the bottom step. 'I don't think I can get upstairs.'

Peter didn't speak. He stood beside her, put his arm around her waist and began to help her up one step at a time. He left her in the bathroom and went down again to make her a cup of tea. He was carrying the tray upstairs when he heard her crossing the landing to the bedroom.

She was standing by the bed in her slip. Peter placed the tray on her bedside table, and undressed her. When he'd slipped her nightgown over her head he lifted back the duvet and she slid in, resting her back on the pillow he'd propped against the bed-head.

While she sipped her tea he got into bed beside her.

'Thank you, Peter, for this.'

'Rehearsal go well?'

'Excellently well. Couldn't have been better. This cup of tea has saved my life. I cannot remember when I have felt so tired, not even when the children were babies.'

'What are husbands for but to pick up the pieces.'

Caroline looked at him. 'What do you mean by that?'

'Nothing. Nothing at all.'

'You do mean something.'

'I don't. It was a perfectly innocent remark. You would do the same for me if our roles were reversed, I know you would.'

Caroline finished the last drops of tea, put the cup back on the tray, turned off her light and slid under the duvet. 'The trouble is I don't deserve you.'

'You do. What's more, you're stuck with me, like it or not.'

'Sometimes I wish . . . '

'Yes?'

'Just sometimes I wish you'd *do* something instead of always being so sure.'

'About what?'

'About . . . me and you . . . you and me . . . about Hugo.'

'That would be ridiculous, your attraction to Hugo being transitory. Which it is, isn't it?'

There was a silence. When she didn't reply, after a few moments Peter repeated, 'It is, isn't it?'

'Am I or am I not a grown woman?'

'You're a grown woman.'

'Then why don't I *know*?'

'Because even grown-ups can't always find the answers.'

'*You* always can.'

'Not always, Caroline. This one has me foxed.'

'Just hang on in there, Peter. Please.'

'I am trying.'

'What a stupid conversation. Why don't we say what we mean?'

'Want me to come right out with it?'

In the dark Caroline nodded.

'I think if I met him on a dark night and there was no one about I'd throttle him. In my most desperate moods that's what I want to do. An absolutely childish thing to be saying, but it's true.'

'I see. He loves me.'

'Does he indeed.' The sarcastic note in his voice didn't go unnoticed.

'That's what he claims. He made me an offer tonight.'

'Did he?' Peter turned on his side so that he faced her, and waited for her answer.

'I don't think the wife is supposed to tell the husband. It's all so ridiculous. I'm two people at the moment. I love you, but I don't want you to touch me, not in that way. And I love Hugo, and want him.'

The silence lengthened and eventually Caroline put her light on and looked at him. 'But is it love, Peter, or lust or just me in need of being told I'm still desirable by someone who doesn't love me unreservedly, like you do?' Her fingers fidgeted with the edge of the duvet cover. She gave a great sigh and then added, 'He wants me to go away with him, you see.'

Despite his shock at her almost casual announcement, very slowly, choosing his words with extreme care, Peter said, 'I wonder if the play is the root of your trouble. Emotionally you're very charged up, you're bound to be, it's a very emotional part. So why not wait until the play is over? It's not sensible to make life decisions when you're on a high and so exhausted.'

Petulantly, Caroline burst out with, 'That's right. Stand back. Leave it all to me, as always. The decision is mine, et cetera, et cetera. Let's all play at being reasonable adults.' Disdainfully, she added, 'It's all so painful.'

Peter's temper erupted. 'Painful! For whom? What do you think it's like for me watching all this happening? I'm not nearly so laid back about it as I give the impression of being. You just *looking* at Hugo like you do causes me such agony. Such jealousy. I hate it. Loathe it. I'm distraught by how I feel about him touching you. But I am determined to give you space, which at the moment is what you appear to me to be in need of most. However, don't underestimate what's going on underneath. It is flesh and blood beneath the clerical collar and the cassock, you know: vibrant, passionate, loving flesh and blood. It is beyond my endurance when you treat me like some kind of holy sounding-board, trying out your problems and indecisions about him on me. A servant of God I may be, but I am also a *man*, and don't you ever, *ever*, forget that.'

His outburst silenced her.

They lay in the same bed. But miles apart.

16

Jimbo's first customer the following morning was a stranger. He bought a newspaper and some chocolate, served himself a coffee, sat on the customer's chair and settled himself for a chat.

It wasn't long before Jimbo realised who he might be. 'You're from the *Culworth Gazette*, aren't you?'

He nodded. 'Eddie Crimmins. Short of news this week, thought I'd call round, see if anything was happening. Like 'Vicar's wife had it away on her toes with the verger', or something of that ilk.'

'Sorry, nothing happens around here. You'd best get back to Culworth and do the courts, or something.'

'Not what I've heard. What's all the posters about the play. Anything there?'

Jimbo shook his head.

'Devastating new talent discovered? Some little milkmaid turns overnight into acting sensation?'

'You're behind the times, there aren't such things as little milkmaids any more. Milking machines, you know, or hadn't you heard?'

The reporter ignored Jimbo's sarcasm.

While Jimbo served his early morning customers, the reporter sat quietly listening to their exchanges. Then to Jimbo's annoyance in came Hugo, up earlier by at least a couple of hours than was his usual habit.

No one but a fool would have failed to recognise his commanding presence. Jimbo saw the reporter go on red alert and then carefully mask his excitement.

Hugo, unaware he'd drawn Eddie's attention, went straight to the bread counter. He called out to Jimbo, 'Jimbo! Croissants. I have a passion for croissants, do you have any?'

His wonderful speaking voice filled very corner of the Store, and the reporter knew he'd met up with his quarry. What luck!

'It's all right, I've found 'em. Brilliant!' Hugo took them across to the till. 'You weren't up when I got back last night. Did Harriet tell you what a superb dress rehearsal we had?'

'She did. She was so fired up she didn't get to sleep till around two o'clock she tells me. By Sunday morning she'll be a wreck!'

'Thanks for these. Need 'em for my breakfast.'

The reporter got to his feet. 'Mr Hugo Maude, isn't it?'

'It surely is.' Hugo eyed the stranger up

and down. 'Mr Crimmins, I presume? Let's do the interview over breakfast. Have you eaten?'

Eddie shook his head.

'Come then.' As he walked towards the door with the reporter in tow, Hugo called over his shoulder, 'Harriet won't mind, will she?'

But before Jimbo could answer the little bell on the door jangled and Hugo and the reporter had disappeared.

The bell jangled again almost immediately and Jimbo looked up to see who'd come in.

It was Willie Biggs. 'Only me!' Having picked up his paper on the way from the door to the till, Willie slapped the exact money down on the counter and said, 'He's not the first. There's two already at the Rectory. What beats me is how they find out? Who tells 'em?'

'In this case I think it was the man himself.'

'Hugo? I 'spect that's quite likely. Folk like them don't hang about when it comes to publicity. Really putting Turnham Malpas on the map. Georgie and Dicky will be doing well out of it, yer know what reporters are like for drinkin'.'

'True. True.'

'Couldn't really expect to get away with it, could we? Stands to reason.'

'Good for trade!' Jimbo laughed.

Willie glanced round the Store, bent over the counter and confidentially whispered. 'What does your dear lady think to this play? My Sylvia's a bit scandalised by it. Really wonders if it's suitable for a village Church Hall.'

Jimbo studied what Willie had said and then declared, 'We have to remember we're in a bit of a backwater here. Compared to some plays in the West End it's quite harmless and Caroline has insisted on some of the bits being cut. No, I think we're on the right lines.'

Willie looked indignant. 'I don't want to be disloyal, my Sylvia being housekeeper there and me verger, but I do think this business with Hugo Maude has gone too far.'

'In what way?'

'The Rector's very upset about it. I know. I can tell. He puts a smiling face on it but when yer catch him unawares he looks grim. Lost his inner peace, yer know, what comes from 'is faith. Course, being 'im he won't lay the law down, but it seems to be it's about time he did.'

'What goes on between the two of them is their affair, Willie, not ours.'

'But when you think about their position in this village . . . The Rector has standards to keep up and she's not keeping 'em, in my opinion. They should be setting an example, not acting like it's for real.'

Jimbo finished writing out a new slogan for the meat counter on one of his white plastic boards, then he said, 'Is that how it looks?'

'Oh yes. Time and again, it feels like for real. It's not right. Not right at all. And there's not only me who thinks that either.'

'Sunday morning it'll all be over. Storm in a teacup.'

'Will it, though? Will it all be over?'

Unbeknown to them Willie had not shut the door properly, so the bell hadn't rung when someone had come in.

It was another stranger, and by the looks of her a reporter. 'Do you do ready-made sandwiches? I'm starving.' She looked innocently at the two of them.

'We do. Above the chill counter. On the left. Freshly delivered every morning. All new in.'

Willie jerked his thumb at the reporter behind her back, pulled a face and left. Jimbo offered the reporter a coffee from the customer's machine.

'Oh! That'll be lovely. Thanks. Early start this morning, too early for me.'

'What brings you here, then?' Jimbo inoffensively inquired.

The reporter struggled to open the hermectically sealed sandwich and, before sinking her teeth gratefully into it, she asked, 'This play, you're doing. Heard it's good and a bit, you know . . . spicy?' She put her head to one side and smiled, inviting his confidence.

'No, no, all very low key. First time we've done anything of the kind so it's bound to be very ordinary.'

'Now come on.' She tried the coffee and approved. 'My word this coffee's good. And the sandwich too. Very good, in fact. Now come on, I've heard you've got Hugo Maude in it, so that's not what the world would call low key, now is it?'

Jimbo tried to be nonchalant about the whole matter to put her off the scent, not knowing how much she'd heard before he and Willie had realised she was there. 'That's correct.'

'Who else? Anyone I know?'

'You're not from the *Gazette*, so where are you from?'

'The *Fulton Examiner*.'

'No! Was it you who ran the big campaign against extending the bypass?'

'Don't try to change the subject! Who else is in it?'

Defeated in his attempt to divert her

attention he replied, 'My wife, for a start. A local accountant and his wife, one of the gardeners from the Big House, a schoolgirl. That's about it.'

'How about that glamorous Rector of yours, is he in it? Bet he is, gorgeous man.'

'No, he isn't. Must press on, stay as long as you like.'

'Haven't paid you yet.'

'On the house.'

'It won't work, you know, giving freebies in the hope that I won't ferret about too much.' She wagged her finger at him and gave him a winning smile. 'My instincts tell me . . . '

'It's a blinking good play and you should stay to see it tonight.'

'Oh, I shall be back tonight. I'm reviewing it for the paper. Just thought I'd get some background detail this morning. What a feather in your cap. Hugo Maude, no less. How did it come about?'

'He's a friend . . . ' He was going to say 'of ours' but changed his mind. 'He's a friend of mine from university. Came to stay and we persuaded him to produce the play. Well, he's acting in it, too.'

While he'd been speaking she'd been making notes. She looked up from her notepad and asked, 'And you are . . . ?'

'James Charter-Plackett.'

'You don't seem quite the sort of person to be running a village shop.'

Jimbo winced. 'That's as may be but I've got to make headway this morning. Will that be all?'

'I'll leave a couple of pounds on the counter for the food. And thanks. I'll just finish eating this.' She waved her half eaten sandwich at him and sat down on the chair. Jimbo disappeared into the back just as Linda arrived to take charge of the post office.

'Oh! Good morning! Haven't seen you around here before, just moved in?'

The reporter picked up on the gossipy tone in Linda's voice and decided to make use of her. 'No, I'm a reporter.'

'No! Well, I never. You can interview me if you like.'

'I like. First of all we'll have your name, then I can quote you.'

'Oh never! Me with my name in the paper! How exciting! First time ever, except once when I was nine and won the egg and spoon at the Brownie sports. What do you want to know?' Excited to such an extent she was eager to throw caution to the wind, Linda propped herself against the counter and awaited her first ever interview.

The reporter got out her notebook and pen. 'First, who's in this play?'

Disappointed that the question she had been asked was apparently nothing to do with her personally, Linda straightened up and made to leave. 'I'm not in it and I've never been to a rehearsal, so I can't help.'

'Oh! I think you can. You're here at the hub of the village, and you seem to me to be a *very* sympathetic person. I expect you know, out of the kindness of your heart, of course, most of what goes on.' She smiled up at Linda and got the capitulation she'd worked for.

Linda resettled herself against the counter. 'Well, of course the highlight is having Hugo Maude here. He's been very ill, and he's come to stay with the Charter-Placketts to recuperate. Him being a friend from university of Mrs Charter-Plackett and . . . ' The tale wound on and before she knew it Linda had told the reporter about how scandalised the village was over the way Hugo Maude and Dr Harris had behaved.

'Dr Harris? Isn't that the Rector's wife?'

Linda nodded. 'Exactly! They've been seen kissing, and not just in the play. I mean, it's not quite the thing, is it? Kissing. What an example to set. Also, they were spotted in the wood together, you know, and . . . '

'Linda!' It was Jimbo coming through from the back carrying a box of butter. 'Linda! It's

329

past nine and you haven't opened up the post office yet.'

'But I was just being interviewed.' She made no move towards the post office and deliberately continued her conversation ' . . . they do say that . . . '

Jimbo banged down the box he was holding and said, 'Linda! I do not want to have words. Please do as I ask. Now!' To the reporter he said, 'Sorry about this but I am a stickler for opening on time. Can I help at all?'

The reporter closed her noteback, smiled sweetly, and left.

As he stacked the butter on the chill counter shelves, Jimbo said, 'Never have I been so angry with you, Linda. Telling a reporter all that. I bet three quarters of it wasn't true anyway.'

'It's no good speaking to me like that, Mr Charter-Plackett, and I was speaking the truth.'

'You were not. You were insinuating all kinds of things.'

'Were they or were they not seen in the wood together? Have they or have they not been seen kissing and holding hands, or him with his arm round her waist and her not objecting?'

Jimbo stopped stacking the butter and

looked straight at her through the post office grille. 'I can't deny it.'

'Well, then.'

'But telling a reporter . . . '

'Well, she kind of wheedled it out of me.'

'It makes me wonder what tales you tell that you hear in here. It should all be absolutely sacrosanct. Taboo.'

'Are you telling me, then, that you never tell anyone what you hear in here?'

Jimbo hesitated.

Triumphantly Linda replied, 'No, you see, you're as bad as me.'

'No, I am not.'

'You are. It's the kettle calling the pan black, that's what.'

'One more word out of you . . . '

'Yes?' Linda came out from behind the grille and, hands on hips, faced him squarely. 'Well, I'm waiting.'

'What you've said this morning is tantamount to putting an advertisement in the paper.'

'It is not. What's more you've no right to speak to me like this.'

Despairing Jimbo said, 'Haven't I? Any more and you'll be sacked.'

'Go on then, do it and then we'll see what the industrial tribunal will say. My Alan knows all about it.'

'I bet he does. Then do your damnedest.'

'Is that it, then?'

'Yes.'

'Right, I won't even trouble to take my coat off. That's it. Eight years of service to you and yours. Well, I can manage without you. And it won't be any good coming round and apologising and begging me to come back like you did before, because I shan't. So there!'

'Right! I'll send your P45 and the money I owe at the end of the month.'

'Right!' Linda flounced out, slamming the door with vigour.

Jimbo immediately regretted losing his temper. Linda might be annoying — she was a stickler for her lunch and coffee breaks — but she did know her job. Damn and blast. Now what? There was one thing absolutely certain, he wasn't going to beg her to come back, ever again. Once was enough. He'd manage somehow. Damn and blast Hugo Maude. The trouble he'd caused. Now this. He finished stacking the butter, threw the empty carton in the rubbish bin and shut himself in the post office with a heavy heart.

★ ★ ★

The reporter went straight across to the Rectory, knocked and waited. She quite fancied cajoling some more information out of the gorgeous Rector. She flicked a comb through her hair while she waited. She knocked again and to her disappointment it was neither the Rector nor the Rector's wife who came to the door.

'Yes?' Sylvia folded her arms across her chest and tried to look intimidating.

'I'm from the *Fulton Examiner*.'

'Yes?'

'It's about the play. I wondered if the Rector's wife would be able to give me an interview. I'm reviewing it tonight for the paper and I thought a little background information would be a good idea.'

'Not in.'

'Oh! That's a pity. I was hoping to see her. The Rector, then. Is he in?'

'No.'

Smiling her most gentle smile, her little-girl-in-need-of-help-and-sympathy smile, she asked, 'Are you in the play? You look as though you might be, you look the adventurous type.'

'I am not.'

'I'll call back later, when they've both returned.'

'Don't bother. They've nothing to say.'

333

'Nothing to say? I can hardly believe that, not with the great Hugo Maude in it. Surely he of all people must have caused something exciting to happen! Such a handsome man, so charismatic. Every female heart a flutter, eh?'

'We're very level headed here, takes a lot to surprise us.'

With a twinkle in her eye the reply came back, 'I've heard one or two things.'

Despite the reporter's persuasive interviewing techniques Sylvia retained her resolve to let nothing slip. 'Well, I haven't and I work here.'

'Oh, I see. You'll know a thing or two about your delightful Rector's wife, then? Bet you've a few stories to tell. Leading lady, I understand. Who could play opposite Hugo Maude without being charmed, and he is a real charmer, don't you think?'

'That he may be, but it's nothing to do with the Rector's wife, believe me.'

'That's not what I've heard in the Store. Apparently, you're all scandalised about what's been going on.'

'I'm shutting the door. Right now.'

'Oh please . . . '

But the door shut with a crash. Knowing when to accept defeat, the reporter went off to the Royal Oak and Sylvia returned to the sitting room where Caroline was flicking through her script.

'Who was it at the door?'

'It's not my place to say it, but I'm saying it.'

'I beg your pardon?'

Sylvia, with her arm fully extended, pointed in the direction of the door. 'That *person* was a reporter. That person was asking me about you. She's found out, goodness knows from whom, what's been going on. I may lose my job over this but I won't stand by and watch the Rector being crucified any longer. You and the Rector and your children mean more to me than anything I can think of. At this moment you are tearing them apart.' Sylvia stamped her foot. 'Just what are you thinking of with this business with Hugo Maude? Tell me that.' She stood arms akimbo and waited for Caroline to reply.

Caroline stood up, her face taut, her eyes blazing. '*Nothing* is going on between Hugo and I. Nothing at all . . . '

'I don't know how you can stand there and *lie* like that. We all know. Every man jack of us in this village knows. You can't fool us, even if you're fooling yourself; which you are and make no mistake about that. I don't know how the Rector faces everybody each day, I really don't.'

'I'm afraid you're overstepping the mark now, Sylvia.'

'It's not me doing the overstepping, believe me, it's you and it's got to stop. Just think what you've got to lose. And the children. God help us, it would kill them if you left.'

'Who said anything about leaving? Not me! It's none of your business, none at all . . . '

'It is though! I've loved those children from the first moment I clapped eyes on 'em. They're like my own flesh and blood . . . '

'But they're not, and the whole business is entirely my concern and not yours. That is enough.'

'Right.' Sylvia began removing her apron. 'This is breaking my heart this is, but you have my notice as of now. This minute. I will not be a party to this kind of behaviour. Perhaps if you have to manage without me you might, just might come to your senses, because at the moment you've no sense left. Not one jot or tittle left. You must be out of your mind. I can't bear standing by and seeing the Rector . . . '

'Always the Rector, what about me? Don't I have a life besides being his wife?'

'When you really get down to it, unfortuntely you haven't. But then you knew that when you fell in love and married him, so it's no good complaining now. You weren't a young untried girl, you knew exactly what you had to face. He's the loveliest man any woman could hope to have, and there's dozens out there who'd jump into your shoes in a trice, but the pity of it is there's absolutely no one else for him, but you. It's the same for the children, no one else for them but you, you're their strength and stay. You're in danger of forgetting that and casting them aside, and all for what? All for *what*, ask yourself that! All for *what?*' Her lovely grey eyes full of tears, Sylvia turned away and left the room.

Distraught, Sylvia went about the kitchen picking up the bits and pieces which were hers; the comb she always left here, the apron she kept for the afternoons, the hand cream she kept by the kitchen sink, the old mac in case it rained. All treasures which she had thought were permanent belongings in the Rectory. Leaving the house quietly, she wandered off to the church in search of Willie to ask for the comfort only he could give at this appalling moment. She sat down on the seat he kept just outside the boiler house door where it caught the sun, and gazed out across the churchyard waiting for him to appear. The morning sun was creeping round casting lovely shadows over the grass. Such a peaceful, restful place and yet her mind was in turmoil, her heart was thumping and her legs felt like jelly. In the depths of despair Sylvia warmed her face with the rays of the sun; a face down which tears were falling.

I should never have said all that. But it's true. She's being led away by that . . . mountebank. That womaniser. Now I've lost my job. Hang the money, I loved it. Willie'll be retiring soon and we definitely need it, but . . . There'd be other places, other people who needed domestic help. The Rector would give her a reference . . . but maybe he wouldn't, not after what she'd said. Caroline always came first with him. Like the reporter had said, he was a gorgeous man.

'Hello, Sylvia! I'm looking for Willie.' It was Peter, the sun catching his red blond hair making it resemble a halo. Sylvia tried to stem her tears.

Peter sat down beside her and quietly asked, 'Can I help?'

There was a silence and Peter waited, then Sylvia admitted she'd given notice.

'I see. Your immediate notice?'

Sylvia nodded.

Intuitively he answered, 'She's having a very difficult time.'

'I know, but so are you.' She patted the hand resting on his knee.

Peter studied Sylvia's face for a moment. 'Indeed.'

'You're being far too kind, far too considerate to all concerned.'

Peter sighed. 'What would you have me do?'

'Go for it.'

'For what?'

'Him.'

'You think so?'

Sylvia nodded. 'Oh, yes, I do. He's to blame. Catching her when she's so vulnerable. Her life up to having that cancer had been all glorious. You know, loving parents, happy family life, good at school, head girl, prizes and such at medical school, high praise in every direction. Then she marries you, then you give her the children and she dotes on them, she truly does, and then she got knocked sideways with the cancer thing. It came as a terrible blow. Really beaten into the ground she's been, and somehow this business is all part and parcel of getting over that.'

'Yes, I know.'

'I love your children, and I don't want to live to see them have their hearts broken. But . . . well, that's what's going to happen if something isn't done and quick. But don't ask me what, 'cos I don't know. The pendulum's swung too far in his favour, and it's to be stopped. You see I can't believe he means all he says to her. At bottom he's a very lightweight person, a child, a kind of Peter Pan. She must be the only person in the village who doesn't know who else he's chasing — well, not chasing, he's already caught her from what I hear. Get my meaning?' Her voice caught in her throat and made her pause. 'I've said much too much and I'm very sorry. She'll never forgive me.' Sylvia wiped away a tear. 'Never!'

'We'll see. Like you, I do now believe something has to be done.'

'Oh yes. And quick, before it's too late.'

Peter stood up. 'I agree. But if she was to make a mess of this play that would be even more damaging. She's got to be successful in it, you see. If I step in right now, today, it could do untold damage. But, yes, you're right, I musn't stand aside once the play is over. Give this to Willie for me will you, please?' He dug into the pocket of his cassock and handed her Willie's wage packet, then walked away.

He'd left his car keys in the vestry so he entered the church by the main door, intending to retrieve them. Peter shut the door behind him and began to walk down the aisle, but paused by the tomb Willie claimed was haunted. Sleeping in his favourite place on the top was Jimmy's dog Sykes. Peter tickled him behind his ear, a practice Sykes adored. His short, stubby tail gently wagged his appreciation. Giving him a final pat Peter recommenced his walk down the aisle, but then stopped in his tracks.

Kneeling on the altar steps was Caroline, her head in her hands. He stood watching her, trying to decide whether or not to go and kneel beside her. Before he had decided what to do for the best she shuffled herself around and sat on the steps, her forearms resting on her knees, her head bowed, totally unaware of his presence. All the love he felt for her coursed through him right to his very feet and he longed to give her the comfort of his arms, to hold her, hug her, heal her. Yet he held back sensing that perhaps it was not *his* arms which could do any of those things at this moment. Space, like he'd said last night — was it only last night that he'd lost his temper? — space was what she needed and that was what he would give her now. So despite his surge of desire to hold her to him he turned and quietly left.

The keys could wait.

★ ★ ★

After an uneventful lunch prepared by Caroline, during which they'd exchanged small talk and nothing more, Peter left for the hospital to visit Jeremy in intensive care.

Slumped in a chair beside his bed was Venetia. She leapt to her feet when she saw who their visitor was. 'Oh, Peter!' She made a hasty and useless attempt to tidy her hair, straighten her sweater, and generally pull herself together. He'd never seen her devoid of make-up, and seeing her now he realised just how devastated she must be about Jeremy's brush with death.

'I'm sorry I look such a mess, I've been here all night. It's kind of you to come.'

'Not at all. Any improvement yet?'

Venetia shook her head. 'Still touch and go. He's not conscious. Damn him!'

'It wasn't his fault!'

Venetia slumped back down in her chair and rubbed her hand across her face. 'I know.' Then she studied Jeremy laid there fastened up to all the paraphernalia of the seriously ill. 'Damn him! I've ignored his existence all the time we've been here. Laughed at him, scorned him, belittled him, taunted him . . . shamed him . . . '

'Shamed him?'

Venetia looked up at Peter and he saw the conflict going on behind the weary eyes. 'Yes, shamed him. I thought he didn't care about me and had never noticed what I was up to, but all the time he had. All the time he knew about me . . . you know . . . '

'No, I don't know.'

Venetia looked surprised. 'You mean that, don't you?'

Peter nodded. Venetia reached forward and took hold of Jeremy's hand, looking at him and not at Peter, she told him, 'I've been unfaithful to him time and again. *Time and again.* This time is the last time, the very last time . . . ' She stopped abruptly, looked at Peter for a moment and then continued. 'But if . . . *when* he comes out of this, I'm going to propose. I never knew until yesterday, when I thought he'd died and it was all too late, how much he meant to me. He's been so loyal, despite everything I've ever done to him, a perfect gentleman all the time.'

'I see.'

'Together we're going to beat this weight business. It's comfort eating, you see, because he thought I didn't love him when he loved me so much. He was right. Well, he wasn't right, I *did* love him but I didn't realise, you see. So his weight is my fault, and my fault alone.' She patted the still hand and then looked at Peter. 'Cruel is the only word to describe me. I've never felt so full of sin in all

343

my life. Do you think God will ever forgive me?'

'God always forgives those who truly regret what they have done.'

He saw hope in Venetia's eyes. 'Then He's even greater than I thought if He can forgive me for what I've done to Jeremy.'

'He is: greater than any of us can comprehend.'

Venetia pleaded with him. 'Will you remember us in your prayers?'

'Of course, we all will.'

'I've been praying all night.'

'Keep at it, he is still here.'

Still gripping Jeremy's hand Venetia said, 'I've had a lot of time to think. This last two years I've lived two lives. One at church and helping Kate with the youth club, and the other as the old Venetia, like I've always been. From now on there's going to be only one Venetia. The nicest and best Venetia, living in the world you live in.'

Peter smiled. 'The world I live in?'

'Yes. I'm going to belong to that respectable, kind, loving world where you and Caroline live. A relationship that's all crystal clear and straightforward with no intrigue and no confrontation. No pretence. No deceit. My world is going to be one where everything is in the open, no secrets, only truth.'

Peter, embarrassed by his marriage being held in such high esteem at this particular moment, simply touched her shoulder in sympathy murmuring, 'I'm glad, so glad.'

Venetia, on the brink of tears, acknowledged his sympathy. 'I'm jealous of the way you and Caroline love each other, do you know that? I'm going to try very hard to love like that. Strong and deep and loyal.' She smiled sadly at him, her lips trembling.

To avoid betraying himself he made to leave.

'Say a prayer for him and me before you go. Please.'

Peter took hold of Jeremy's other hand, said a prayer and made the sign of the cross on Jeremy's forehead and then on Venetia's. 'God bless you both.' Before he let go of Jeremy's hand he was almost sure he felt a very slight squeeze of his fingers.

17

Although the play did not open until half past seven everyone involved was at the hall by six o'clock. First night nerves were very apparent, from the stage hands scurrying about checking and rechecking to Mrs Peel worrying about her music, from the actors themselves to Sheila Bissett fluttering around checking her flowers.

'What do you think, Dr Harris, are they all right?'

'They're wonderful, Sheila, I told you so last night. Absolutely right. Even the vase.'

'Hugo likes them, too, in fact he raved over them, so I suppose they must be. The dear man. He's so thoughtful, isn't he?' She tidied the angle of one of her gladioli then stood back and admired her arrangement. 'So lovely, we shall miss him when he goes. You will too, I expect. Ron and I have been thinking of buying tickets for Stratford when he's on. We've never been, ever. Do you think it would be a good idea?'

Caroline agreed it would, and would Sheila mind if she left her to it as her first night nerves were at breaking point.

Sheila turned to look at her. 'Of course, off you pop, I've done here now anyway.' She glanced round to see if anyone was within hearing distance and then whispered confidentially, 'I don't blame you at all for falling for him, you know. We all have. I'm quite envious of you.' She gave Caroline a meaningful wink; a wink which bordered on lewd.

It served to categorise Caroline's passion for Hugo at the lowest level imaginable. What had been fine and beautiful and fullfilling was reduced in a moment to tawdry and commonplace by Sheila's gesture. She spun on her heel and went back to the minute dressing room she shared with Liz, Harriet and Michelle. All there was for her to sit on was a bathroom stool someone had brought from home. Caroline sat on it with her hands clenched, without speaking, letting the excited conversation of the other three swirl around her.

Harriet, knees bent so that she could see into the mirror she'd propped up on the narrow windowsill, broke off from combing her hair to admire Michelle's dress. 'Oh, that does look lovely! I'll say this for her, your grandmother knows her stuff.'

Michelle pirouetted in front of them in the dress she would be wearing in the first act.

'Just wish I felt as lovely as it looks! I don't know what made me agree to do this. It's not my scene at all. I've only kept going because Mum's so thrilled at me having the chance.'

Harriet wagged her finger, 'Who's leg do you think you're pulling! Rhett's the draw and no wonder! I can't believe he's the same boy, young man I should say.'

Michelle blushed. 'He is doing brilliantly, isn't he?'

'And so are you, isn't she, Caroline?'

Caroline looked up. 'Sorry, I wasn't listening.'

'And no wonder. You're going to do really well too, you know. Don't worry.' Harriet gently hugged Caroline. 'Hugo will see you through. He's an old hand at this kind of thing.'

There came a loud rap on the door and, as it opened slightly, they heard Hugo saying, 'Everyone respectable, can I come in?'

He cut such a dashing figure in his slacks, high at the waist in the nineteen twenties' fashion, an open-necked shirt with a dark cravat at his neck and his hair sleeked down with gel, they quite forgot they'd seen him the previous night at the rehearsal dressed just like this. Somehow there was an extra vitality about him, an added buzz which made him larger than life. The small room seemed scarcely large enough to contain him.

'All my favourite ladies prospering, are they?' But his question was really aimed at Caroline and the other three knew it.

She fell under his spell immediately and began to glow. 'We are.'

'Excellent. Fifteen minutes to blast off. Good luck!' He held Caroline's eyes for a moment and smiled especially for her.

'Good luck!' The four of them called as he closed the door.

Caroline acted stupendously well that night. Her performance was way beyond anything she had ever expected of herself. Congratulations flooded in, from villagers, from the press, from friends. When she finally arrived home at the Rectory she was on a high.

'Peter! Oh, Peter! It was brilliant! Marvellous! Wonderful! I can't find words to describe how well it's gone. Hugo is in his seventh heaven.'

Peter held his arms out wide and she went into them and he hugged her. 'I'm so glad! I can't wait to see it tomorrow night. I am prepared for being very impressed!'

She held her head away from his chest and looked up into his face. 'Oh! Make no mistake, you'll be impressed all right. We all of us acted our socks off! We really did.

Michelle, Rhett, Liz, Neville, Harriet! The hall was full, every seat taken and the press were there, too,' she thumped his chest in her excitement. 'National and local! Hugo got them there in droves! What it is to be well known!' She flung herself down on the sofa and kicked off her shoes. 'I'm desperately thirsty.'

'Tell me what you fancy and it shall be yours.'

'Water. Cold, cold water. A jug full!'

After she'd drunk two glasses she said, 'We had one *faux pas*, that was all, but Hugo got us through it. There isn't any wonder that he's at the top of his profession! I can't wait to see him in *Hamlet*. He'll make a perfectly splendid one, I know. It's only because of him that we've done so well. Thank God for Hugo!'

'Indeed.' Peter sat down in the other chair and fidgeted with his wedding ring. 'I'm truly glad it went well, Mr Fitch will be glowing tomorrow night. He's quite childish sometimes about how his money can achieve things. He said to me last night how impressed he was with Rhett Wright. He made it sound as though it was he, Craddock Fitch himself, who'd got Rhett to act so well.'

Caroline sat up. 'Where did you see

Craddock Fitch? I thought he'd only got home yesterday?'

'He did. He popped in to see me.'

'What did he want?'

'This and that.' Peter stood up. 'Finished? I'll clear away.'

'Well?'

He looked down at her and thought about Venetia believing that everything between him and Caroline was clear and open. 'Came to tell me he's dropping the prosecution.'

'That's a relief, he must be mellowing in his old age!'

But Peter had gone towards the kitchen. She followed him in. Her two cats were settled for the night in their basket so she kissed them on the tops of their heads, tickled their stomachs as they rolled over to wallow in her attention and then looked at Peter's back as he rinsed out her glass and got out a clean tea towel.

'Peter!'

'Yes?'

There was a pause. 'Oh, nothing. I'm going to bed.'

'Won't be long.'

'You deserve first prize for your . . . ' He turned to face her. ' . . . loving patience.'

He turned back to the sink, put the well dried glass in the cupboard above the draining board and said, 'I'll follow you up in a while. Tell me more about the play tomorrow, you look completely whacked right now.'

Disappointed he hadn't taken up her remark she said, 'I'll say goodnight, then.'

'Goodnight. I'm so proud of you. God bless.'

'And you.'

Caroline fell asleep almost immediately and never realised that it was more than an hour before Peter, having spent an anguished time thinking over his situation, climbed the stairs to bed. He'd sat at his desk, head in hands, mulling over how he would handle the situation the following night. He'd smiled wryly to himself when he thought about the notion he'd had that morning of dramatically strangling Hugo in the wings at the end of the play as the final applause faded away. No, that wouldn't do! The publicity! And he didn't fancy a stretch in prison.

Appeal to Hugo's better nature? He didn't have one.

Threaten him? Not a suitable action for a pacifist to take.

Cajole him? Hugo would simply laugh.

Thump him good and hard? Even less of a good idea.

But somehow his exit from Turnham

Malpas had to be brought off with the minimum of harm to Caroline.

Peter picked up the photograph he kept on his desk. It was the one he'd taken of her and the children on their first seaside holiday. She had a twin nestling in the crook of each arm and was nuzzling her cheek against Alex's head. He remembered how the people in the hotel had commented on how like him Alex was, and how Beth had a look of Caroline, hadn't she? He owed her so much. Her forgiveness alone was something he would never be able to repay, not if he lived a thousand years. Who was he to feel so desperately injured at this moment?

Peter replaced the photograph and knelt to pray for guidance.

★   ★   ★

On the Saturday night the play received a rapturous reception at the end of the first act. Mr Fitch's guests were incredibly impressed and told him so when they gathered for coffee during the interval.

'God! Fitch! You've boasted about this village of yours often enough, but bless me it's come right up to scratch and no mistake! It's like as if it's for real. Amazing!'

'Fitch! Where in heaven's name have you

found such talent? Can't quite believe it in a village this size.'

'How come you cornered Hugo Maude? Even I've heard of him, so he must be good. Damn me! Introduce me, would you? My Angela will be green as hell . . . Beg yer pardon, forgot I was in a Church Hall.'

'Congratulations, Fitch! Most impressed with the leading lady. Who is she?' The speaker bent his head to hear, balancing his coffee precariously within striking distance of Mr Fitch's country suit. Mr Fitch whispered in his ear. The inquirer was so astonished he shouted his reply. 'The Rector's wife! My God! The Rector's wife? Since when have Rectors had wives like that. Bet he needs to keep her on a tight rein.'

Peter, at Mr Fitch's request, had just come to join the group and overheard the last remark. He ignored the comment and tolerated being introduced to everyone with as good a grace as he could muster. Inside he seethed with despair. Accepting their congratulations on his wife's wonderful performance as cheerfully as he could, he longed for the interval bell to go so that he could slide back into anonimity in the darkness of the Church Hall and lick his wounds. He couldn't take much more.

When it came to the scene when Caroline

told her lover that it was all over, Peter's flesh crawled.

'I cannot go on. I have the children to think of. I suspect that Julian is ashamed of me, and I am too if I really think about it. Daisy hates it, too. She loves her father, you see, and knows how hurt he is. As a mother I have my duty to do. They didn't ask to be born, and they are flesh of my flesh and as such deserve the best of me. I have a husband who deserves none of this anguish . . . '

'But what about love? You haven't mentioned love. Surely it deserves a place in our lives. You've said yourself you don't love him any more.'

Marian turned angrily on him. 'I've never said I don't love him. You're putting words in my mouth. What I am saying is I will not divorce my children's father, I will not. For their sakes, I will not!'

Leonard went to sit beside her on the sofa and, taking her hand in his, he asked, 'Taking this course of action will slowly but surely destroy you. No one should have to make this kind of sacrifice. I'm offering you love, doesn't that count for something?'

Marian kissed his lips greedily. 'Oh yes, of course it does, but it's not enough.'

'Not enough? What more can one ask? I shall love you to my dying day.' He brushed her hair from her face and held her head between his hands, looking closely at her. *'If he loved you like I do he'd let you go, if that was where your happiness lay. It's all so easy, just come.'*

'And live a life in corners, hardly daring to acknowledge each other. Perhaps in thirty, forty, fifty years things might be different but now I'd be classed as a wicked woman, make no mistake about that. I can't live that kind of life and he wouldn't divorce me anyway.'

'Make him.'

Marian shook her head. 'It's against his principles.'

Leonard mocked her. 'Divorce might be against his principles but torturing his wife isn't, then?'

'You're being ridiculous. In any case living your kind of life from one house party to the next wouldn't be my kind of life. I need stability, a structure, security. It sounds pathetic, I know, but it's true.' She took his hand from her face, kissed the palm and whispered, 'Don't, please, don't make it hard for me to say goodbye. I love you like life itself. Since I met you . . . Before you, he and I trudged on, going through the motions but you . . . ' she traced his features with a trembling finger ' . . . you've made each moment of every day throb with life. The sun

356

is brighter, the sky more blue, the world more entrancing. That's been your gift to me . . . '

'But, darling . . . '

Marian placed a finger on Leonard's lips. 'So I shall have that gift for the rest of my life. I shall keep it locked away and take it out from time to time, unwrap it and enjoy it again and again. Kiss me, and then I'll leave. I shan't look back or I might weaken and take you in my arms and fly away with you like you wish.' With great longing in her voice she added, 'You will be in my heart for ever and a day, my dearest.'

Peter listened to the dialogue going back and forth between the two of them and writhed inside. There was still the scene to get through when she heard from the maid that there'd been a shooting accident at the Big House and did madam know it was Mr Leonard who'd died. He wished Hugo Maude in hell and longed for the play to finish.

When the curtains did finally close on the last line an audible sigh went around the hall, and then the applause began. Most of the audience stood to clap and they had curtain call after curtain call, until finally Hugo stepped forward to say his thanks.

With arms outstretched he opened his speech with, 'What can I say? Without your support where would we have been? You dear, darling people. Weren't the cast absolutely splendid?' He flicked his hands in the air, beckoning applause. When it had died down he continued. 'I came to Turnham Malpas a broken man, wounded by the hurly-burly of life. I leave to go to Stratford, refreshed, renewed, revitalised, re . . . '

' . . . charged?' Someone from the audience called out.

Hugo laughed, 'That's right. Recharged. I love you all . . . '

A voice from the back whispered hoarsely, 'Some more than others', and was instantly hushed by his neighbours. Hugo ignored the comment and followed on with, 'There are so many people to thank for this production, not least Mr Fitch who has sportingly lent us his piano and provided the wherewithal for the production. I give you Mr Fitch!'

Mr Fitch stood up and from his place in the front row turned to acknowledge the thanks.

Hugo quickly drew everyone's attention back to himself by signalling to one of the front of house helpers to step forward. They carried a bouquet. By West End standards it was huge, by Turnham Malpas standards it was colossal.

'For my leading lady!' Hugo leant down to

take the bouquet into his arms and he dramatically kissed Caroline, handing the bouquet over to her. Massively stimulated by the success of her performance she thanked him with a big kiss. The audience cheered. This bouquet was followed by others from husbands, from families, from Mr Fitch, from well wishers. And then Neville stepped forward.

'I should just like to say how much everyone in the cast, and all the backstage helpers to whom we owe an enormous debt of gratitude, have learned under Hugo's tutelage. Me in particular. I know I'm considered a cold fish and that it's time I let my hair down and relaxed more, well now I well and truly have in this play and I quite like the experience!' Muted cheers came from the body of the hall. 'All our lives have been enriched by his work here and we're grateful for the time he has carved out of his busy life to work with us. He's a hard task master, believe me. He's kicked us, cajoled us, ordered us, badgered us, shouted at us, persuaded us, until finally we got it right. Hugo Maude, a present from us all.' He stepped to the wings and emerged with five bottles of champagne in his arms. 'With all our love and best wishes for the future.'

Hugo's eyes filled with tears as he accepted

the champagne. 'What can I say, but thank you so very, very much.'

The speeches went on until finally Hugo called a halt. 'Goodnight! Goodnight! The cast still have a party to go to! Goodnight, everyone, and thank you once again from the very bottom of my heart for all your love and kindnesses. Goodnight!' He waved vigorously to everyone as they began to leave and then signalled for the curtains to close.

Turning, he enfolded Caroline in his arms and said, 'My darling!' He looked into her eyes and saw behind the excitement and the sparkle an unexpected wariness which he decided to ignore. 'Caroline! You were wonderful! Wonderful! Completely stupendous!' Bending close to her ear he whispered, 'Have you decided? Are you coming with me? Say you are!'

'Move over, Hugo, it's the husband's turn now.'

It was the sharp tone of Peter's voice which startled Hugo. Peter had only ever been polite and generous in his dealings with him, despite the delicacy of their relationship, so he released Caroline and looked up at Peter wondering what was afoot. 'Mr Fitch is anxious to introduce you to his guests, so you'd better go play your I-am-humble bit and accept their admiration.'

Hugo looked at Caroline but could read nothing from her face, he half thought of suggesting she went with him to see Mr Fitch, but changed his mind when he couldn't interpret her feelings. So he meekly did as Peter suggested. After all if he was to take *Dark Rapture* to the West End then he would need backers and all Mr Fitch's guests were influential people. It was only politic to go. Suddenly a sweet *au revoir* to Caroline didn't seem like a good idea and he left without a word.

'Brilliant! Quite brilliant. You were right. I was impressed.'

Eyes bright with success Caroline looked up at him. 'I told you you would be. And it wasn't just me. Michelle and Rhett and Harriet and Liz and Neville were brilliant too. Life will never be the same, will it? So I'm determined to enjoy every last minute of this day. You can stay for the party? Willie doesn't mind, does he?'

'He's sleeping in the spare room, so we can stay as long as we want.'

'Oh! I didn't know. Sylvia's not . . . '

'No.'

'Peter . . . '

He bent down and tentatively kissed the

top of her head. 'Yes?'

'Nothing. This make-up feels uncomfortable. I'm going to remove it.'

'I'll help clear the chairs, then. Make space for us all.'

★　★　★

Apparently from nowhere, a trestle table was erected, and food and drink appeared as though by magic. Hugo, secretly extremely excited by the great impression he'd made on Mr Fitch's guests, having laid the seeds to take *Dark Rapture* to the West End, donated his gift of champagne to the party and opened a bottle. They all gathered round with their paper cups and waited for him to pop the cork. He gave the bottle a vigorous shake and the cork fired out, narrowly missing Caroline's face. She leapt aside, stumbled over Neville's feet and only saved herself from falling by grabbing Sylvia's arm.

'Sorry!'

'That's all right.'

'Sylvia!'

'Yes?'

'I'm really sorry, you know, about . . . '

Sylvia's eyes filled with unexpected tears. Caroline kept hold of her arm and said quietly, 'I'm so sorry. One day perhaps you might . . . '

'I'll see. I can't bear . . . It's the children, you know, I miss them.'

'I understand.'

'And you.'

'Yes?'

'And the Rector.'

Still holding her arm, Caroline kissed her cheek. 'We'll have a talk sometime. Yes?'

Sylvia nodded. 'Well, all right then.'

Hell's bells! Would nothing ever be right again? She'd accepted the maternity leave stand-in job, she desperately wanted to do it and now she might just have no one to see to the children. But would she be here anyway? Hugo caught her eye and smiled that special smile he kept for her. Her heart felt as though it was spinning in her chest, her blood pumped faster and faster and all she could see through the haze was Hugo's beautiful features and the smile which was only for her. For a moment they were the only ones in the hall. His glorious dark hair, his widow's peak, the strong beautifully moulded forehead and those eyes! Were there ever such expressive eyes as his? Then their moment was broken by someone standing in front of Hugo. It was Peter, blocking Hugo completely from view. Peter. Peter's children. Her children. Her darling Alex and Beth. They'd survive her going. Children were remarkably resilient and with her gone surely Sylvia would come back to give a hand.

The noise of the party grew, everyone was talking, running over the high points of the play, laughing, teasing, making plans for another production, returning borrowed jewellery, clothes they'd lent, pictures commandeered for the stage, her Indian throwover was returned to her, plans were made for storing the costumes Mrs Jones had run up, the chatter and the noise and the excitement went on. Someone had put on a tape and the music added to the excitement.

Then the door burst open with a crash and silence fell as they all turned to see who had come in. It was Don Wright. But not the Don they'd known all these years, for this Don was the worse for drink and unsteady on his legs. An audible gasp of surprise went round the hall.

'Wel-l-l now. Champagne, ish it? Don'll 'ave one!'

'Now, Don, is this a good idea?' This from Mrs Jones.

''Ello, Greta! Give us a kish.' He went forward weaving his way between the chairs. 'You've known me a long time, but it doeshn't give you the righ' to tell me wha' to do. Come on, then, I like a nicesh plump woman I do. Round, like, and cuddly.' He lurched forward and grabbed her, giving her a resounding unwelcome kiss. His hands clutched her bottom. 'My word, but you're a . . . ' Mrs Jones fought him off and then smacked his face.

'Oh now come on, that'sh not kind to an upright good living man li' me. My Vera never lifted a hand to me.' His bleary eyes peered at everyone. 'Where ish she? Where'sh my Vera?'

But Vera was hiding behind Rhett. 'Don't let him see me, Rhett, please.' Rhett stood his ground. 'Oh, Rhett! Whatever have I done? I've driven him to drink, that's what. Him that's never done me a wrong turn all these years.' Vera peeped out from behind Rhett and, seeing him, realised he was still the same old Don. 'He won't change for me though, will he? It's just a load of sentimental old tosh he's saying. His problem is he's got no one to wash his socks and iron his shirts. But I shouldn't have done what I've done.'

When Don couldn't spot Vera, he said, 'Anyway it'sh not only her I've come to shee, it's that Mr Hugo Maude. I've come to knock his block off.'

Hugo pushed forward into a gap and faced him. 'I'm here.' Summoning all his acting techniques, despite the prospect of a physical attack, he assumed an air of authority and said, 'I suggest you toddle along home, Don, and sleep it off.'

'Home? I haven't got a home no more. Not now my Vera'sh left. You've driven me to drink! Me, a lifelong teetotaller! Thish champagne's good, gi' me some more.' He held out his cup and someone dribbled a drop in to pacify him. 'That's not enough, fill it up, go on fill it up. That's better!' Don staggered slightly, steadied himself, took a slurp of champagne from his paper cup then pointed with his free hand at Hugo. 'This is a toast to that shnake in the grassh. Mr Hugo Maude. The man who parts women from their lawful husbands. He started with my Vera. Thirty-six years of married bliss we've 'ad, and he comes along and whizz bang wallop she leaves me. Three daysh and it feelsh like three yearsh.' Don placed his champagne on the trestle table and, taking out a grimy handkerchief, mopped his bleary eyes.

'Oh Rhett, he really is missing me. What have I done?' Vera whispered.

Don put his handkerchief away and continued with his tipsy monologue. 'But he wasn't content with just one woman, was he? Oh no. When my Vera left me because of him,

366

he didn't tell her he already had another string to his bow, did he? Oh no! Up at the Big House getting his oats, he was. She was only too ready and willing; anything in trousers, that's her motto. He's a two-timing blackguard. Now 'er 'usband's had a 'eart attack! It was the shock that did it! Lucky if he lives.'

'Someone get him out!' Hugo snarled his request, but no one moved to comply; Don's performance had mesmerised them all.

Don picked up his cup again. The champagne appeared to have cleared his head, for now his speech was not nearly so slurred and his eyes were taking in everything: the blank, horrified faces, the incredulous ones, the embarrassed ones, and in Caroline's case the appalled one.

Don went to stand in front of her. 'It's you my heart bleeds for. You're a lady, and he shouldn't have done it to you. You've been duped.' Don liked the sound of the word and said it again, 'Absolutely duped. How many more he's had while he's been here I don't know, but he's rubbish, he is. Don't take no notice of him,' he jerked his thumb in Hugo's direction. 'Don't listen to his sweet talk, it's all acting. Go home to the Rector and them lovely children of his, 'cos all that rat will do is drag you through the mud, believe me.'

Peter, horrified by what Don was saying, at last mobilised himself as Don paused to toss the last of his champagne down his throat. He forced his way through the crowd, pushing aside those rooted to the spot by the horror of what they were witnessing. He intended to take Don by the arm and frog-march him out, but as he reached him the door opened again and everyone turned to look at the newcomer. This time it was Venetia.

Unaware of her arrival, Don pursued his point, emphasising it by stabbing the air with a shaky finger. 'Yer see it's all right for Mr Hugo Maude to mess her about, 'cos that Venetia's a . . . tart. An out and out *tart*. But not you!'

Someone switched off the tape and in the profound silence which followed everyone stared at Venetia.

The evening was full of shocks, for this was a Venetia they'd never seen before. A broken reed battered by life's storms, she wore a grubby sweater, wrinkled trousers, no jewellery. Her hair was straggly and unkempt and, for the first time since they'd known her she wore no make-up. She looked completely done in. It was Venetia who spoke first.

'Thanks for the character reference, Don. That's all I needed to hear, tonight of all nights.' No one answered her, all they could do was brace themselves for her news. 'I saw the lights on and I had to talk to someone before I went to bed.'

Harriet broke the spell by walking towards her. Assuming the worst, she said, 'Of course you did. We're all so very, very sorry about Jeremy. Such a great loss for you . . . and for us. Look, come and sit down here.'

Venetia shook her head. Looking directly at Hugo she said quite steadily, given the circumstances, 'From this day forward I shall not be the Venetia everyone's always known. I regret deeply all the things I've done which have caused harm, and from now on things will be very different because, hopefully, I've been given a second chance. I may have been a . . . tart, like Don said, but not any more.

'My Jeremy's not dead, you know.' An audible sigh of relief went round the room. 'I proposed to him tonight. I don't know if he realised what I was saying, I hope he did. I hope it gives him the strength to keep on fighting because I want him to live. It's still touch and go, you see.' Venetia half lifted her hand in a sad farewell. 'Goodnight. God bless.'

No one spoke for a while after the door closed behind her. Peter's first concern was Caroline. He looked down at her and knew he'd never seen her so distressed. She visibly trembled. Her eyes were closed. Sweat beaded her top lip. Her hands were clenched so tightly the knuckles were white. Peter didn't know what to say or what to do. One wrong move and he could blow it for ever.

He stood beside her watching people self-consciously begin clearing up: saying nothing, just busily occupying themselves to cover their embarrassment. Slowly they began to exchange a few words. Don weaved his way across to the collection of empty champagne bottles and, putting the top of one of them to his mouth, he sucked the last drop from it and from the next and the next. He staggered wildly and then lurched forward, falling across the end of the trestle-table. It collapsed with a mighty crash and he with it.

The noise caused Caroline to open her eyes. She looked up at Peter and said softly, 'Please take me home in as dignified a manner as possible.'

★　★　★

'There's just one question I want to ask you. Did you know he was seeing Venetia?'

Peter shook his head. 'Not until yesterday when something Venetia said at the hospital made me think he just might, you know . . . '

'Because if you'd known and said nothing . . . '

'I truly didn't know.'

'It wasn't news to everyone else. They all knew, I could tell from their faces.'

'Apparently so. Here, drink this.' He handed her a small brandy. 'You need it.'

Caroline placed the glass on the coffee table. 'Not now, I need a clear head. I never thought it would be Don Wright who would cut me down to size.'

'It's been a night of surprises.'

'You can say that again. What I can't understand is why I never guessed, why a grown woman like me, well experienced in dealing with people from all walks of life, never realised. Not a glimmer. Not a hint.'

'He's a very complex character.'

'I can't believe he didn't mean what he said to me. He can't have done, can he?'

'I think he did at the time he said it.'

She looked up hopefully. 'You think he did?'

'Oh yes.'

'I see. Can I be honest?'

'What else?'

'That phrase Marian used in the play, 'throb with life', every moment. That's how it was for me.'

'I know.'

'Every moment to be treasured. It was gloriously reckless. Miraculous. Enchanting. He cast a spell over me.'

Peter knelt on the hearthrug to put himself on a level with her.

'Now, damn him, all that fine, uplifting love is smashed to smithereens. All those wonderful times ground under his heel, like the finest crystal, shattered and never to be, no more.'

She sat quite still for a moment just looking at Peter, remembering gratefully how, despite her crying need for him, she'd told Hugo she couldn't in all conscience sleep with him until she'd definitely left Peter. At least she didn't have that stumbling-block to face. Then she thought of Hugo and how he'd captivated her and she asked pleadingly, 'It was true what Don said, was it? About Venetia? It wasn't just him being drunk for the first time in his life?'

'Judging by Hugo's face it was true.'

'Damn! Damn! Damn! How could he do it to me? How could he?'

'I'm sure that when he was with you he did love you.'

'If he did, how could he go from me to her?'

'Because he's several people all at once, and all of them crave adoration. It feeds his genius, you see.'

The door bell rang.

Caroline's eyes were wide with pain as she begged, 'Peter! Don't answer it.'

'I must. It could be someone in need of help.'

'Not at this time of night.'

The bell rang again. Peter stood up.

'Please don't answer it.'

They heard Willie coming down the stairs, complaining.

Peter went into the hall.

'Oh, you're back, sir. Thought it was you forgotten your key. Will you see who it is?'

For the first time in his ministry Peter decided to ignore what might be a call for his help. 'No. Ignore it. Go back to bed, it's half past one. Whoever it is can wait till tomorrow. Thank you.'

Willie turned back and climbed the stairs. Peter went to the sitting room window and moved the curtain slightly so he could see clearly. He could just make out Hugo's silhouette walking away down the road back to Jimbo's. 'Whoever it is has gone away.'

'It would be him coming to apologise. Full of remorse. I can't bear to take any more of his sweet talk. Never any more of it. I must have been the only one completely taken in by it. Perhaps I needed to be taken in, needed to believe he loved me. It was so . . . let's face it, it was so flattering. It inflated my ego, boosted my morale, gave me such a kick. What a fool I've been!'

Peter shook his head. 'Don't, don't. You're being too hard on yourself.'

'Not hard enough. To think I nearly threw everything away, everything . . . You. Alex. Beth. When I think of their distress if I'd gone, I can hardly believe I could even *think* of putting their happiness in such jeopardy.' She was looking down at her hands, twisting them together back and forth in her lap when she said this, so she didn't see the searing pain in Peter's face.

She raised her eyes and looked straight at him. 'Because of my job I thought I knew the human race, but I don't. I'm an amateur, a complete amateur. You're streets ahead of me in that. I've made an utter fool of myself. I wish he'd never come here. The damage he's done!'

'He's done some good too, you know.'

Scathingly Caroline asked, 'Such as?'

'He's made Venetia, for one, think about herself and her lifestyle and made her put Jeremy first. He's brought Mrs Jones to heel; she had far too much pride, far too much self-importance. Mr Fitch has been humbled and about time, too: he's almost sick with worry about Jeremy. Vera's struck out for a better life for herself all because of her disappointment over the costumes. Don has learned Vera's value to him, to the extent that he is most probably going to do as she wants. People working on the estate have had a salutary lesson, which was sorely needed, about appropriating estate property. I'm also completely certain that Sylvia will be back. It might take a week or so, but she will. And when she is back, your regard for each other will be strengthened not diminished. And look at the cast of the play! Who would have thought that Rhett and Neville could act like they did? Superbly too! Their lives will never be the same again. So, in a way, the village is a better place for him having been here.' He smiled at her, one of his gentle encouraging smiles: full of strength and support.

She was silent for a while, then raised her eyes to his, and with a voice clearly at breaking point, asked, 'How can you ever want me back?' Having dared to ask the question uppermost in her mind Caroline began to cry. It was like a storm breaking. Peter daren't even touch her in case his embrace would be unwelcome, so he sat on the rug waiting. She howled like an injured animal caught in a trap, desperate with pain, and it cut his heart to pieces, but he knew he must wait for her; for her to show her need of him. Wait and wait for her.

He heard Willie creeping down the stairs. He came to stand in the doorway, clutching his clothes, and signalled he was going home for the rest of the night. Peter nodded. 'Goodnight and thanks. See you in the morning.'

Willie nodded towards Caroline. 'She'll see things straighter tomorrow.'

'I know. I know.'

It was fully ten minutes before Caroline held out her arms and begged him to hold her. The time he'd sat waiting for her to ask for his help was the most tortured he had ever known.

'Oh Peter! I'm so sorry! Can you ever forgive me for what I've done to you?'

'There's nothing to forgive.'

'Where would I be without you?'

'My darling! You won't ever need to be without me.'

We do hope that you have enjoyed reading this large print book.

Did you know that all of our titles are available for purchase?

We publish a wide range of high quality large print books including:
Romances, Mysteries, Classics
General Fiction
Non Fiction and Westerns

Special interest titles available in large print are:
The Little Oxford Dictionary
Music Book
Song Book
Hymn Book
Service Book

Also available from us courtesy of Oxford University Press:
Young Readers' Dictionary
(large print edition)
Young Readers' Thesaurus
(large print edition)

For further information or a free brochure, please contact us at:
Ulverscroft Large Print Books Ltd.,
The Green, Bradgate Road, Anstey,
Leicester, LE7 7FU, England.
Tel: (00 44) **0116 236 4325**
Fax: (00 44) **0116 234 0205**

ACKNOWLEDGEMENTS

The Society wishes to thank all those
who have contributed in any way
towards the production of this play.
Most especially our thanks go to
Mr Craddock Fitch, our President,
without whose enthusiastic support this
play would not have been presented.

Stage Manager Dean Jones

Lighting Willie Biggs

Scenery Barry Jones and Ronald Bissett

Costume Greta Jones

Flowers Sheila Bissett

Music Dora Peel

Publicity Ann Parkin

Sound effects Barry Jones

Box office Ann Parkin

Refreshments Charter-Plackett Enterprises

CAST

Marian Latimer	Caroline Harris
Charles Latimer	Neville Neal
Julian Latimer	Rhett Wright
Daisy Latimer	Michelle Jones
Leonard Charteris	Hugo St John Maude
Doris Jackson	Liz Neal
Celia Tomkinson	Harriet Charter-Plackett

Produced and directed by

Hugo St John Maude

The action of the play takes place
in the drawing room of Rocombe Manor,
home of the Latimers.

ACT ONE
Scene 1
A Summer morning
Scene 2
The following evening

Refreshments will be served in the interval

ACT TWO
Scene 1
Sunday morning four weeks later
Scene 2
The same evening

Turnham Malpas Amateur
Dramatic Society

presents

DARK RAPTURE

by

Digby Clarke-Johnson

on

Friday 10th and Saturday 11th July

in

ST THOMAS' CHURCH HALL

at

7.30 prompt

Tickets £5 including refreshments
Concessions £4